Something Terrible

Wrath James White
&
Sultan Z. White

BLOOD BOUND BOOKS

ISBN 978-1-940250-16-8

Artwork by Andrej Bartulovic

Interior Layout by Lori Michelle
www.theauthorsalley.com

Printed in the United States of America

First Edition

Visit us on the web at:
www.bloodboundbooks.net

ALSO FROM BLOOD BOUND BOOKS:

Contents :

TO DAD.

And special thanks to Paul Goblirsch for taking a chance on me. Thanks to my teachers Dr. Daves, Ms. Ro, Ms. Page, and Ms. Lazure. Thanks to my ex-girlfriend Emily who supported me throughout writing this. Thanks also to the men of Webster Hall 2012-2013. Thank you to my mother and father for continuing to inspire me.

Something Wondrous
by Brian Keene

Probably the most common advice given to beginning writers is "write what you know." It's excellent advice, but too often it gets misinterpreted. Writing what you know doesn't necessarily mean that if you're a steelworker, your character should be a steelworker, too, nor does it mean that if you grew up on the streets of North Philly, all of your stories have to take place in that same location. It is okay to do these things, of course, but writing what you know goes deeper than that.

Do you remember your first kiss? How about your first heartbreak? The first time you disappointed your parents? The first time you disappointed yourself? Writing what you know encompasses all of these things. Everyone remembers their first kiss, but your memory of the experience is different and unique from everyone else's, and when you put that experience into words, it helps others remember their own. Writing what you know is just that—writing what you know about life. Everything that happens to you, both the good and the bad, the important and the mundane, is grist for the muse, and a writer's job is to wade through that grist and pull things out and show them to others, thus evoking an emotional response from the reader.

I write a lot about being a father, because that's what I know the most.

There are many things I suck at. I cannot, for example, fix a car, hammer a nail, install drywall, or recite stats about various sports teams or athletes. Fellow author Geoff Cooper, who used to make his living as a mechanic, once told me that my car's timing belt ran the dashboard clock, and I believed him. My last attempt at building a bookshelf resulted in me smashing my thumb with a hammer after constructing something that looked vaguely triangular. Installing drywall? I'm not even sure what drywall is. And my knowledge of football, basketball, NASCAR, etc. can be summed up by the fact that, until my fortieth year on this planet, I was certain that a field goal was a baseball term.

Some people say I'm good at writing (others think my writing skills are akin to my knowledge of professional sports). But one thing most everyone seems to agree on is that I'm a good father. I love my sons. That's what I know. And thus, that's what I write about a lot. Sometimes this is a conscious effort. Other times, I'm not even aware of the subtext until someone else points it out.

My oldest son is twenty-four as I write this. He's a social worker, and I'm proud of him. My youngest son is six, and depending on which day you ask, he intends to be either a lumberjack, a scientist, or a writer when he grows up.

I'm not the only author to thematically feature fathers and sons (it's a predominate theme in the works of Tom Piccirilli, for example), nor am I the only horror author whose child has expressed an interest in following in their father's footsteps (Richard Christian Matheson, Joe Hill, Leah Moore, Christopher Rice, Trent Zelazny, Kasey Lansdale, and dozens of others come to mind). I'm also probably not the only writer to be paralyzed with fear at the thought of my child choosing this vocation.

Writing is a hard fucking job. I've had hard jobs. I've worked in foundries and on loading docks. I've driven long-haul trucks and worked as a roofer (the latter came to a quick end when my lack of prowess with a hammer was revealed). I even worked as a telemarketer, which is a thankless, psychologically demoralizing profession. I know hard work, and I'm here to tell you, writing for a living is fucking hard.

There's no 401K or retirement. We never get a tax refund and always owe more. Regular, timely paychecks are nonexistent. It wreaks havoc on our relationships (would you want to live with somebody who spends most of his waking hours inside his own head?). And at the end of the day, after you've written for eight hours straight and given yourself carpal tunnel syndrome, a bad back, and hemorrhoids—all in an effort to entertain the folks who buy your books and thus enrich their lives a little bit more—there's some jackass talking shit about you online.

With all that in mind, I think you can understand why I might be pensive about my youngest son's potential interest in following my footsteps.

But I also know how proud I would be if he did.

There are all kinds of collaborative moments to be shared between a father and son. But to share the writing experience, to jointly delve into the process and uncover truths together and communicate them to the world? That is something wondrous.

And so is this collection you are about to read.

I first met Sultan White when he was just a kid, and it unnerves me to realize that kid—a kid who loved zombies and especially loved his Uncle Brian's zombie novels—is now a man. It unnerves me even more that he is following in his father's footsteps, because if his efforts here are any indication, within a few years he may very well put both his father and his Uncle Brian out of business. And if that happens, I doubt I can get a job hammering nails or fixing cars . . .

To paraphrase Rush—children grow up and old friends grow older. That's simultaneously wonderful and terrifying. Just like the stories you are about to read.

Brian Keene
Somewhere in the backwoods of
Pennsylvania
April 2014

iii

Something Terrible
Wrath James White

1.

Eddie opened the door and stood there . . . smiling.

Gil wondered what Eddie intended to say, planned to do, but that smile changed everything. A rage surged within him like a tidal wave, the kind that destroys entire coastal towns. It erupted violently, and his fists were suddenly hurtling toward Eddie's smiling face. Knuckles met flesh and bone with a wet smack and thud, like a meat tenderizer pounding a thick cut of steak.

Eddie crumpled to the floor like a marionette that had its strings cut.

Gil followed him to the floor, still punching. Each blow increased his anger rather than assuaging it. Gil was dimly aware that he was yelling, roaring, as he beat Eddie senseless, trying to destroy the man who had once been his best friend.

"Dad! Dad! You're going to kill him!"

Gil heard his son's voice. He knew what the words meant. What they meant for him, his future, his family. He would be a murderer on death row, or endure life imprisonment. A man's death would be on his conscience. Gil knew all the implications of his actions, all the repercussions, but he didn't care.

Killing Eddie right then and there, in his own entryway, was exactly what Gil wanted. He switched from punching

Eddie's face to strangling him with both hands. He sat on Eddie's chest and squeezed with all his might until his friend's eyes rolled up in his head and he stopped breathing.

Then Gil rolled off him and collapsed. He stared at the wall, feeling numb, empty.

"You okay, Dad? Is he dead? Is Eddie dead?"

"Dada?"

Gil looked up and saw Eddie's baby boy toddling out of the kitchen, his face smeared with crushed carrots and creamed corn.

Gil looked back at Eddie and saw his friend take a huge breath and start coughing. He wasn't dead—yet—but he would be. Gil was certain of that because killing him had felt good. Thinking that bastard was dead had felt better than anything Gil had felt since coming home tonight. It almost felt like he'd righted a wrong, fixed what was broken. Deep down he knew it wasn't that simple. It would take a lot more than this to fix everything, to put it all back to normal. It would take years of counseling and group therapy. But it was a start.

Killing the bastard who had raped his daughter was the least Gil could do.

2.

Gil and his wife had a rule. Men were not allowed to babysit their daughter. Not alone. It didn't matter if it was a friend, neighbor, family member; not even Natalie's father or Gil's brother were allowed to be alone with little Selma. There were no exceptions. It often made for some uncomfortable moments. Trying to explain to his boss that his son wasn't allowed to be alone with Selma on the slim chance the kid might secretively be a pederast had been . . . difficult. When Gil tried to explain it to his stepfather, the man had been so offended he'd stormed out of the house. His mother had given Gil that accusatory look, believing he had deliberately hurt her husband's feelings.

"You know your stepfather would never do anything to hurt Selma. He loves that little girl! Why would you say something so hurtful?"

"I'm not saying he would, Mom. I'm just saying you never know. It's better to be safe than sorry."

That hadn't helped. Gil's relationship with his stepfather had been chilly ever since. In his parents' minds, Gil had accused him of having pedophiliac tendencies. And wasn't that what they were really saying with the rule? Any man, no matter how well they knew him, no matter how nice, how kind, how normal he appeared, might be a pederast. Many people had been offended by the suggestion over the years, and Gil couldn't blame them, but what else could he do? If anything ever happened to his baby girl, Gil would never forgive himself. Even worse, Natalie would never forgive him.

Natalie had been molested by a cousin when she was young. His name was Tony. He was five years older than Natalie, and he'd always been first to volunteer to babysit her and the other children. Everyone in Natalie's family used to remark about how good Tony was with kids. That's why no one believed her when she told them how he'd tried to force himself inside her and then made her watch while he masturbated on her belly. She had only been five years old and hadn't had the vocabulary to describe the things he'd done to her. Tony had been allowed to continue babysitting her, and the abuse continued and progressed. He had also continued babysitting all her other cousins, her sister, and even her niece before he was finally caught in the act by her stepbrother, Wayne. Wayne went to jail for almost a year for putting a bullet in her cousin's head after he'd caught him sodomizing his daughter in a coat closet during a Christmas party. After years of being ignored, Natalie's family had finally believed her, but by then it was too late. The number of loved ones who'd been abused by Tony had reached nearly a dozen, but Natalie had been the first. She'd never trusted another man after that until she'd met Gil. Even after they'd had a child together, their son, Kai, it had taken Natalie months before she was comfortable leaving Gil alone with him. And then, when she'd gotten pregnant again five years ago and given birth to their daughter, she'd wept for days, afraid she wouldn't be able to protect her. Afraid her daughter might one day suffer the same abuse she'd suffered. That's when they came up with the rule.

Gil parked the Ford truck in the driveway and hopped out to unstrap Selma from her car seat.

"We going to Eddie's house?" Selma asked. An Elmo doll was tucked in a stranglehold under her arm, and the doll giggled and shook when she squeezed it.

"Yup, sweetie. Eddie and Amy are going to watch you for a while, while Mommy and I go out."

"I want to go with you and Mommy!"

"Sorry, sweetie. Mommy and I need some alone time."

"Why can't Kai watch me?"

"Your brother is out with his friends. Kai's a teenager now. He wants to play with other teenagers. You'll have fun with Amy. You can play with their dog, Coco. And maybe, if you're a good girl, Eddie will make ice cream."

"Chocolate?" she asked, her hazel eyes sparkling with an almost religious rapture at the mere mention of her favorite desert.

Gil chuckled. "Maybe. If you're a good girl."

The front door opened and Gil's best friend, Eddie, bounded out the door full of vigor and enthusiasm.

He smiled when he saw Gil, then rushed over and gave him a big hug. "What's up, man? Good to see you. We need to hook up for another run soon. You still running?"

"When I can."

The man was an endless source of energy and always seemed to be in a good mood. He was only eight years younger than Gil, but when it came to vitality, he seemed to have Gil beat by twenty years. Of course Eddie was nearly half Gil's size. At only five foot, nine inches and a hundred and sixty pounds, Eddie was six inches shorter and almost a hundred pounds lighter than Gil. Eddie was half-Korean and half-Dutch. His wife was half-Cuban and half-Swedish. Neither looked Dutch or Swedish, though Eddie didn't look particularly Korean either. He was a generic brown that, in Texas, usually got interpreted as Mexican. His amazingly curvaceous wife looked deliciously Cuban. Gil found it hard to look at the woman without blushing. Luckily, being African American, blushing was more figurative than literal.

"Where's my girl? Where's that pretty little girl?" Eddie crooned as he raced around to the car door and snatched Selma out of her car seat. "There she is!"

Selma exploded with giggles as Eddie hoisted her in the air and twirled her around.

Gil always thought he might be just as animated as Eddie if he were carrying around a hundred pounds less. It didn't matter if it was fat or muscle. Weight was weight. And he had to admit, these days it was more fat than muscle, though Gil wasn't exactly in bad shape for a forty-five-year-old. He was in better shape than most guys he knew who were half his age. Just not the shape he wanted to be in. He always felt tired. No matter how much sleep he got, after nine or ten hours at work, an hour in the gym, then two or three hours with the family before bed time, he always felt like he was on the brink of exhaustion. When the weekends came, all he wanted to do was sleep. He didn't want to go on a picnic or to the pool or the playground like he saw so many other parents do. He wanted to collapse in front of the TV until Monday arrived and he had to do it all over again. That, however, was a recipe for divorce and resentful kids. Yet, no matter how much time he spent with his daughter, it was never enough. His wife practically accused him of being a bad father for not spending more time with the little girl. He wished he could be more like Eddie.

Eddie had just had his first kid last year and spent every waking second with his young son. He was every bit the proud, doting papa. Gil had been the same way when his first child, his son, was born fifteen years ago. But age and a stressful job had leeched the life out of him. It had sapped his energy and his general enthusiasm. He loved his daughter every bit as much as he'd loved his son when Kai was the same age. But when Kai was born, every day had seemed like an adventure, wondering what the boy was going to do next. The reality was that Selma just seemed like work. He knew he needed to change that, alter his perspective, find strength in his love for his daughter to push through his fatigue and general malaise to be the kind of father she deserved before she wound up on a stripper pole or worse in fifteen years. Spending more time with his daughter had been his New Year's resolution for the past five years, and here he was passing her off on a babysitter again. Goddamn father of the year.

Gil smiled as Eddie swooped Selma off the ground and up onto his shoulders. Eddie was the only man Gil trusted around his daughter. They worked out at the same gym. Gil was just trying to stay in shape as middle-age loomed large over the horizon. Eddie was trying to put some muscle on his habitually lean but flabby body. He wasn't the type of guy who was thin and ripped with wiry muscle. He was thin but still had a paunch, and were it not for the gym, he'd have no muscle tone at all. When Gil first met Eddie, the man's arms had looked like tubes, with no discernible biceps or triceps. The shoulder blended right in with the biceps which blended into the forearms. He'd been fumbling around with some weights, on the verge of hurting himself, when Gil had taken pity on him and started showing him how to lift properly. As it was, he still didn't work out hard enough to look athletic, but at least he didn't look weak and sickly anymore.

"Man! She has gotten so big!"

"She's in the ninetieth percentile for height," Gil

answered proudly, following Eddie through his front door and into his house.

"I believe it," Eddie replied, setting Selma down in the kitchen. Selma immediately took off in search of their little "min pin," Coco. "Cocoooo? Cocoooooo!"

"Where's Amy?" Gil asked, looking around the kitchen.

"She went out to get some snacks."

"She'll be back soon though, right?" Gil's smile cracked. His eyes shot nervously from one side of the room to the other. He and his wife had reservations in forty-five minutes and it was a thirty-minute drive to the restaurant. That left just enough time for Gil to drive home, pick up Natalie, and get on the road. No time to wait for Eddie's wife to get home, but Natalie would freak if he left Selma alone with Eddie. *Fuck.*

"She should be home any minute. Just go. I'll take care of Selma until Amy gets here."

The hairs on the back of Gil's neck stood on end.

"Uh, umm. That's okay. I'll wait."

Eddie cocked his head and wrinkled his brow. Staring hard at Gil's face. Gil squirmed under his friend's naked appraisal.

"You don't think I can handle your daughter by myself? Go ahead and take your wife to dinner. I got this," Eddie said with that lopsided grin that made him look cute and harmless and slightly retarded all at the same time.

Gil fidgeted, shifting from one foot to the other and looking everywhere but at his friend. "No, man. I-I'll just hang out until Amy gets back."

Eddie stepped closer to Gil, forcing eye contact. "What's going on, man? You don't trust me with your daughter?"

Gil let out a sigh. "It's not that. It's just that Natalie and I have this rule—forget it. It's nothing. Amy will be home soon, right?"

Eddie smiled and patted Gil on the back. "She just went to the store, man. She'll be right back. Stop trippin'. You know I wouldn't let anything happen to your pride and joy. I'll protect her with my life."

Gil smiled and nodded. "I know you would, man. I'm sorry. Thanks for watching her for me. We all need to hook up for dinner soon."

"Definitely. See you in a couple of hours. Tell that sexy wife of yours I said hi."

"You too."

Gil left, feeling guilty and worried, and guilty for feeling worried. He drove the six miles back to his house to pick up Natalie. She looked gorgeous when he stepped through the door. Natalie was not a small woman. Not fat but not skinny either. She had a small paunch left over from two pregnancies, the last one having taken place when she was already in her thirties. Luckily it was shadowed by a voluptuous bosom. Her bra size had gone up two sizes when she was carrying Selma and had never diminished. She had wide hips but thin, muscular legs and a small but round ass that looked a bit out of proportion; it almost made her look top-heavy. To Gil, Natalie's incongruous curves were irresistible, sheer perfection. Even after fifteen years of marriage, the sight of her still took his breath away.

She was wearing a simple black dress with a plunging neckline and a slit up one side that accentuated her thin, athletic legs and tan wedges with braided straps that increased her height by another five inches and almost brought her eye to eye with Gil.

"Hey, beautiful!"

"Hey yourself. I look like shit. I don't have anything to wear."

"Are you kidding me? You look gorgeous!"

"I'm going to change."

"What? But you look so sexy in that dress."

"I don't feel comfortable in this."

"We don't have time for you to change. We'll be late for our reservation."

"Sorry, I'm changing."

Gil followed her into the bedroom and watched as she ripped through her wardrobe in a frenzy. Her low self-esteem clouded her vision and turned the image she saw in the mirror into a funhouse distortion. He knew what she was seeing. Those thighs that he loved were thick, elephantine pillars in her mind. Her voluptuous hips that drove him wild were just mounds of unwanted adipose tissue to her. Gil never understood why the fact that he loved her body wasn't enough for her. What did it matter if she didn't live up to the media-created standard of beauty if her husband was happy with her looks?

"Why is it that every time I say something looks sexy on you, you change your clothes?"

"I'm a mother. I'm not supposed to look sexy."

"You're still a woman . . . and a wife."

"Come on, Gil. Don't give me shit. I wasn't comfortable."

Gil checked his watch again and tried to calculate how much time he had to get downtown before their reservations ran out. Forty-five minutes. Downtown Austin was twenty-five minutes away. Thirty in traffic.

"Okay. Just find something else quick."

It took exactly fifteen minutes and three more changes of clothes before Natalie finally left the house wearing a dress that was far less flattering than the one she'd taken off. Gil didn't care. As long as she was happy with what she was wearing, and they weren't late for their reservations, she could have been wearing a potato sack for all it mattered.

"You look gorgeous," he said, kissing Natalie on the cheek and opening the car door for her.

"You sure this dress doesn't make me look fat? I feel like it makes my hips and ass look too big."

Gil rolled his eyes. "I'm an ass man, darlin'. Trust me, yours is just lovely. Shall I get down on my knees and prove it?"

Natalie smiled. "And how would you do that?"

"I'd lick the stank off you."

Natalie shook her head and scowled.

"You are disgusting!" she said, laughing.

"You married me. So what does that make you?"

Gil stuck his tongue out as far as it would go until it touched the tip of his nose.

"There are so many better places you could put that tongue than my ass, you know?"

"Anywhere you want it, darlin'."

"How did I ever wind up with such a pervert?"

"You love this pervert though, don't you?" Gil asked, leaning in for a kiss.

"I love you very much," Natalie responded before touching her lips to his.

They kissed for several long seconds. It was a deep, passionate, soul-stirring kiss that left them both breathless.

"You sure you don't want to stay here tonight? A couple of hours without the kids could be put to some good use."

"I'm hungry."

"Yeah, me too."

"Can I have a rain check on you licking the stank off me?" Natalie asked, kissing Gil again as he shifted the car into reverse and pulled out of the driveway.

"Of course."

"Does my ass really stink?"

"Not at all. Your asshole smells like roses."

"You're a jerk."

"You love this jerk."

The drive to the restaurant was quick. Gil checked the rearview mirror obsessively as he tested the speed limit, trying to make it to the restaurant before their reservation ran out. They made it with four minutes to spare. He parked the car and rushed around to open the door for Natalie, something he only did when they were dressed up for a night on the town. Natalie smiled and held out her hand for him. He took it and helped her out of the car. Together they walked into the restaurant, a Brazilian steakhouse they had been dying to try for months. The evening was off to a wonderful start.

It was late when they arrived back at Eddie's house. They were both slightly tipsy. They'd had wine with their meal and then had gone out for more drinks at a wine bar on Congress Avenue that also served appetizers and desserts. They'd shared a bottle of cabernet and a piece of chocolate cake almost as large as Natalie's head.

The house was dark when they arrived. Gil stepped out of the car and rang the doorbell. After a few moments, Eddie came to the door in his pajama pants without his shirt. He looked sweaty and out of breath, like he'd been working out or having sex.

"Did I interrupt something? You and Amy in there gettin' busy when you're supposed to be watching Selma?"

"Nah, man. Amy's sleep. I was just doing some pushups in the living room. Come on in."

Gil walked in, frowning, looking around for Selma. The TV was on in the living room and Selma was sitting on the couch, still awake.

"She wouldn't go to bed. I've been up with her all night," Eddie said.

Gil felt ill. Eddie had been alone with Selma for God knew how long.

"And you were just in here doing pushups? Since when do you do pushups?"

"I used to do a hundred in the morning and a hundred at night. So I've slacked off the last couple of months. Don't give me shit about it. You ain't exactly Brad Pitt either, motherfucker."

Gil laughed. "It just seems weird. You're down here doing pushups in the living room while Amy's upstairs asleep and Selma's down here watching *Family Guy*. Wait—*Family Guy*?"

Eddie shrugged. "It's a cartoon. She's too young to get the adult humor. As far as she's concerned it's just a bunch of funny characters bouncing around on-screen saying goofy shit."

"She's five. She's not retarded. Don't let her watch that shit."

"Okay. Okay. My bad."

"Don't worry about it. Thanks for watching her." Gil reached out for Selma and lifted her off the couch and onto his broad shoulders.

"Come on, Princess. Mommy's waiting. Time to go home. Say good night to Eddie."

"Good night, Eddie."

"Good night, Selma."

Gil shook Eddie's hand. "Thanks again for watching her, man. I appreciate it."

"No problem, man. You guys are family."

"Oh, and you need to do more pushups. Your tits jiggled when I shook your hand. You're like fat and skinny at the same time."

"Fuck you, man!"

Eddie punched Gil in the arm.

"I'm just fuckin' with you. Good night."

"Drive safe. Tell Natalie I said hi."

3.

"He made me touch his penis." She pointed at Gil's crotch. "Down there."

Gil felt like he could feel the earth rotating under his feet. The heavens spun like he was on a carrousel. He felt cold and then flush with rage as he began calculating myriad ways to punish the man. But this had to be a mistake. He knew Eddie. Eddie wouldn't do something like that.

"How did he make you touch it?"

"With my mouth."

Gil's stomach threatened to revolt. His muscles tightened, hardened, eager for something to destroy. Instead, he gathered Selma into his arms.

"Oh, baby. I'm so sorry. I shouldn't have left you alone with him. Daddy's so sorry."

"Where was Amy?" Natalie asked, and Gil felt pangs of guilt like physical pain as Selma answered.

"She wasn't home yet."

It must have happened right after Gil dropped her off—when he knew Amy wasn't home.

Gil looked back at his wife. Natalie's expression wounded him where he never knew he could hurt. It felt as if something had pierced his flesh and cut deep into the cells, wounded his very life force. She looked betrayed. Not by Eddie but by Gil. Eddie was Gil's friend. Gil had vouched for him repeatedly. But, worst of all, Gil had broken the rules. He knew that, in his wife's eyes, Gil had betrayed her every bit as much as Eddie had betrayed them both. He had practically delivered his own daughter into the hands of a pedophile. He could see her reliving her own assault from decades ago, when she was just a few years older than Selma. Gil felt miserable, wretched, had never believed anyone, certainly not his best friend, could rape a child so young. Of course he knew it had happened, but he still found it inconceivable. He couldn't imagine someone sexualizing a child. His child! He couldn't think of anything more horrible, more inhuman.

"What did you do?" Natalie said through clenched teeth, her face twisted into a rictus of pain and outrage. "What did you do?" She punched him several times and then snatched Selma from his arms.

"What's going on?"

Their son, Kai, walked into the room. He must have just gotten home. If he had been home last night they wouldn't have needed a babysitter. But it wasn't his fault either. The fault rested solely on Gil's shoulders. He had to make it right.

"His friend molested your sister!"

"What? What did Eddie do?"

"He made her perform oral sex on him."

"What the fuck? That sick son of a bitch!"

"Watch your mouth, Kai."

"Well, let's go get his ass! Let's go fuck his ass up!"

Gil looked at his son's angry face, a lighter, cappuccino-colored version of his own, and then at his wife's beautiful, blonde, fair-skinned regal features, now distorted in anguish. The pain on her face increased Gil's fury until it was like a living thing clawing inside him, trying to get out and tear shit up.

"I'm going over there."

"I'm calling the cops!" Natalie said.

"Not yet," Gil said, and something in his face communicated his intentions to Natalie, broke through her own tidal wave of emotion.

"Don't . . . don't get arrested. Don't go to prison, Gil. Don't . . . don't . . . "

Gil nodded. He knew what she meant. She didn't want to say, "Don't kill him," because she wanted him dead. She wanted Gil to kill Eddie. She wanted that sick, twisted fucker to pay. She just didn't want Gil to get caught. She didn't want to lose her husband. Gil wasn't sure what he was going to do, but he wasn't going to rule out murder.

"I won't go to prison. I won't get caught. Just don't call the police. Let me handle this. I promise, I'll make it right. I'll fix it."

Natalie shook her head. Tears flowed freely down her cheeks as she squeezed Selma tight against her.

"You can't fix this, Gil. Nothing can fix this."

Gil nodded. "But I can fix Eddie."

"I'm coming with you, Dad."

"No. You stay with your mom and your sister."

Kai stepped in front of Gil, barring his way to the front door. "I'm coming with you, Dad. She's my sister. It's my job to protect her too. Let me help."

Gil hesitated, but he couldn't think straight. He tried to figure out what a good parent would do in this situation, but this wasn't something they addressed in any of the parenting books Natalie had made him read when she was pregnant. This was outside the rulebook. Gil struggled to think of every reason for or against, but he couldn't discipline his mind to the task. It kept wandering back to the pain on his wife's face. She had been devastated. And he couldn't get Selma's words out of his head. Words no father should ever hear. His little girl telling him that Eddie had made her touch his penis.

With my mouth.

"Come on."

4.

Eddie was still alive and Gil was going to make sure he wouldn't be happy about it.

"What about his kid?" Kai said. "We gonna do this in front of his kid?"

Gil's anger came surging back. "I don't give a fuck about that damn kid! He raped my little girl! I should kill this piece of shit right in front of his kid."

"We should kill his kid too then. We should kill him and make Eddie watch. That would really fuck him up."

He said it so coldly, so callously, Gil wasn't sure he'd heard the boy right.

"What did you say, Kai?"

"We should kill his kid. We should torture the little bastard. I mean, he hurt Selma, right? An eye for an eye, right?"

Gil looked over at the little toddler and shook his head.

"No, we aren't touching his kid. Take him back in the kitchen."

"Don't hurt my boy." It was a hoarse, phlegm-choked croak. Barely more than a whisper gurgled from cracked and swollen lips and a mouth full of blood. Eddie was staring right at Gil, trying to sit up. His eyes were glazed and unfocused and kept drifting from one side to the other, unable to focus. He looked like he was extremely inebriated, but Gil was pretty sure the problem was brain damage. Lack of oxygen from being choked, combined with the severe beating he'd taken. He was lucky he wasn't a vegetable.

Kai led the boy into the other room. Just before he closed the kitchen door, he turned to Eddie and smiled. Gil did not like the look of that smile. It was wrong, inappropriate. It was as if Kai was enjoying this. Gil found himself worrying about what Kai might do to Eddie's kid.

We should kill his kid. We should torture the little bastard. I mean, he hurt Selma, right? An eye for an eye, right?

The words still hung heavy in the air.

"Kai! Don't hurt that boy! You hear me? Don't do anything until I say so!"

"Yeah, Dad. I won't," Kai said quietly. His words barely penetrated the door, barely reached Gil's ears. There was little conviction in them.

"I'm serious! Don't you do anything!"

"Yes, Dad." Again Kai sounded almost distracted, like he was barely listening.

Gil looked down and saw the fear in Eddie's eyes too.

"I didn't do anything! Don't let him hurt Little Eddie! Please! We're best friends, for Christ's sake! Whatever you think I did is bullshit! You know I wouldn't hurt Selma. I wouldn't do that!"

That Stygian rage, like a volcanic explosion, erupted to the surface once more. Gil grabbed Eddie by the throat and began choking him again.

"She told me! She told me what you did! You sick fuck! She told me herself!"

"Use these," Kai said. He was standing above Gil and Eddie holding duct tape, a drill, and a palm sander. "I found them in the garage. We should torture his ass for what he did. It's only right. Selma's going to be suffering for a long time. Just kicking his ass ain't enough. Killing him ain't enough. This piece of shit needs to suffer!"

"Watch your mouth, Kai! I'm still your father."

"Sorry, Dad."

Gil felt stupid correcting his nearly adult son for his language under the circumstances, but with everything spiraling out of control, his boy and his responsibilities as a father were things he could still control.

Gil stared up at his son, glancing from the murderous gleam in the boy's eyes, eyes that looked just like Gil's, to the power tools he held in his hands, and questioned how much control he really had over the kid. Even through his own rage he knew there was something wrong with Kai. The boy seemed eager to make Eddie suffer. *Is that normal? Is he just angry? Is he just doing what anyone would want to do in this situation?* After all, Gil had been about to strangle the man to death himself. *But torture?* Gil couldn't help but wonder at this sadistic streak emerging in his only son. Justified or otherwise, it was troubling. Gil reached up and took the tools from his son's hands.

"Go back in the kitchen, Kai."

"I want to watch. I want to see what you do to him. I want to see his ass suffer for hurting my little sister."

"I said go back in the kitchen, Kai! You don't need to see this shit."

"I'm not going anywhere! She's my sister, Dad!"

Gil looked back at Eddie, whose eyes were now clear and focused on him.

Gil's shoulders slumped and his head dropped. He nodded. "Okay. Okay, then help me hold him down."

Together they wrestled Eddie back onto his stomach and pulled his arms behind his back. Kai held his arms while Gil duct taped his wrists behind his back and then his ankles. Finally he rolled him over and put a strip of tape over his mouth.

"Do you know how many times I've thought about what I would do to a motherfucker if he ever hurt my kids? I even talked about it with you, remember?" Gil said to Eddie, whose eyes were wide in terror. Eddie shook his head and tried to speak through the duct tape. Gil ignored him.

"What did *you* say you would do? You said you would castrate the guy and shove his own cock down his throat. You remember saying that?"

Again Eddie shook his head violently, and this time he began to scream for help, his cries muffled by the tape.

"Do it, Dad. Cut his fucking balls off!"

"Didn't I tell you to watch your damn mouth?"

"Sorry, Dad. Sorry."

"I'm not cutting his damn balls off. That's what he said he would do. That's not what I said I'd do. I said I'd take the guy somewhere and torture him for hours, days, weeks. And that's what I'm going to do to this motherfucker. We've got to get him out of here before Amy comes home. She didn't do anything. No reason she should have to see this. Besides, we'd wind up having to duct tape her too to keep her from calling the police, and that wouldn't be right."

"How do you know she's not involved?"

"Selma would have said so. Besides, Amy wasn't even here. It probably wouldn't have happened if she'd been home. They've babysat before. That's why we have that rule. I fucked up. I should have never left her here with him. I broke the rules and now my little girl—my angel—this son of a bitch raped her!"

And I allowed it to happen. I put her in his hands. I broke the rules. This was all my fault, Gil thought.

"I should have never trusted you, Eddie. Natalie was right. You can't trust men around little girls. And now I'm going to hurt you, just so I feel better about myself. You're going to help absolve me of my guilt, Eddie. I know. That shit's fucked up. But this is how it's got to be. Kai?"

"Yes, Dad?"

Gil tossed him the keys to his F-150 and then began looking around for Eddie's keys. He found them on the kitchen island, shook them in his hands like loaded dice, and then shoved them into his pocket.

"I want you to drive my truck over to the WalMart parking lot and wait for me. I'll be driving Eddie's car. It's going to be a while. I need to carry him to his car and clean this place up."

Gil watched Kai leave and then began cleaning. He removed a mop and bucket from the closet in the laundry room and scrubbed the floor, washing away Eddie's blood. A small end table had been knocked over at some point during his brutal beating of Eddie, and Gil set it back in place. He knew where everything in the house went. He knew Eddie's home as well as he knew his own. He'd always felt at home here. Never again. That was all ruined now.

He walked toward the front door and removed Eddie's keys from his pocket. Eddie lay on the ground bleeding and moaning. Gil squatted down and lifted the man to his feet.

"You can walk or I can drag your ass. You gonna fuckin' walk?"

Eddie nodded and then began whining and pleading incoherently through the tape around his mouth. Standing next to Gil he looked even smaller than usual, bleeding and crying.

"Save your strength, Eddie. I can't hear you anyway. And you're going to need every ounce of it."

Gil half-dragged Eddie to the car, who did his best to hop along beside him even with his legs duct-taped together. Each time he began to fall, Gil caught him and dragged him forward until they reached Eddie's car. Gil popped the trunk.

Eddie adamantly shook his head, refusing to get in. Gil punched him in the gut, doubling him over. He had aimed for the solar plexus, and by the way the air expelled from Eddie's lungs in one big *whoosh*, Gil was pretty sure he'd hit his target. Eddie's body folded around Gil's fist. Gil watched his best friend wilt and drop to his knees. He knelt down beside him.

"I can keep you right here, Eddie. It doesn't matter to me where I do it, but I am going to hurt you. I have to. That's just the way it's got to be. The question is what I'm going to do to Amy when she gets home or to Little Eddie. You saw how Kai looked. I know you did. Well, I don't know if I can control him. And if Amy sees us, well . . . you know what I'll have to do to her. It's probably best for everyone if we're as far away from your family as possible, don't you think? Now get the fuck in the goddamn trunk!"

This time Eddie complied. Gil lifted him to his feet and met no resistance as he hefted him into the trunk.

"I can't say this will all be over soon. You and I both know it won't. I'm going to hurt you until I get bored or you die. Enjoy the ride, my friend."

Gil slammed the trunk and walked back into the house to find Little Eddie. "Eddie?" Gil called as he walked into the kitchen where Kai had left him. The boy was nowhere to be found.

"Eddie!"

He rushed into the living room, looked outside in the yard, and then dashed upstairs to check the bedrooms.

"Fuck! Where the hell did he go?"

Then Gil had a dark, terrifying thought. *Kai, what did you do?*

Gil retraced his steps, checking the house room by room, but this time he checked smaller places where a little scared boy could hide and even smaller places where the body of a dead child could be folded up and stashed. Then, feeling guilty, he checked even smaller spaces where body parts might fit. He checked the walls and floor for blood spatter and was relieved when he didn't find any. *But strangulation doesn't draw blood*, Gil thought. *If Kai strangled him and hid his body . . .*

Kai took him with him. Of course.

That made Gil feel only slightly better. He didn't want to think about what Kai might do without him there to intervene. Kai had a scary temper. It was one of the things he was working on in counseling. He'd been sent there after breaking a kid's leg in a fight. He said the kid had been bullying him. He had been jumped by three boys and was defending himself. That wasn't why he was in counseling. The fight was over. Two of the boys had run away and the last boy was lying on the ground holding his face that Kai had split open with a rock when Kai walked over and stomped on the kid's kneecap, deliberately breaking it. He'd been suspended, and therapy had been strongly recommended. Gil had gone along with it, even though he didn't believe in shrinks, because Natalie had been concerned. Now he was sure he'd done the right thing. In fact, he was worried he hadn't done enough. Kai needed serious emotional help. Gil pulled out his phone and dialed Kai.

"Hey, Dad. You on your way?"

"Is Little Eddie with you?"

There was a pause.

"Y-yeah, Dad. You didn't want me to leave him there by himself, did you? Then Amy would have definitely called the cops right away. She knows Eddie wouldn't leave his son alone. Besides, what if he got into something? Drank ammonia or bleach or something or got out of the house? And this way Eddie won't get out of line either. He'll be too afraid we'll hurt Little Eddie."

"You haven't though, right?"

Another long pause. "Haven't what, Dad?"

"You haven't hurt Little Eddie, right?"

"Of course not."

"You sure?"

"Dad, I wouldn't hurt a kid. I'm not some pervert like Eddie."

"Okay. I'll see you in a few. I'm leaving now."

Gil felt guilty for not trusting his own son, but something

just didn't feel right. Everything Kai said had made perfect sense, of course. Taking Little Eddie with them was probably the best move. Amy would think Eddie had taken their son to the park or the movies or something, which would give them a good head start. No one would be looking for him for several days, which meant no one would be looking for his car. Plenty of time to drive somewhere and stash the vehicle. A person wasn't considered missing unless he or she was missing for more than forty-eight hours unless there was evidence of foul play or it was a child younger than fourteen. Little Eddie was with his father, as far as anyone knew, so there would be no reason for anyone to call the place for at least a day. After that, it would be at least another twenty-four hours before the cops did much of anything but take a statement and do a cursory investigation. They wouldn't start taking it seriously until the second day that Eddie didn't come home, and even then they were likely to treat it as a parent abducting his own child. They would send out an Amber Alert, but they weren't likely to start going door to door or launch a manhunt. That would give Gil all the time he needed.

Gil walked back into the garage, opened the car door, and slid into the driver's seat. After fastening his seat belt and starting the ignition, Gil took a deep breath, let it out in two quick, shallow exhalations, and then hit the garage remote to raise the overhead door. He backed out of the garage and down the driveway.

He could hear Eddie thumping around in the trunk. It sounded loud, so loud he worried people on the street could hear it, but he knew better. It was loud to him because he was nervous and because he was in the car. To people outside it would be inaudible over the sound of the engine and the normal car sounds. Gil worried about Eddie kicking out the taillights and then remembered it wasn't possible to do that on most newer cars. There was nothing Eddie could do but make his feeble little noises.

Gil drove the short distance to where Kai waited for him

in the parking lot. He spotted his black F-150 in the back of the lot, Kai's head sticking up in the driver's seat, and Gil looked frantically for a second head. Not seeing one, he began to panic, imagining the worst. He left the car running as he hopped out and dashed over to the truck. Little Eddie was there, strapped in the front without a car seat. His head wasn't visible above the car door. Luckily there was a car seat in Eddie's vehicle.

"Let's go," Gil said, opening the truck and taking out Little Eddie.

"Where's Eddie?" Kai asked.

Gil looked around cautiously. Kai had parked far away from the other cars. There was no one within earshot.

"He's in the trunk," Gil whispered. "Let's go."

"Where are we going?"

"I know a place. There's an old warehouse in Austin by the airport. It's abandoned. I used to work there. I still have the keys on my old key ring. It's in the glove box. They never changed the locks."

Gil buckled Little Eddie into his car seat in the back and then slid behind the wheel as Kai took shotgun.

"Buckle your seat belt, son. The last thing we need is to get stopped for some dumb shit like that when we've got Eddie in the trunk. It's a twenty-minute drive to Austin."

5.

The warehouse was full of old rusted machine parts, covered in a thick layer of dust and cobwebs. There was a strong smell of mildew and motor oil along with animal scents, musk, urine, feces, and perspiration. The building had been abandoned for more than half a dozen years, yet still had the appearance of something recently abandoned. It hadn't been vandalized. There was no graffiti on the walls and even the windows were still intact, which was rare even for an occupied building in this part of town. An old calendar from 2007 still hung on the wall. Here and there a rusted power or hand tool could be seen as if it had been casually discarded in some worker's haste to put this building behind him. It was still daylight outside, but the few windows at the top of the nearly twenty-foot walls let in only a few scant rays of sun, so the room never got brighter than a dim twilight. Here and there a light bulb burned. The oddity of a building that had sat empty for so many years still having power was not lost on Gil. It made him nervous. He felt like they weren't completely alone.

Gil didn't know if he had the stomach for this, but he didn't want to seem weak in front of his son. Even if Kai was a sociopath, as Gil was beginning to suspect, he was still his son, and Eddie deserved this. After what he'd done, Eddie deserved every ounce of pain and suffering they could conceive. And he was sure Kai had a pretty extensive imagination from all the violent video games he played, the graphic novels he read, and the cheesy, grade-B horror movies that were little more than torture porn. Gil wanted to prove himself just as creative, just as willing to take this thing to its conclusion. He just hadn't yet decided what the conclusion would be. The punishment had to fit the crime. Eddie would have to feel it for a lifetime, just as Kai said Selma would. Even in this, Gil still wanted to be his son's hero. He wanted his boy to be proud of him. And the only thing that would make him proud now, was hurting Eddie . . . hurting him really bad.

He picked up the drill and saw that disturbing gleam in Kai's eyes. He tried to ignore it, but he couldn't deny it. He immediately looked down at his son's pants and saw an unmistakable bulge. Kai was aroused. He was getting off on this. Gil's stomach did a little flip.

Oh, God. I can't do this!

He felt like he was going to vomit. His hands and legs

trembled. Gil felt hot. The saliva in his mouth dried up. Sweat bulleted down his face. He swallowed hard. Eddie looked terrified.

Eddie's my boy. I can't do this to Eddie. I can't fuck my boy Eddie up like this.

But Eddie fucked up your daughter, some cold and vengeful part of Gil whispered back. *He fucked your daughter! You gonna let him get away with that? You gonna let Kai see his father act like a little pussy? So what you kicked Eddie's ass? What's that gonna do? He'll be raping some other kid tomorrow. Even if you call the cops, he'll get out of jail in a few years and be back at it. These kinds of perverts don't ever stop. You know that.*

And a new thought came to Gil's mind. What would he say to his wife? She had been through sexual abuse. She knew what it felt like to wake up to recurring nightmares of being powerless before some pervert's lust. She counted on Gil to protect her. She was confident that if anyone ever tried to hurt their family, Gil would make him rue the day. Rue the day. Gil laughed. He didn't even know what those words meant, really. Not literally. To him, they meant that whoever hurt his family would suffer. What would she say if he didn't punish Eddie? He'd seen the look in her eyes when he left. She wanted Eddie dead. What would she say if she knew he'd let the man who raped his daughter off the hook? Eddie wasn't the only person Gil had boasted to about what he'd do to anyone who hurt his daughter. He'd told Natalie as well.

"I'ma get medieval on his ass!" Gil had joked in his best Marsellus Wallace voice. "I'ma call a couple of hard pipe-hittin' niggas to go to work on homes with a pair of pliers and a blowtorch!"

They had laughed, and their laughter had eased the tension. But there had still been pain in Natalie's eyes. Pain and anger and something that hurt Gil to his core. Her eyes were distant and afraid, remembering her own abuse. He had felt helpless then, unable to protect her from her past or avenge her. But he had the chance now. He could avenge his daughter. If he didn't do this now, how could he ever face his wife again? How could he look his daughter in the eye?

Protect and provide. It was the sole purpose of the male species. That was the responsibility a father and husband was imbued with by nature. It was instinctual. When he was arrested, maybe he'd bring in experts to testify to that, biologists or anthropologists or some shit. They would tell the courts that Gil had no choice. It was his paternal instincts that made him do it. Maybe they'd try to pack the jury with fathers and his lawyer would ask them what they would do if someone molested their child. That would at least make them think. It might make them hand down a lighter sentence. Maybe he'd get probation. Gil could almost see himself getting acquitted. What father wouldn't understand? If he were sentenced, there would be protests outside the prison. He imagined his case spawning a movement. It didn't matter either way. Even if he was caught and sentenced to death or life in prison, he had to do this. He had failed to protect his daughter. The least he could do was avenge her. He would make sure she never had anything to fear from Eddie again. That she knew Daddy had made Eddie pay for what he'd done to her. That he would hurt anyone who ever tried to hurt her. At least that was something.

Gil tried to steel his nerves and quiet the pounding in his heart, the shaking in his hands. He wiped the sweat from his eyes and took a deep breath. He reminded himself that he wasn't doing this just for Kai. He wasn't doing this for himself, so he'd feel like some kind of big man. He was doing it for his daughter and all the other unknown girls Eddie had molested and was likely to molest in the future if he wasn't stopped.

The drill whirred and Eddie's eyes widened to the size of golf balls.

"I'ma get medieval on your ass," Gil said.

Again Eddie shook his head vigorously and screamed

against his tape. He was duct-taped fast to the little metal folding chair. Kai had practically mummified him. Shiny, gray strips, two inches wide, wound up Eddie's legs to the kneecaps and covered his torso from shoulders to waist. Gil avoided looking at his eyes, tried to forget that Eddie had once been his best friend. He took the drill, aimed it at Eddie's kneecap, and pushed.

"MMMmmphf! MMMMMmmmmmphf!" The tape around his mouth was not enough to mask the cry of agony that pealed from Eddie's lungs as the drill bore through skin and muscle into cartilage and bone, spraying blood and skeletal fragments. Skin and meat wrapped around the bit like the skin of a fruit around a peeler. Eddie jerked and convulsed, nearly toppling the chair, but the duct tape kept him firmly in place.

"Oh shit! Look at him! He's freaking out!"

But Gil wouldn't look at him. He didn't want to see the pain Eddie was experiencing. He didn't want to see what he had done.

"Use the sander next! Skin that motherfucker!" The enthusiasm in his son's voice made Gil feel even more wretched. This wasn't right. None of this was right. It had gone way too far, but now, stopping wasn't an option either.

Gil was in a fugue state as he put the gore-covered drill down on the floor between Eddie's legs and picked up the palm sander. There was a piece of fifteen grit sandpaper on it. Extra coarse. Gil ripped off some of the tape covering Eddie's torso, unraveling it until part of his chest and stomach was visible, but enough tape remained to keep his arms immobile and his back tight against the chair. Then Gil took the sander and placed it to Eddie's nipple. Blood and skin spattered Gil's face as he abraded the skin and fat from his friend's pectoral muscle. Eddie's nipple disappeared in seconds. The sander sheared it away millimeter by millimeter while Eddie screamed and thrashed, eyes bulging from their sockets, wild with terror and anguish. The sandpaper was now soaked with blood.

Gil paused to wipe the blood from his face, change the sandpaper, and pick out the pieces of flesh and gore that threatened to clog up the sander.

Once he'd cleaned it out and affixed it with a new sheet of sandpaper, he took a deep breath. It was time to hurt Eddie some more.

Gil closed his eyes as he stood. His hands were shaking again. Eddie was moaning and shivers ran through his bloodied and battered form like he was in an ice bath. Gil bit down like a dog trying to bite through a rawhide chew toy. His eyes were still closed as he tried to block the sounds of Eddie's torment from his mind and clear his thoughts to prepare for more carnage.

He brought the sander down on Eddie's forehead. Eddie thrashed and bucked in the chair, but Kai was already behind him, holding him steady as Gil sanded the skin from his best friend's skull, spraying blood, skin, and flesh in a red mist onto the wall behind him and all over Gil's face, arms, and upper body. Eddie thrashed violently against his bonds, trying to avoid the sander, but the duct tape held him fast until the sander shredded through the tape around the lower part of Eddie's brow as it continued to rasp away his skin. Eddie's screams were horrible, even with the tape still in place.

Blood washed down Eddie's face in a steady stream, obscuring his features and blinding him. Gil watched Eddie gag, sputter, and spit his own blood to keep from choking on it, gasping for air. His nostrils were caked in blood. He was being water-boarded with his own fluids.

Kai grabbed Eddie's head, one hand on his jaw and one on the top of his skull to hold him still, when the sander cut the remaining duct tape away from his forehead and Eddie jerked his head away from Gil. Gil was having a hard time trying to hold him.

He brought the sander from Eddie's forehead down to his face, grinding away on his right cheek. When he finally released him, Eddie looked like something from *Dawn of the Dead*. All the skin was gone from his forehead and the white bone was visible, as was his right cheekbone. Gil felt a wave of nausea wash over him. He dropped to his knees and began to vomit.

Gil staggered back to his feet, picking up the roll of tape. He walked back over to Eddie and began to wind the tape around him again, replacing the tape he'd removed or cut with the sander, once again securing him firmly to the chair. Kai stood by, watching.

There was an old coffee maker in the corner, sitting in what once had been the break area. Even the old water cooler was still there. Empty water bottles were strewn haphazardly around it.

"Make us some coffee, Kai."

"What? In that old thing? It's filthy. It has dust and spiderwebs in it. I don't think there are any filters or anything in it either, and where am I supposed to get coffee? You want me to go to the grocery store?"

Gil locked eyes with his son. "Just boil some water, please."

Kai nodded slowly, and a predacious smile slithered onto his face as what Gil was planning, or some version of it, filled his imagination. Gil didn't like that expression. It was wrong. Where there should have been horror and revulsion, there was mad glee. It could have been a defense mechanism. Certainly revenge feels good. Even Gil was feeling rather proud of himself for avenging his daughter's assault, but he also felt sick to his stomach, disgusted by what he'd done to his friend and what he was about to do. Whatever Kai was feeling, didn't appear quite so ambiguous.

Kai brought the coffee maker over to an old rusted utility sink in the corner and began to fill it up. Once it was full, he plugged in the coffeemaker and sat on a work bench, waiting for the water to boil.

Gil was surprised the electricity was still on. As far as he knew, the place had been closed for years. Someone must have still been using it for something. He didn't know what and didn't want to know. If it was something illegal, that was even better. It meant they had probably taken care to keep the place off the police radar and wouldn't be eager to call the cops if the owners did happen to stumble across this violent little scene. It might also mean whomever owned this place now would want to kill all three of them, but Gil didn't think that was likely.

"The water's hot."

"Bring it here."

Kai handed Gil the coffee pot and Gil walked over and poured it directly onto Eddie's face, scalding his open wounds and searing his skin with third-degree burns.

"Arrrrhhhhh! Arrrhhhhh!"

"Shut the fuck up!"

Gil handed the pot back to Kai. Eddie's face was red and puffy. The skin was blistering up like bubblegum and looked loose on his face, like it could slide right off. Even his eyelids were scalded, suppurating with little translucent bubbles of cooked skin. Gil wondered what was wrong with him that he could do this to another human being.

He hurt my daughter. That's what's wrong with me. I'm just doing what any father would do. But he wondered. Would any father do this, or would they have just called the police and let them handle it?

But leaving it to the police felt almost cowardly. At best it was impersonal. It didn't show his passion for his child, his love, his fury that someone had dared use her, dared hurt her. Gil thought about all the women he'd known over the years. All the women he'd been in a relationship with. All the women he'd fucked. As many as three out of five had been raped or molested at some point in their lives, including his wife, Natalie, and it had left scars on them. It had wounded them and, in many cases, had utterly broken them. Most became extremely promiscuous. Some were submissive, looking for a daddy to take control of them, and continue the abuse they had come to believe they deserved and had learned to enjoy. Some had become drug addicts and alcoholics, manic depressives. Some had bipolar disorder or some other psychological issues. All had low self-esteem. None had survived the experience intact.

Maybe doing this will spare Selma from that life, Gil thought. Maybe she wouldn't wind up spreading her legs for every swinging dick who showed her an ounce of kindness or begging some sadistic fuck to spank her or whip her or shove his entire fist up her twat like some girls he'd met. Maybe she wouldn't go looking for a daddy in the men she dated, because she would know how much her real daddy cared. He had tortured a man for hurting her. Daddy loved her that much.

"What are we going to do to him now?" Kai asked.

"Nothing," Gil said, turning away from Eddie's mutilated visage and his own thoughts.

"Nothing? But—"

"We have to go home. If we disappear and Eddie's missing, people will put two and two together. He's not going anywhere."

"But what about Little Eddie? We can't just leave him here."

"Yeah, I thought about that. He can't talk yet. He wouldn't be much of a witness. We could bring him with us. Say Eddie asked us to watch him."

Kai shook his head. "But Mom knows what Eddie did. Mom will know we did something to him if we show up with Little Eddie and Eddie ain't with us."

"I'm not killing a kid."

"I didn't say kill him. I just said we can't take him home and can't take him to our house either."

"I'm not just going to turn him loose to wander the streets and get molested by some pervert or something."

"Someone like his father? For all you know, Eddie could have been molesting his own kid," Kai said.

Gil shuddered. The thought repulsed him, angered him, almost as much as the thought of that piece of shit messing with his daughter. *That sick fuck!*

Taking Little Eddie by the hand, Gil led him outside to the car. Kai followed close behind.

"Put him in his car seat. I'm going back in there to clean myself up. There's a bathroom in the back. You've got blood all over you too. When I come out, you should probably go in and get cleaned up."

There were so many things Gil still needed to figure out. Revenge was more complicated than just fucking a guy up, especially if he wanted to stay out of prison. There were so many loose ends to tie up. Any one of them could be the thing that led the cops to his doorstep.

A small utility sink was affixed to a wall in the corner. When Gil worked there years ago, when it was an air conditioning company, this sink had always smelled like urine. His manager had vowed to catch whoever was pissing in the utility sink. He never did, as far as Gil knew.

Gil took off his shirt and washed it. He splashed water on his face, neck, chest, and arms, scrubbing away his best friend's blood.

"I need to go to the hospital, Gil."

Eddie's words were gurgled through a mouthful of blood. Gil wondered how Eddie had managed to avoid choking on it. The duct tape had fallen away from his mouth and was draped around his neck like a bandana. There was too much blood for the adhesive to stick.

"Shut up, Eddie. I ain't taking your ass to the hospital. You'll stay right here until I get back."

Eddie looked like shit. A quarter of the skin and muscle on his face had been sheared away by the sander. His forehead had been ground down to the bone. The rest of the skin was covered in blisters. A cascade of red washed down his face from the various wounds. Eddie's pupils were completely dilated and he was shivering. He was going into shock. If his blood didn't clot soon, he'd bleed out. As it was, he was almost definitely going to get an infection. For a brief moment, Gil considered taking him to the hospital, but he was in no hurry to go to jail. He was feeling a little guilty for what he'd done. Eddie had been his friend. But friends didn't rape other friend's children.

What if he didn't do it?

The thought burst into his mind like a thought bubble from a comic strip. It seemed to hang in the air between the two of them. Gil tried to ignore it. He put the question out of his mind. Madness lay in the entertainment of such thoughts. He was already fully committed. There had been no reason for Selma to lie about it. That wasn't the type of thing a five-year-old would have just made up. How would she even know people did such things unless someone had shown her? Unless what she said Eddie did was true.

"I didn't do it, Gil. I didn't do it! I didn't do it! *I didn't do it! I didn't do it!*"

Gil rushed over and grabbed the coffeepot again. He grabbed Eddie by the head, feeling his fingers slip against the bare, bloody bone of Eddie's forehead, and then poured the remaining boiling water down Eddie's throat and nostrils, water-boarding him. Eddie was screaming, struggling for air, gurgling up the scalding fluid, drowning even while his mouth and nose boiled. When Eddie ran out of water, he threw the coffee pot across the room, shattering it against the wall, and then wrapped Eddie's swollen mouth in duct tape again. He had to go around several times, sticking the tape to itself more so than to Eddie's skin, of which there was less to use.

"You think I expect you to fucking confess, motherfucker? Of course you'll lie. Why the fuck would you tell the truth? Either you'll go to prison or I'll murder you. You know that. You have every goddamn reason to lie. That's why I don't want to hear shit you have to say. You just sit there and keep your fucking mouth shut until I get back!"

Gil rinsed his shirt out a few more times, but it was hopeless. The blood wouldn't come out. At this point, prison was practically inevitable, but Gil planned to delay the inevitable for as long as possible. He walked out to the truck and rooted around in the back for his gym bag. He found an old T-shirt that had probably been there for weeks. It was stiff with dried sweat and smelled like the essence of a used jockstrap, concentrated and distilled. It was overpowering, but Gil had no choice. Either he smelled like a homeless person or looked like a serial killer.

He looked up in the front seat where Kai had the radio blasting an incoherent rap song in thick country slang.

"Turn that down and go in there and wash the blood off your hands. And don't touch Eddie! You understand?"

Kai nodded and smiled. "Yes, Dad. I won't."

Kai had always been such a good kid. He was smart, well-mannered, obedient, and could even be charming and funny when he thought it was worth the effort. But there was a coldness to him, an emotional detachment that had always felt like a barrier between them. Gil had thought it was his fault, his own failure to connect with his son. He often wondered if he'd been too hard on the boy when it came to discipline and if that was what had kept them from connecting, but he had seen Kai display the same apathy toward his mother and even his sister. And seeing the ease with which he embraced the idea of torturing Eddie, the delight he seemed to take in it, Gil questioned if Kai could connect with anyone. He knew what he suspected his son of having: an antisocial personality disorder . . . in other words, a sociopath, but why did he think that? Because the kid was quiet? Kept to himself? Or because he brought the kid with him to torture a guy and Kai didn't hesitate, and even enjoyed it? For all Gil knew, Kai may have been trying to bond with him right now, through this act of violence. It was demented but possible. They had never built a tree house together or spent a weekend camping and fishing. This was the most personal thing the two of them had ever shared and probably would ever share, and that was truly fucked up.

Gil looked at his son with new affection and a bit of sorrow and regret as the boy lumbered out of the warehouse in his burnt-orange Abercrombie & Fitch T-shirt and black, skin-tight Aeropostale skinny jeans, looking like any teenage boy anywhere, except that there was a smear of blood on the T-shirt and Kai's eyes looked glassy and hollow. He had seen too much. At seventeen years old, he had already seen too much, lost his youth in one blood-soaked afternoon, and it was Gil's fault. This day would change Kai forever. It would change them both.

"We need to go shopping for some new shirts before we go home. These shirts need to go in the trash."

"Jesus! Is that you?" Kai said, as he climbed into the truck and the smell of fermented sweat assailed his nostrils.

"I accidentally left this T-shirt in my gym bag. It's probably been in there for a couple weeks."

"Aw! That smells awful!"

"Okay. I'm driving to the outlet mall right now."

"Ugh! They may not even let you in stores smelling like that, Dad. Open a window!"

"Is it really that bad?"

"Seriously?" Kai waved his hand in front of his face and then hung his head out the window.

Gil started to laugh, and Kai began laughing too. They chortled and snorted as the absurdity of it all overtook them.

"Come on. Give me a hug!" Gil said, wrapping his arms around Kai and pulling him tight.

"Ewww, don't! Awww! That's horrible! I can't breathe!" Kai said, desperately trying to pull away from his father. When Gil let him go, Kai stuck his head out the window again and panted like a dog.

"That wasn't funny! That was awful!" Kai said, in between laughter.

Gil laughed harder. Tears squeezed out the corners of his

eyes and his stomach ached. He started the car and together they pulled out of the parking lot and headed toward the freeway. Behind them, Little Eddie began to cry.

"Shit! I almost forgot about him. What do we do with him?"

Gil's laughter stopped. He reached up and adjusted the rearview mirror so he was looking directly at the kid's face. There was so much of Eddie in the child's features. Same slightly slanted eyes and high cheekbones but with skin that was slightly darker, owing to his mother's Cuban background, and full lips and curly hair that made him look more like a light-skinned black kid than Korean or Dutch or Cuban or Swedish or whatever else his parents were mixed with. His parents' nationalities had blended into a child that looked like it could have been Kai's younger brother. He could have been Gil's own son.

"Fuck." Myriad scenarios ran through Gil's head, but they all resulted in some type of injury to the kid or, at the very least, the possibility of it.

"We could leave him at a fire station or a hospital?"

"What?"

"In school, they told us that fire stations, police stations, and some hospitals are safe havens. You can legally drop an unwanted child off there and they take them in," Kai said.

Gil considered it. He remembered hearing something similar. "But someone would see us. They would have cameras or something. We'd get caught."

"Then we drop him off near there and tell him to walk in himself."

Gil shook his head. "He's only a year old. He can barely walk."

"If we drop him off close enough, he could make it. I think that's the best we can do."

He was right. This was the best plan. Anything else would end with one or both of them getting a lethal injection. Gil wished he hadn't brought Kai. He wished he hadn't gotten him involved. He hadn't been thinking straight. The idea of Eddie raping his daughter had clouded his judgment. Deep down, he'd been hoping Kai would stop him from doing anything too bad to Eddie. Instead, the boy had egged him on. When he first showed up at Eddie's door, he had intended to talk to him, get his version of the story, maybe kick his ass if he had to. Seeing the man's face, smiling, had set him off, enraged him. It had been all downhill from there. Nothing anyone could have said would have changed a thing. Once he threw that first punch, the rest had been inevitable.

"Okay. Let's find a fire station."

They drove around for twenty minutes before they found one nestled in a quiet residential area, where two guys and a kid would go unnoticed. It was across the street from a park where there were lots of kids playing, mothers and couples with strollers, people walking dogs. All of them were potential witnesses, but they were also the perfect camouflage. Gil wasn't sure if this was the best location or the worst.

"What do you think?" Kai asked.

"I don't know. Could be a lot of witnesses."

"We could park around the corner, by those trees," Kai said, pointing to a small copse of trees on the other side of the park, opposite the playground and slightly further away from the fire department. There was a small parking area there with six parking spaces, only two of which were occupied. Everyone else had parked in the larger parking lot closer to the community playground.

"That's a long way for Little Eddie to walk by himself," Gil said.

"Yeah, but it's the only place that isn't exposed and where there aren't a lot of people."

He was right. It was the only place they could let Little Eddie out of the car without being seen. Gil's head swiveled back and forth, scanning the park, the street, the sidewalk, checking to see if anyone was looking their way as he piloted the truck to a halt in the parking lot.

"Okay, let's get him out."

"He smells like shit!"

"Well, I'm sure that's exactly what happened. He's not potty-trained yet. Just get him out of his car seat."

Kai unstrapped Little Eddie from the seat and placed him down on the asphalt.

"How are the firemen going to know who he belongs to?"

Gil shook his head. "They probably won't. Not until Amy manages to track him down. They'll take him to Child Protective Services and he'll spend a few nights in foster care."

"What if she never finds him? I mean, what if no one ever realizes he's Little Eddie?" Kai looked genuinely concerned.

Gil felt bad for thinking the kid had no feelings. But he didn't have an answer either. Gil shrugged. "I guess we could write it on his clothes somewhere."

"Can't they match handwriting?"

Gil didn't know. "He'll be fine. Let's just send him over there before someone sees us."

Kneeling down so that he was eye to eye with Little Eddie, Gil pointed toward the fire station. "See that building over there? That's a firehouse. That's where firemen work. Mommy is waiting for you over there with the fire engine. You like fire engines?"

Little Eddie nodded.

Gil felt wretched, but he continued. "Run over there and the firemen will give you a ride on their fire truck and they'll take you to Mommy, but you have to be quick. Go ahead! Run!"

Gil aimed Little Eddie toward the fire station, and off he went. He and Kai watched the little toddler stumble across the field. The park seemed even bigger than it did before, watching Little Eddie waddle his way to the sidewalk and into the street. *The street!*

"He's going to cross the street!"

Gil started after him, but Kai held him back.

"Someone will see you. I'm sure he'll be okay. The cars will stop for a baby. There're hardly any cars on that road anyway. He won't get hit."

Gil watched with his heart in his throat as Little Eddie teetered out into the street . . . and a bright, canary yellow Hummer H2 came rolling down the road, just a hair over the twenty-five mph speed limit, still slow enough to stop, as long as the driver saw Little Eddie. The driver was a woman with bright red hair that had been dyed so many times it looked like cotton candy. Even from halfway across the park, Gil could tell she wasn't paying attention to the road. She was staring at something in her hand, probably a phone. She was probably texting some equally vapid friend. Gil thought how ironic it was that Hummers were such big, testosterone machines, yet he almost always saw women driving them. It was quite rare, in fact, to see a man driving one. Perhaps men were worried people would think they were overcompensating. Not worried enough to stop driving big Ford and Ram trucks with lift-kits on them though.

"Oh no."

She never hit the brakes. There was no squeal of tires. There was just that strangled cry and a thump like a vehicle bottoming out at the end of a driveway or coming off a curb. A dark smear stained the street. Silence rushed in, crushing the sounds of children's laughter that had echoed from the playground just moments before.

Gil turned away. "Let's go."

"Shouldn't we see if he's okay?" Kai asked.

"He isn't."

6.

As they had planned earlier, Gil and Kai drove to the outlet mall to buy new shirts. They wound up buying entire outfits. They drove all the way to Georgetown to dispose of their bloody clothes. They threw them into a drainage ditch. Gil hoped the steady stream of water trickling through it would wash away any evidence if anyone were to find them.

Father and son barely said a word to each other as they drove back home. Any pride they'd felt for doing what needed to be done to Eddie was lost when that Hummer rolled over Little Eddie's tiny body. The sound of that thud, Little Eddie's head hitting the bumper and falling under the wheels, that sound would haunt them both forever.

"W-what's Amy doing here? D-do-do you think she knows?" Kai stammered.

"How could she? If she knew what we did, the cops would already be here."

"Maybe they're on their way."

Gil looked up and down the lush, tree-lined street with the nearly identical brick and stucco houses. Kids played on the front lawn of one house. A man in his sixties applied coat after coat of wax to his aging Buick Regal. An overweight bleached blonde jogged by dragging a small, heavily panting collie. A Mexican couple pushed a stroller while their son, no older than five, teetered on a small bike with training wheels that were bent at such an angle that only one wheel touched at a time. A warm, moist breeze blew through the Monterrey oak in front of his house. A bird sang. All was calm.

"I don't think so, son. Just relax and don't say anything. Let me do all the talking."

Gil and his son stepped out of the truck and headed up the front walkway. Before he could put his key in the lock, the door opened. Natalie stood in the doorway with Amy. They were both smiling.

"It was all a mistake," Natalie said.

"What?" Gil asked. "What are you talking about?"

"Eddie didn't do anything. Selma made it up."

Gil's legs went weak. He put one hand against the red

brick veneer to steady himself. For a moment, everything threatened to go dark before coming back into vivid focus.

"What the fuck do you mean she made it up?"

Natalie visibly recoiled form the hostility in his voice. "She-she said Eddie didn't do anything. They just sat and watched cartoons all night. She made up everything about him touching her. I called Amy and told her what Selma said and she came right over and we asked her together. She said she made it all up. I tried to call you on your cell phone, but you wouldn't answer."

"I-I had it on silent."

Gil looked at his cell phone. There were eleven missed calls. "You sure she wasn't intimidated? Maybe she changed her mind because she didn't want to upset Amy?" Gil said.

Natalie shook her head. "I don't think so. You can ask her yourself, but it might just make her more confused."

Gil closed his eyes, tilted his head back, and ran both palms down his face. "Oh. My. God."

Natalie's smile faltered.

"What is it?" Amy said.

"But-but why? Why would she make something like that up?" Gil asked.

He turned and looked at Kai, who was standing directly behind him with a smug, arrogant grin on his face and he knew. He knew without the slightest shred of doubt. Kai had told her to say it. Gil's eyes were wide as his mind worked through the implications.

"Why? Why did you do this, Kai? Why?" He grabbed his son by the shirt and pushed him against the wall, slammed him against it.

"I wanted you to care," Kai said. Defiance bristled in his voice and in his furious eyes. "You haven't given a shit about this family in years. You work all day and then you spend half the night at the gym with Eddie. When you come home, you're too fucking tired for your own goddamn family! You eat and go straight to sleep. I wanted to see if you still gave a shit about us!"

"Where's Eddie?" Natalie asked.

Gil shook his head.

"I tried to tell you," Natalie whispered. Her voice was trembling now. Along with her bottom lip.

Gil let his son go and turned to the two women. A tear rolled from the corner of his left eye followed by one from his right. He wiped both away quickly.

"I-I did something terrible," Gil said. He thought about what happened to Little Eddie. He could still see the boy's little body going under the wheels of the bright yellow Hummer, the blood . . . and that sound. Gil dry heaved, remembering what he'd done to Eddie. He could taste his own bile scalding the back of his throat. He swallowed it down and shuddered. He wondered if Eddie was still alive. He hoped he wasn't. It would be easier for all of them if he was dead. Eddie's injuries were grotesque and painful, but Gil didn't know if they were life threatening. There was the risk of him dying from shock. He'd looked pretty bad when they'd left him. And if he did survive, he would probably be horribly disfigured, physically and emotionally. He'd never be the same again.

"Where's Eddie? Where's my husband? Where's Little Eddie?" Amy cried out, looking from Gil to Natalie to Kai and back to Gil.

"I did a terrible thing."

"What did you do? *What did you do?*" Amy cried. "*Where's my baby!*"

"I—" But there were no words.

Sins of the Father

Wrath James White and Sultan Z. White

*T*est. *T*est. *I am at One Schroeder Plaza in Boston, speaking with Officer Walter Knox of the Boston Police Department. Officer Knox was first on the scene at the horrific massacre at the Mercy General nursery. Can you describe what you saw, Officer Knox?*

It was fucking terrible! Excuse my French. This fucking nut job was just going from one bed to the next, twisting these babies' necks like he was slaughtering chickens. Little newborn babies! He bashed most of their skulls open with a fire extinguisher, and then I guess he got bored with that so he started strangling them with his bare hands. I didn't even know what I was seeing at first. He'd already killed two orderlies and three nurses who tried to stop him; he snapped their necks like he was doing to the babies. So the doctors, those fucking cowards, were just standing there outside the nursery, three of them, watching him murder those little newborn babies. Not doing shit to stop him. I mean, I know they were scared. That fucking lunatic had just murdered five people in front of them, but they could have, I don't know, they could have done something. Those fucking nurses, God rest their souls, were heroes. They tried to stop him. So, I shows up, and these doctors are standing outside the door to the nursery, watching this guy, and they point to him. I look in there and I see him holding this little baby. I feel terrible.

I just couldn't believe what was happening. He killed another baby while I was standing there like a fucking idiot trying to figure out what was going on. Then I took him down.

How?

I didn't bother going for the Taser or my baton, if that's what you're asking. I pulled my gun. And I was just hoping this piece of shit resisted. I was hoping he would go for the next baby, because I wanted to kill him so bad. I wanted to kill this fucking nut job so bad my dick was hard. I mean literally. I had an erection I was so hot to kill this piece of shit. You'll edit that part out right?

Sure. Then what happened?

The guy just smiles, puts both hands behind his head, and kneels down on the floor. And he's just staring me right in the eyes and smiling the entire time. I cracked him one. I kicked the crazy son of a bitch right in his smug little face. I couldn't help it. I didn't care who was watching. I just couldn't stand that crazy bastard staring at me like that.

And how did he react?

He didn't. Crazy fuck never stopped smiling. His nose was busted and blood was running down his face, turning his teeth red, and he just kept fucking grinning at me. I tell ya, it made my fucking skin crawl. I cuffed him, and me and my partner, Vinnie, hustled him out of there as fast as we could. You want to know something crazy? When I said he was going from bed to bed, killing those little babies one after another, that wasn't entirely correct. He skipped some of them. It was like he was choosing between them. I talked to Detective Monroe, and he said there was no similarity between the ones he killed. You know, he wasn't picking them based on race or gender or anything like that. He killed white, black, Asian, Hispanic, red-haired, blonde, brunette, blue-eyed, green-eyed, brown-eyed little girls, boys. It didn't seem to matter. You know, these kind of nuts usually have a type they go for. Not this guy. But what he did say is that the ones he didn't kill all looked the same. Black hair. Dark brown, almost black eyes.

Just like him.

Yeah. Just like him.

How has this affected you, Officer Knox?

You mean mentally? They made me go see a shrink. It's standard procedure after something like this, but you just tell those guys what they want to hear and they clear you. But I still have nightmares. About the babies. You know what I dream about the most?

What?

That one baby. The last one he killed. The one he murdered while I was standing there, just staring at him, before I pulled my gun. I thought it was a doll. It was so small. I didn't know it was a baby. I mean, who would think someone would do that? Who would expect to see something like that? He saw me. That fucking lunatic saw me. He made eye contact. And that's when he first started smiling. He was smiling, looking me right in the eyes, while he wrung that little baby's neck. I still have nightmares about that.

Bush Correctional Institution. First interview with Adam Horrowitz, convicted serial murderer. The date is July 9, 2014.

How are you today, Adam?

Are you flirting with me? You want a date?

What? No.

Are we going to be neighbors? Are you looking for a friend?

No.

Then let's forget about the small talk. Agreed?

Agreed. Point taken. So, how about you just tell me about yourself. Tell me about your parents. What was it like for you growing up?

It is a cliché to blame all my crimes on bad parenting. I know. It makes me sound like I'm trying to avoid taking personal responsibility for my actions. I am not. I know what I did. I also know that I would not, could not, have done any of it were it not for my father.

My father believed that it was his, that it was every father's responsibility to make sure his son was a better man than he was. A noble sentiment, but my father took it too far. He was not content to simply provide me with a better education, a better upbringing, better job opportunities. He wanted more. See, my father was a biological engineer. Starting to get the picture? He didn't believe that nurturing alone was the key to better parenting. For him, a better child meant better genes. So he went directly to the heart of the matter. He began "improving" my DNA, altering my genetic code.

I remember hearing him lament marrying for love. He said it was selfish. That he had failed me in this regard. He should have married the woman who would have given him the best genetic offspring. My mother was short, of average intelligence, average educational achievement, slightly above-average looks but no beauty queen. That's where my father believed he had failed me. He thought he should have married a woman who was tall, athletic, with above-average intelligence and beauty. It was an insult to my mother, who was perfect to me, but I said nothing in her defense, and this is where I take full responsibility. I never spoke up for myself. I never told my father to stop. I let him do whatever he wanted to me. See, I didn't want to disappoint him. I guess part of me wanted to be the superman he always told me he would make me, stronger than a locomotive, faster than a speeding bullet, smarter than Einstein. I wanted it too. Who wouldn't? And I trusted my father implicitly.

It was not just a matter of trust. That makes me sound like some naive patsy. We both know that was not the case. The real reason I let him do all those things to me was that I was afraid, afraid of disappointing him. To say he would have been disappointed were I ever to object to one of his experiments, if I had told him I was happy with who I was and didn't need any more "improvements" is an understatement. He would have been appalled. To him, it would have been the same as someone who was desperately poor turning down a million dollars. And I do believe that is how he saw me, at least in the genetic sense: desperately poor.

So what exactly did he do to you?

I'll get to that. This is my story, and if you don't mind, I'd like to tell it my way. You need to know who my father was as a person if you're going to write my story. I could sell this story to anyone, you know? I know everyone's curious. The whole world wants to know what I am, what I can do, why I did what I did. I get their letters. Scientists. Psychologists. Journalists. I chose you because of that article you wrote about designer genes in *Scientific Discovery*. It showed not just an understanding of the science but of the motivations behind it. And that's why you have to hear the entire story, to understand my father's motivations as well as my own, because, after all, we are co-conspirators, my father and I. In the same way Dr. Frankenstein was complicit in his creature's crimes.

Can I ask one question before you get into the rest of your story? It will help give me the proper perspective, I believe, as I listen. (He slid a newspaper over to me. The headline read THIRTEEN INFANTS KILLED IN HOSPITAL NURSERY RAMPAGE.) Why murder? Why did you murder all those innocent people? Men, women, children? Why?

When most parents look at their children, all they see is perfection. They don't see the asymmetries and abnormalities. All they see is beauty, no matter how ugly their child truly is. Not my father. All he saw when he looked at me was something imperfect, something that needed to be fixed. There are at least a billion parents who would have looked at me and seen a perfect, beautiful child, but not my father. After he had changed me, I began seeing things through his eyes. When I looked at the rest of humanity, I saw all the flaws and imperfections.

Do you know the first thing a male lion does when he takes over a pride and becomes the new alpha male? He kills all the cubs sired by the former head of the pride. Do you suppose that when *Homo sapiens* supplanted Neanderthal man as the new dominant human species, Neanderthals simply took their inferior genes and shuffled off quietly? Or do you imagine there was wholesale warfare, an epic slaughter? Do you imagine *Homo sapiens* completely wiped out their inferior brothers, a mass genocide of Neanderthals on a scale that would have made the Holocaust look like a post office shooting? You see, in order for my genetic line to survive and flourish, your flawed, imperfect genetic line must end. You all must die. But again, we are jumping ahead. Let me tell you about my father.

My father was not a perfect man. His imperfections were his own personal obsession that he'd spent a lifetime trying to overcome. From track to gymnastics to boxing and wrestling, he'd tried and failed to excel in athletics even as he made a name for himself in science and academics, winning awards and research grants over scientists decades his senior. But this was not enough. He threw himself into art and music with the same zeal with which he'd attacked athletics, with similar results. He spent more than a decade laboring at the piano and the violin and nearly as much time smearing oils and watercolors over a canvas. He even wrote several dozen abysmal poems before conceding defeat somewhere in my tenth or eleventh year of life. I can still recall the joy I felt at no longer having to watch him curse and swear over some hideous mockery of a landscape or having to cover my ears as he drudged his way through Beethoven or Mozart, making a soulless cacophony on the piano. That was, until he refocused his obsession with perfection on me.

My father could not accept his limitations. He could not

accept the idea of limitations as a human condition. He believed deep in his soul that anything could be achieved with hard work, that a man's will could bend and shape time and space. He believed in the limitless potential of the human spirit. In that sense, he was an idealist, a romantic, you might say. His perfect human was intellectually, creatively, physically, and aesthetically gifted, Nietzsche's the Übermensch. It tortured him that he had only mastered the intellectual, but I believe his greatest disappointment was his appearance, his eyes.

My father had been brought up on westerns. His childhood heroes were hard, chiseled cowboys with piercing eyes and square jaws. Then he looked in the mirror and saw a round-faced boy with sad, puppy-dog eyes that seemed to predict the worst possible fate, instead of the fierce, confident eyes of a warrior. That was the first thing he changed about me. My appearance.

Isolating the precise strand of DNA that controls such things as symmetry, hair color, eye color and shape, and even height, weight, and bone structure, that was brilliant. Do you have any idea how difficult that is? There are more than twenty thousand genes in the human genome. In order to identify those genes specifically associated with something like bone structure or height you need to compare genetic differences among individuals. Then, once you have found the gene that makes one person tall and another short, one with high cheekbones and a strong jaw and another with a weak chin, you need to isolate it. Do you know what years of study have determined to be the perfect face? An oval face. Why? Because it is symmetrical. Humans are drawn to symmetry. An oval face will have wider cheekbones and then narrow down to the jaw line and chin. Oval faces will narrow up toward the forehead. There are ten hallmarks of physical beauty across all times and cultures. Big eyes, small nose, tall and lean, well-defined muscles or an hourglass figure with breasts proportional to the hips and a small waist if you are a female, symmetrical face and body, thick hair, large hands, smooth, glowing, blemish-free skin, full lips, light skin with dark eyes, or light eyes with tan skin. In other words, me.

You are quite handsome. Are you claiming your father did all this? You mean to say he changed your face and body?

You don't understand. I am not merely handsome. My features are perfectly symmetrical. Look at my eyes. The vertical distance between them and my mouth is approximately 36 percent of my face's length, and the horizontal distance between my eyes is approximately 46 percent of my face's width. My head is exactly five-and-a-half inches from ear to ear and seven inches long from hairline to chin. There are two-and-a-half inches between my eyes and another two-and-a-half inches between my mouth and my pupils. It is what they call "the golden ratio." That ratio represents the ideal human facial proportions across all cultures.

Why was that so important to your father? Something like beauty would seem to be beneath someone of your father's genius. It seems trivial, even a bit shallow.

That's because you buy into all that liberal bullshit about beauty being in the eye of the beholder, of social and cultural biases that are forced upon us rather than an inherent part of our nature. Everything in our culture is determined by beauty, from the car you drive, the house you buy, your clothes, and even your job prospects. How many beautiful homeless people do you know? The economic, social, romantic, and even political opportunities are exponentially higher for more attractive people.

Those who are born with all the universal hallmarks of beauty—tall, lean, muscular, perfectly symmetrical faces and bodies—are inherently adored. They are trusted and admired. We elect them to rule us. We pay for them to entertain us. We idolize them and try to emulate them. They are our leaders, our gods. Did you know there were two studies conducted in the mid-1980s that independently demonstrated that infants as young as two- and three-months old stared longer at symmetrical faces, faces you and I would consider the most attractive? More recent experiments with newborns less than one week old show significantly greater preference for faces with a higher degree of symmetry. Another study showed that twelve-month-old infants exhibited more observable pleasure, smiling, giggling, a higher degree of attentiveness and involvement, less distress, and less withdrawal when interacting with strangers wearing attractive masks than when interacting with strangers wearing unattractive masks. They also play significantly longer with facially attractive dolls than with facially unattractive dolls. No matter how much we may want to believe beauty is subjective, studies have shown again and again than it can be reduced to a simple matter of mathematical symmetry. Newborns and infants have not had time to learn and internalize cultural or media-created standards of beauty. What these studies suggest is a human genetic predisposition to beauty, to symmetry. We worship and adore it because we are instinctively programmed to do so. In that case, the perfect man must be beautiful as well as intelligent and powerful.

Okay, so how did he do it? How did he get these genes into your system to change your physical appearance?

He injected them. He isolated the genes he wanted and injected the DNA directly into my skin cells, bone marrow, intramuscularly. He even injected DNA into my brain cells.

You're talking about naked DNA?

Yes.

You are aware there are no studies that show direct injections of naked DNA into a fully formed, mature adult as having any significant effect whatsoever? There has been some minimal success with treating cancer with naked DNA, but even this is highly controversial. As far as altering the DNA of mature cells, there has been no proof that injecting DNA leads to this type of gene expression.

I am the evidence.

How so? How else do you believe these treatments changed you?

How didn't it? I am stronger, faster, smarter than a normal human. I told you about the brain injections?

Yes.

Well, the day after he began the injections, I could already feel myself changing. I could read a book and retain everything. I understood things more clearly and I could read people's minds.

What? Did you say—

Telepathy. Yes. I could hear what people were thinking.

Can you still? (Smirking)

Yes.

What am I thinking?

You are thinking about your pregnant wife. You're wondering if you will be a good father. If it will be a boy or a girl. You are concerned about your marriage and what will happen to your child if you were to ever get divorced. You can't wait to get this interview over with so you can go be with her right now. I believe you have an ultrasound appointment.

Wrong. (Squirms uncomfortably in his chair and begins gathering his things.)

Am I?

Yes. (Turns recorder off.)

Testing. Testing. Second interview with Adam Horrowitz, convicted serial murderer. The date is July 10, 2014. The time is 4:10pm. We are at the Bush Maximum Security Correctional Facility.

How are you today, Adam?

Fine.

Yesterday we were talking about the injections your father gave you.

Yes.

Can we talk some more about those?

What would you like to hear?

The injections must have been painful.

Yes. Very.

But you never protested?

No.

How old were you when the experiments began?

I must have been twelve. Maybe thirteen.

Twelve?

Maybe. Maybe thirteen.

That must have been hard, being subjected to these painful treatments at such a young age.

It was necessary. I won't say it was for the good of humanity. My father did it for me.

Tell me about your first murder?

You mean murders? Or do you mean what I experienced in the minutes between when I murdered that first inferior creature and the second, third, fourth, and fifth? They were all pretty much the same, part and parcel of the same holistic experience.

Your first murders were at the fertility clinic?

Yes.

Why there?

Because they were reproducing, spreading their inferior genes.

How do you know they were inferior?

Because they weren't me. I am the only perfect human. I am the alpha male.

And these men were challenging you?

No. They couldn't possibly have challenged me. They were spreading their genes. I wanted to spread mine. They were in the way so I removed them.

How old were you at this time?

I had just turned twenty-one.

How did you kill them?

I was at the fertility clinic—
To donate sperm?
Yes. To donate sperm. There were five other guys there. The room was very clean and formal. That's what struck me. It looked like a furniture showroom. The couches and chairs were new. There was a tall fern in the corner, two high-def TVs on the walls at both ends of the room, one playing sports and the other playing soap operas, a coffee maker that also made espresso, and the usual coffee tables, of course. There were pamphlets on in vitro fertilization and the freezing of sperm and ovum for later use, right next to maternity and gardening magazines. There were a few sports magazines for us guys and a *Wall Street Journal*. The carpet was plush with thick padding. That place must have made millions.

I looked around at the guys there waiting to donate sperm. They had us in a different waiting room than the one for the women and couples who came there for fertilization services. That would have been awkward otherwise, don't you think?
I'd imagine.
I could hear their thoughts.
Whose thoughts?
The other guys there to donate. I could hear everything that went through their silly, untidy, disordered minds. Two of them were graduate students, donating sperm to make a little extra beer money. One was a lawyer who just liked the idea of dozens of little "hims" running around. It was an ego boost and yes, I am aware of the irony. One was a guy donating sperm for a lesbian couple who wanted to have a child, and the other was a serial donator who came in three times a week. He was a recent high school graduate and first-year psychology student who was convincing himself that he was doing it as research for some future thesis, but he was really just sick of eating Ramen noodles and frozen pizza and saw this as a way to combat the usual student poverty.

As was to be expected, they were all taller than six feet

and relatively attractive. All but one was white. The other was an Asian man. They all came close to the idealized standard of beauty—tall, lean, and relatively proportionate. But they all had flaws. One had a nose that was too large for his face. The Asian had one eye that opened wider than the other. The blond, the lawyer, had ears that were too large for his head. Another had unusually small hands for a man, women's hands. These flaws alone didn't mark them as inferior. It was their vain, petty, selfish, and immature thoughts. None of them had ambitions that went beyond buying a smartphone, HD TV, or sports car, the best way to cheat on the next midterm exam, or what job or client would make them the most money. Do you think any of them would contribute in any significant way to the advancement of humanity? Do you think the cure for cancer was sitting in one of their heads? The end of world hunger? The solution for world peace? Do you think any of them even cared about any of that? They were all pathetic.

I watched all five of them, studying their mannerisms, listening to their conversation, sizing them up. Obviously I couldn't kill them right there, but I had already decided they had to be eliminated. I could not allow their ridiculous gene lines to survive and flourish. First I had to kill them, and then I had to return and destroy all of their "donations."

I engaged them all in conversation. You may not know this, but before my father's treatments, I was painfully shy. Since the improvements, I was a master conversationalist. These guys were easy and our shared experiences made finding common ground simple. I plucked the one thought going through all their minds.

"I hope they have good porn in there."

That's all I needed; they took it from there.

"Hell yeah!" the two graduate students said.

"I heard it was all pretty vanilla," the lawyer said.

"Really? Shit. I was hoping for something a bit more hardcore," the freshman said.

"Hey, ever seen those bukakke videos?" the Asian guy whispered, looking around as if afraid his mom would overhear him.

"Hell yeah! Like German Goo Girls? That shit is crazy! That would do it for me."

"I bring my own," the frequent flyer said, holding up a DVD with the title *2013 Cum Shots.*

"Are there really 2,013 cum shots?" I asked.

He shrugged.

"How the fuck would I know? I never make it past the first twenty or thirty."

Everyone laughed.

"What's your name, man? My name's Adam."

"I'm Kent."

"Brad. Pleased to meet you, Adam."

"Name's Roger."

"Charles. Good to meet you, Adam."

"My name's Henry," the lawyer said, holding out his hand for everyone to shake.

I obliged him, putting on the warmest smile I could fake. "So what brings you all here," I asked, and then listened to them all lie.

All except the guy who was here donating his sperm for the lesbian couple. He was the only one who told the truth.

I invited them all out for a drink afterward. To celebrate our immaculate conceptions. They all laughed and pretty soon I had talked them into meeting me at a bar around the corner.

One by one we were called up and ushered into different rooms for a physical, a blood test, a semen sample (to make sure we had swimmers), and then into the little room with the TV, the stack of porn DVDs, and the wet wipes. The porn was as vanilla as the lawyer had said and it took me quite a while to get in the mood staring at women with fake tits, letting out fake moans, as they faked orgasms. Finally I filled my specimen jar and left. You want to know what finally did it for me?

What?

Imagining killing those assholes. Of course, the things I imagined doing to them were far too extravagant for me to ever really do, but it was all fantasy. Just to help me fill the cup.

When I was done, I raced out to the lobby. I thought about driving somewhere, to a gun store or even a cutlery store. See, I didn't exactly carry lethal weapons around with me. Not back then anyway. All I had was my genetically enhanced strength, and I decided that would have to do. There was no time to buy a weapon. I was afraid some of them, or all of them, would leave.

The bar was only three blocks away. I walked there. I didn't want anyone to get my license plate and connect me to the place where I was planning my minor massacre. If I needed to make a quick getaway, I would simply take one of my victims' car keys.

When I arrived, three of the guys were already there. They cheered as I entered and asked me what kind of beer I wanted. I ordered a martini that I sipped for most of the night. Alcohol muddles the mind. I wanted mine clear. The lawyer kept buying everyone rounds, and when the two grad students arrived, he started ordering shots of tequila for everyone, showing off, flaunting his money, trying to purchase our friendship the way he'd purchased his $2,000 watch or the $300 jeans he wore. But he was making my job easier. By the time the Asian guy, Brad, left, he could barely stand. He was my first kill.

I excused myself to use the restroom and then followed him to his car. I had to dispatch him quickly. He smiled when he saw me behind him. Brad waved at me. He was happy to see me. "What's up, dude?"

I looked around. It was already getting dark by that point, and he had done me a favor by parking by the back fence where there was no light. I was sure no one could see us. I smiled.

"I forgot to tell you something," I said, and then I punched him as hard as I could.

I felt the jolt travel up my arm at the moment of impact, and he just dropped like he'd been short circuited. I picked him up. Picked up his keys. Unlocked his car door, and dragged him inside. If someone had spotted me at that point, he or she would have thought I was just helping a drunk friend into his car.

Once we were in the car, I pressed my thumbs into his eyes, puncturing them into his brain. He screamed and fought for a couple of seconds before falling silent. Those screams. How do I describe them? They were the most terrified sounds I'd ever heard. Shrill, piercing. He even sobbed. It was like the cries of a child knowing his father was coming to punish him.

I had never felt so powerful before.

I could hear his thoughts slipping away. Once he stopped screaming, once he knew he was dead, the fear lessened. That was the peculiar thing. He was at peace even as I dug my thumbs into his brain matter. The things he lamented were as trivial and petty as you would have expected. Never getting married or having kids or buying a house. Never having the opportunity to visit Europe. Pathetic.

I checked for a pulse. None. I wiped my bloody hands off on his clothes and walked casually back to the bar. But not before checking his vehicle for some kind of weapon to use against the others. Nothing. I hoped the two grad students didn't leave together. That was going to be hard.

The freshman kid left next. I was waiting for him. I pulled him into Brad's car and choked him unconscious on the back seat and then held my arm across his throat, squeezing until he stopped breathing. I held the choke until I was certain he was dead and then shoved his body down behind the front seats. I was practically panting. My head felt light. The exertion and the adrenalin rush were taking their toll. My nerves were jangling like live wires when I walked back into the bar.

"Where'd you go, man? We thought you left."

"I helped Brad into a taxi. He was way too drunk to drive."

"Yeah, I'm getting pretty wasted myself. I've got to try a case in the morning. Big corporate finance scandal. I can't talk about it, but I'll bet all of you have their products in your homes right now."

"Hey, thanks for the shots, man. Are you guys going to stick around for a while?" I asked the two graduate students. "Next round's on me."

"Hell yeah, then."

"Let me walk Henry to his car. I need to ask him something. Don't worry, I'm not going to hit you up for free legal advice. I just want to see if you think I need to hire a lawyer and if this is something you would handle or maybe you could recommend an attorney."

Henry squinted suspiciously at me, but then his ego took over and he shook his head and smiled. "Sure, Adam. Let's talk. What've you got goin' on?"

We headed toward the parking lot. "My father is a genetic engineer."

"Uh huh."

"He has isolated a few strands of DNA. My DNA. He has found, for example, the exact genetic strand that determines an individual's height. This is a find that could make him millions. The problem is that a recent Supreme Court ruling determined that you can't patent genes. I'd like to challenge that ruling."

"Wow. That's a pretty big case. Going up against the Supreme Court. That's . . . wow. You said it could be worth millions?"

"Hundreds of millions. Here. Walk with me to my car. I'm leaving too."

It was too easy. I knew exactly what bait to set to lure him in. Money. That's all it took. He followed me to the back of the parking lot, to Brad's car. Again, I looked around to see if anyone was watching us, but it was completely dark by now.

This one didn't go as smoothly. Henry was a fighter, and he knew some kind of martial arts. Jiu-jitsu, I think. I punched him hard in the jaw. I felt it unhinge. I was pretty sure it was broken. He staggered but didn't drop. I tackled him, tried to lift him off his feet, take him to the ground, so I could get an arm around his throat and choke him out. It wasn't that easy. Henry knew what he was doing.

We scuffled there between two parked cars. I punched him several more times, splitting his nose and swelling his left eye. He never yelled for help, never screamed. He was confident right up to the end that he could take me. He almost did.

He had his legs around my neck and was hyperextending my arm in some combination—I've since learned—of a triangle choke and an arm bar, when I picked him up and slammed him down on the concrete. He almost broke my arm before I bashed his head open on the ground. His head struck one of those little concrete parking curbs and blood sprayed from the wound. His eyes rolled up in his head. The whites of his eyes shined in the moonlight. I grabbed him by the head and smashed his skull onto the curb again and again until it split open. His brains spilled out like someone had broken a casserole dish filled with spaghetti. That's what it looked like to me, anyway. Like spaghetti.

I sat there for a moment, trying to catch my breath. I considered just leaving him lying there. I was so tired by this point. But those two students. There was no way I could let those two idiots live. Besides, fighting and beating Henry had been so satisfying. I was ready to take on those two guys.

I searched Henry for his keys after I dragged him into Brad's car, and then I went to his car, a red Jaguar convertible, and searched it for weapons. I found the gun in the glove box. A couple was climbing into the big SUV parked next to it. They were a professional couple. You know the type. They probably met at work and started a kind of office flirtation that had just now blossomed into some drunken romance. They both looked over at me as I pulled the Glock 9mm out and shoved it in my waistband. I smiled at them and waved, hoping they hadn't seen the gun. I considered shooting them both. The only thing that prevented me was the noise and the very high likelihood of being caught, and I still needed to kill the two grad students and get back to the sperm bank to destroy all those donations and replace them. The couple smiled back at me and gave me a halfhearted wave that likely saved both their lives.

The two grad students, Roger and Charles, were both staggering off their bar stools when I walked back into the bar.

"Sorry I took so long. You guys still up for that drink?" I smiled excitedly and I could see them hesitating, considering it.

"Naw, we both have classes tomorrow. Fucking Saturday classes."

"No problem. I understand. Hey, can you guys give me a lift back to my car? I left it back at the clinic."

I patted them both on the back and draped an arm around their shoulders, warm, friendly, inviting.

"Sure."

The minute we were out of the parking lot, I pulled the gun. I ordered them onto a side street. I wanted them off the main street where they might be able to signal a passing cop.

"We don't have any money, bro," Roger offered immediately.

"I've got $20," Charles said. "It's yours, dude. Just don't hurt us."

I didn't reply. I just aimed the gun at his forehead and pulled the trigger. I blew the entire top of his head off. Blood sprayed the windshield, the passenger window, me, and Roger. The sound of the gun going off inside the small car was deafening. My ears rang. Roger was freaking out. He tried to get out of the car while it was still moving. I grabbed him by the back of his shirt, pulled him into the car, and shot him in the back of the head. The bullet exited through his face and shattered the windshield.

I reached over, put the car in park, and then hopped out to walk back to the clinic. I was only a couple of blocks away. I wiped off the gun and the one door handle I had touched and left the gun in the car. I didn't need it anymore. It would just be more evidence. The reality was, even my prints would be useless. I wasn't in the system anywhere. I had to be arrested for something before they could find a match.

The clinic was closed when I made it back. I broke in after doing a search on my smartphone on how to disable alarm systems. I was able to find information on the exact brand and model the clinic used. I shut it down in fewer than five minutes and picked the back door lock in fewer than two. Then I spent the next two hours destroying and replacing sperm samples. I don't know what I would have done without Kent's DVD. You know, there really were 2,013 cum shots on there.

This is the first interview with Maria Horrowitz, mother of convicted serial murderer Adam Horrowitz. We are at her private residence. The date is July 15, 2014.

Can you tell us a bit about Adam's childhood? Tell us about his father. All we have is Adam's recount of his father, who seems a bit cruel, though Adam doesn't seem to think so. Maybe you can paint a better picture of your husband. (He shuffles through his bag, takes out some pocket tissues, and hands them over.) Here, these will help. Wipe your tears. Take your time. When you are ready, tell me.

I don't want anyone to sympathize with my husband. If anyone deserves sympathy, it would be me. Me. You know I've always wanted another child, right?

I was raised Catholic. My parents were strict, always enforcing their traditional values. I never thought there could ever be parents worse than them. When I turned eighteen I left the house and the religion, almost certain I'd never look back. If I ever acted in a way that my parents or God, apparently, didn't agree with, I'd get beat. So I received a ton of beatings. More than I'd care to remember. I grew up hating God, in all his hypocrisy and evilness, and envied my friends at school with atheist or nonreligious parents. I promised myself I'd never raise my child Catholic. I thought there was nothing worse. I was wrong.

When I was young, I fell in love with a scientist, Victor. He was so charming. He swept me off my feet. I knew he was the one, so I married him, without my parents' blessing.

When I was pregnant, we agreed he'd handle raising the child. I didn't want any influences from my upbringing affecting how I raised my own kid. So I let him take care of it. That was my first mistake. I shouldn't have given him that much control. It ended up taking over his life. He became obsessed with making little Adam the best he could be. It was awful. He was always doing these experiments on him. Oh, I couldn't explain them in the least to you. It was all way over my head. I just knew Adam would always run into my arms crying. He was so young.

Victor made me do something I thought I'd never do again. I started going back to church. I needed to get out of the house. I needed an escape. I fell back to my roots. I turned to God. For a long time, God had no answers. He was silent. But then he told me to bear another child. That it would complete the family and save Victor from his spell, his evolutionist nightmare. It's funny how God told me that. I remember I used to draw pictures in my diary when I was a child of my future self, living in a big house with a loving husband and two kids.

When I proposed the idea to my husband, he was outraged. Of course, I never revealed I was going back to church because then he might have actually hit me. Every time I'd bring up the idea of having another kid, he'd throw a fit. We'd argue for hours. He'd yell at me, saying I wasn't beautiful enough, smart enough, strong enough to bring another being into this world, and that it was selfish of me to even think of it. He'd curse himself, that he wasn't perfect enough. That he would always be doomed to create babies with the same faults as his. He refused.

This is the man I loved, that I thought was the greatest person to enter my life, and he dismissed himself as if he were the world's litter. I am the woman he loved, the object of his fantasies and desires, and he scorned me like I was just some filthy slut looking for a lay. And poor Adam would sit and listen to us argue, and as time went on, I think he began convincing himself that he was ugly, dumb, weak, and needed to be fixed. As time went on, he began allowing his father to experiment on him. He didn't argue. He never disagreed with his father.

It was terrible. I stopped having sex with Victor. I figured that if he didn't do what I wanted, I wouldn't do what he wanted. And that bastard hated me for holding out on him. If he was so fixed on the natural order of things, that religion is unnatural, then why wouldn't he create life with me? That's the most natural thing there is. Contraceptives and birth control are artificial, manmade. Just like religion. The hypocrisy goes both ways. But men will be men. They only have one thing on their mind, those animals. Our relationship was stripped of all love, only held together by the mutual desire to care for Adam, and the not-so-mutual desire to fuck. Every night at ten o'clock, Victor would stand next to me at the bathroom sink, arms folded, foot tapping, and watch me as I swallowed down my birth control pill. Some nights he'd lead me to the bed, slowly sliding the bands of my nightgown off my shoulder, as he pulled down his underwear. He'd always keep his shirt on because he was self-conscious of his scrawny physique. There was a time when I loved him and didn't care about his appearance. But he ruined that feeling. He'd whisper things to get me in the mood. But not like he used to when we were young lovers. He'd whisper that it was my wifely duty, that I was expected to sleep with him if I truly loved him. He sounded exactly how my dad did to my mom. There was no difference between that radical Catholic man and this radical Darwinist man. He'd pretend to love me only when he wanted to get into my pants. But I wouldn't fall for his advances anymore. The foreplay was forced and there was no fire in the bed. I couldn't get wet for him anymore. He'd make me suck him off, either that or he'd lather himself with the strawberry lubricant he kept in his nightstand drawer. Then we'd have bland, impassionate sex for a couple of minutes.

I'll censor that part.

No, I want you to publish it. I want to humiliate my husband. He deserves it. Just like I was humiliated in front of all my church friends.

How did he humiliate you? If you don't mind my asking.

I started replacing my birth control with placebos. Eventually I was blessed with the second child I always wanted. At first I was afraid to tell Victor. But I finally worked up the courage to tell him. I thought he'd understand, be kind again. When I told him about Adam, my first pregnancy, he was so happy he almost cried. I expected the same reaction. But this time was different.

"How could you?" he screamed. "How could you be so selfish?"

I couldn't respond. I couldn't believe he could hate something most people would consider a miracle.

He trudged over to the bathroom and ripped apart the packaging to my birth control. "Where is the phone number to this damn company? I'm suing." He had so much trust in modern science, it was almost cute. He always insisted on finishing inside me, it was some weird fetish of his. I would have gotten pregnant sooner or later. He was so naive for how smart he claimed to be.

"It was me. Not the company."

He fumbled with the folded up white paper with the instructions. "What? No, I watched you take them. We followed the directions precisely."

"No, I've been replacing the pills with sugar pills. I haven't been on birth control for a while now." It was too late to take back my words.

He grabbed me by the wrist and dragged me through the house. I was glad Adam was at school and didn't see his father act like that. His grip was tight and left my skin red when he let go like it was sunburned. He dragged me out to the car, opened the passenger side door, and tossed me in.

"We're going to the abortion clinic." He started the car and backed it out of the driveway before I could voice an opinion.

"What? No, baby, no!" I remember holding my belly, even though there was no noticeable size to it yet. "I can't!"

"Well, you damn sure are!"

He drove silently, ignoring my protests, just staring out of the windshield.

We arrived at ABC Women's Help Center. "Get out."

"Let's talk about this first," I begged.

"Get. Out."

He yanked the parking brake and then folded his arms over his chest, just like he did when he waited for me to swallow the birth control. He had no intention of leaving. At least not until the mistake was removed from my body.

I quickly walked across the sidewalk with my head down. This was against my moral code. I was a God-fearing woman. I was being forced to sin.

When I entered the clinic, the stale scent of an overly sanitized hospital room hung drearily in the air. The waiting room was typical, office chairs lined the wall, fake plants, old magazines. No one else was there, so I walked directly to the woman at the reception desk.

"Maria?" the woman asked.

"How did you know my . . . oh my god!" It was a woman

from my church. I'd seen her every Sunday. What was she doing here?

"You've come to get an abortion?" She spoke carefully, almost hesitantly.

"Yes. Yes I have."

The woman looked down and sighed. She looked disappointed. "Come with me," she said.

There was something off about the clinic. I didn't get it right away, so I let her lure me into the back room. I walked down a hallway with other patients' rooms, and it looked like an average doctor's office.

A doctor greeted me at the end of the hall. He looked strangely familiar. He asked me to take off my pants and wait for him inside the room. I really didn't know what was going on. It didn't even click that it wasn't common procedure—no paperwork signed or anything. I was still shocked that my own husband had kicked me to the curb in front of this damned place. So I did what the doctor told me.

"The nurse will be with you shortly," he said. I undressed and waited on the bed.

The same woman at the receptionist desk walked in. No nurse uniform. Nothing. She picked my pants and underwear off the floor without a word and left. It wasn't until she locked the door that I realized where I was. ABC Women's Help Center. I knew the name sounded odd. I read an article about places like this once. They're fake abortion clinics run by pro-life fanatics. They build their centers around actual abortion clinics in hopes that women accidentally stumble into the wrong building. They usually name their center with a beginning letter of the alphabet so they are in the front of all the phone books. It's all a ploy so that when the unsuspecting women walk in, they can bombard them with their religious propaganda, false scientific studies, and "slut-shaming" schemes.

I shuffled uncomfortably in my seat, looking for something to cover my naked lower body with. Before I could find anything, more people entered the small room. They were all people I knew, or at least recognized from the church I attended. I was scared.

Do you want to know what happened next?

Yes. (He leaned forward in his seat.)

They all fucking harassed me. They forced me to watch a hideous video of dead babies, aborted fetuses, some late-term abortions with the babies still moving after they were aborted. It was disgusting. And they were shouting at me the whole time.

"Whore!"

"Slut!"

"You'll go to hell for this!"

"You're a traitor!"

"Sinner!"

"Skank!"

"How could you murder your own child? You evil woman!"

Okay. I get it. (He takes back his pocket tissues, wipes the spit from his face, and then leans back into his seat.)

Sorry about that. I just got a little emotional.

No worries. I completely understand. Please, continue. What happened next?

Okay. Let me think. Oh, yes. The woman who took my pants, she wouldn't give them back. Instead, she thrust a clipboard into my face with an agreement on it. They wanted me to agree to carry out my pregnancy until the end. They wanted to legally bind me to birthing my child. And they wouldn't give me my pants back until I signed it. At that point, I wasn't sure whether to agree with them or not. I knew I wanted to have my child, if not to save my husband then at least to spite him. But after what they did to me, these people, who just a few months prior took me back into their church, into the religion with open arms, how they could treat me with such cruelty. Why would I ever want to bend to their will after that?

I slapped the clipboard from her arms, pushed her aside, and ran through the group. I kicked open the door and ran half-nude and crying down the hallway. When I made it outside, I was actually relieved to see my husband. I covered my private parts with my hands as best I could and tiptoed across the sidewalk barefoot. I climbed into the car and wrapped my arms around Victor. But he shrugged me off. I was still crying, but he didn't wipe my tears away. He didn't seem to care that I was scared, confused. He didn't even seem to care that other men saw me naked.

"What?" he said.

"Baby, it was horrible. That's a fake abortion clinic!"

"I know." His face bore no emotion. "I wanted you to feel the pain of your mistake."

I froze. I had no words. I just stared at the man who called himself my husband.

"I know you've been sneaking off to church every Sunday morning. Those are the people you call your friends. They are ridiculous. Evil."

He put the car in drive, drove a block to the real abortion clinic, and then parked right in front. He took the keys out of the ignition and folded his arms over his chest. "Get out."

Testing, one, two, three. This is the first interview with Scott McNeil, the warden at Bush Correctional Institution. The date is July 16th, 2014. At 11:55am.

There's a lot of debate as to what we should do about Adam. What should be his punishment? Scientists want him alive for tests. The public wants him dead. What do you think?

When I first saw him, I thought he was just some punk, some Ivy League yuppie prick. In person, he didn't look like that at all. Not how I originally pictured from reading the news reports, you know? He was harder somehow. I expected my boys would teach him a lesson, knock him off his pedestal a bit. I heard what he thought of himself, that he was the most evolutionary advanced being on the planet, the goddamn alpha male. He definitely didn't look it, at first. In here, the real tough guys are big bastards, like body builders. He was lean. Had like a swimmer's body, you know? And he's got those movie star looks and that real proper speaking voice. He looks like he'd be a mark. But there's something hard about this guy. You could feel it right away. He was like the mafia dudes we get in here. The hired killers who've seen so much violence the shit don't affect them no more. Nothing affects them. Fucking sociopaths. He was like that. Calm, cool, like he could slit your throat and his pulse wouldn't raise a tick, you know? We get guys like that in here all the time. They don't care about themselves, so they damn sure don't care about you. Those are the really dangerous ones. Those are the guys you have to watch.

He went through the booking process without saying nothing. Which is kind of fucking weird for a new guy. Usually the guys who've never been to prison are kind of nervous, talkative, trying to make friends with the guards, or just asking a bunch of questions about what it's like in here. They usually want to know about the stories they hear about prison rape. They want to know what to do to keep from getting raped, and I just tell them to be a man. Act like a man and you won't get raped. Then, when we start to do the cavity search, that's when guys show their true colors. We typically see two reactions. You get the tough guys who won't cooperate with the guards, throws an attitude, and fight back every chance they get, and then you get the guys who break down, start sweating, their eyes tear up, butt-hole clenches up. See, they start realizing they ain't in Kansas anymore. That reality hits 'em and they freak out.

Not this guy.

It was eerie in a way. The way he never reacted to anything. The way he answered questions concisely, without stuttering, like he already knew what my nurses were going to ask. He acted like he'd been in and out of prison his whole life, like he'd been institutionalized, you know? Not like a guy doing his first stint. The booking process went smoothly, it finished earlier than usual. By the time we finished, the prisoners were still in the yard. After we got him situated in his cell, he walks out into the yard. That's where the real fun began. With most new prisoners, I usually book them and then go back to my office to finish paperwork. But this time I figured I'd stick around and watch how he interacted with the other inmates. I was up on the wall with the snipers, watching Horrowitz walk out.

He walked right to the center of the yard and just stood there, watching everyone. He'd stare at someone for a while, then seem to lose interest and focus on the next guy. And he was only looking at the meanest bastards. The real tough guys. But how the hell would he know who they were? It ain't like these assholes wear signs. He was just sizing them up. It was freaking everyone out. But rather than getting pissed off and going up to him and challenging him, you know, "What the fuck you lookin' at? You got a fucking problem?" that sort of thing, these guys are doing all they can to get out of his line of sight. I swear to you. They acted like he was aiming a gun at them.

I'd heard about what he did, everyone had, but this was the Special Isolation Wing, and everybody in there is bat-shit crazy. Special Isolation is where we put the child molesters, serial killers, mass murderers, and homosexuals, along with some of our more high-profile convicts, domestic terrorists and that sort of thing. Then there's some guys in there that are just out of their fucking minds and should be in a mental institution, but the crimes they committed were so heinous the public wants to see them punished, not talking about their feelings and sucking down drugs at some mental facility. We keep them out of general population where they might be targeted and killed by the other inmates. What I'm saying is these ain't your normal inmates. It's a whole ward full of fags and lunatics, and this guy is just watching them all. Guys walk past him and don't even look at him. I swear, they were walking around him. Nobody challenged him, nobody tried to talk to him. Nothing. They stayed as far away from him as they could. And I know, you think I'm exaggerating. Maybe this is normal or I was imagining it. And I'm telling you, I've seen hundreds of guys walk through these doors and some are immediately embraced, some are immediately challenged, and some the other cons approach cautiously, try to feel him out, you know? Try to get a read on who he is. Nobody gets ignored. Nobody. People want to know who they're living with. But this guy would look at someone and the other guy would look away. I'm talking serial killers and mass murderers trying to avoid making eye contact like some kind of nervous school girl blushing over a handsome quarterback.

I'll tell you something else weird, the COs act weird around him too.

COs?

Corrections officers. The guys who work for me—they're good guys, but they're human, and by that I mean some of them can get a little mean, a little overzealous. A con pushes one too far and he's going to get his head cracked. You know? It's going to happen no matter how much you council them to use restraint, and frankly, in my opinion, it should happen. There's more of them then there are of us. Fear is the only thing that keeps them at bay. You crack a couple skulls, and that helps keep everyone else in line. But they were all scared of Horrowitz.

Give me an example. How did you know they were afraid of him?

Well, we've got one CO, Martin Hightower, big bull of a man. Black dude, about six foot six and nearly three hundred pounds with a temper just as big. He's put a few inmates in the hospital. An inmate threw a handful of feces on him once, and Hightower nearly killed the guy. He beat the guy so bad he was in the hospital for a month. Now he has severe brain damage, memory loss, slurred speech. Hightower did a number on this guy. Fucked him up for life. I hated to do it, but I had to suspend him for two weeks. He almost got fired over it, but come on, what would you do if someone threw human shit at you?

Anyway, we were doing a random cell check and Hightower and a couple of SORT team guys—SORT stands for special operations response teams; I figured you wouldn't know? Anyway, they're searching Horrowitz's cell, you know, for drugs, weapons, that sort of thing, tearing it apart. Hightower finds a bunch of letters from Horrowitz's dad, and he starts going through them. Then he starts reading one. Horrowitz snatches them out of Hightower's hands and smacks Hightower right in the mouth. Smacks him hard, and then turns his back on him and sets his letters back on the shelf where they were. The SORT team guys could've taken Horrowitz down, but Hightower just walked away. Now Hightower is twice this guy's size. He could have killed him. But he didn't say anything. He didn't do anything. He just walked away. Just like that, he walked away. The SORT team guys were so confused they left him alone too. I'm telling you, there's something different about that guy.

July 18, 2014. 6:30p.m. Office of Dr. Kristophe Tompkins, court-appointed psychologist for Adam Horrowitz.
Good evening, Dr. Tompkins.
H-hello. Who are you with again?
No one. No publication, that is. I'm a freelance writer writing Adam Horrowitz's authorized biography.
Authorized? You've interviewed him then?
Yes.
What did you think?
I'm more interested in your professional opinion.
But what did you think of him? How did he strike you?
He's scary. If I was a religious man, I'd say he was evil. But I'm not. So, to me, he's just one deeply disturbed individual.

What if I said you were right the first time? That Adam Horrowitz is evil, pure evil.

That's your professional opinion?

My professional opinion is that he suffers from an antisocial personality disorder and narcissistic personality disorder. He's a sadist with delusions of grandeur; he's manipulative, deceitful, mistrustful, arrogant, and callous. But aren't I really just saying the same thing in fancier words? Isn't what I'm really saying is that he's evil? There is no cure for him. I am not talking about a disease of the mind. I am talking about the character of the man. He doesn't suffer from these disorders. We suffer from them. The public. Those babies he murdered suffered from his disorders, all those people he murdered.

And that's why you refused to treat him?

Because it would do no good. He's not Jeffery Dahmer. He doesn't want to stop doing what he's doing. He didn't want to get caught. He just didn't care if he got caught. He was single-minded. Like a . . . a suicide bomber. His life wasn't as important as destroying the lives of those children.

Why?

If you've interviewed him, then you know why.

But why do you think he did it?

I think he did it for the exact reason he has repeatedly stated. He was making room for his genetic offspring, eliminating competition. The same reason he killed those men at the fertility clinic—and something else you may not know, that the police haven't released to the press. Those five men he murdered, they weren't the only ones. There were at least twenty sperm banks that he visited under different aliases in twenty different cities. By now, there may be hundreds of unsuspecting women carrying his children. They're keeping it quiet because they don't want to cause a panic. Imagine if you were to discover that the baby inside you wasn't conceived with your husband's frozen sperm or the handsome, blond-haired, blue-eyed PhD student you picked out of a profile but with the sperm of a notorious serial killer? That would fuck up your day, wouldn't it? It would cause a panic. Of course they can't let that information out. And that nursery wasn't the first one he visited either. He's killed dozens of babies. Smothered them. In hospital nurseries all over the country. It's going to take a long time to sort out all the murders he's committed.

And you know this . . .

Because he told me.

Let's go back to your diagnosis of Adam Horrowitz. You said he suffers from antisocial personality disorder and narcissistic personality disorder. So he's a sociopath?

As I said, Adam Horrowitz doesn't suffer from anything. He wouldn't know the slightest thing about suffering. He is incapable of experiencing many of what we would consider to be normal human emotions. Things like sympathy, compassion, even fear to a large degree are foreign to him. Do you know there was a study done that theorized you can tell how violent a kid is going to grow up to be by testing his pulse rate when he is a toddler? See, getting your pulse taken by a doctor when you're a baby is a strange, unfamiliar, and frightening experience for most babies. It's stressful. Their pulse rates shoot up. But some babies show low resting heart rates when tested. Heart rates in the forties and fifties. Those are the kids, the study suggested, that grow up to be violent. They lack the normal fear response.

That fear is what keeps many of our more aggressive tendencies in check. Eliminate that fear and what's to stop you from taking a swing at, a shot at, or a slice out of anyone who pisses you off? Adam's pulse rate was forty-two when he was examined following his arrest. Forty-two. A normal heart rate, under those circumstances, would be in the nineties at least, even the low to mid hundreds.

What else did you discover during your examination of Adam Horrowitz?

There's a dimensional system of general personality structure developed by psychologists called the Five-Factor Model of personality, or FFM, that we now apply to personality disorders. The FFM is comprised of five bipolar domains of personality functioning: labeled surgency, or extraversion versus introversion; agreeableness versus antagonism; conscientiousness versus disinhibition; neuroticism versus emotional stability; and intellect or openness versus closedness to experience. I was curious to see where Adam was on this FFM. He rated highly in the domain of extraversion. Adam is assertive, active, and thrill-seeking, although also extremely low in the extraversion facet of warmth and compassion. Adam scores extremely low on all facets of neuroticism, with the exception of anger and hostility. In other words, he doesn't experience normal negative emotions like anxiety, depression, and self-consciousness, but he has great difficulty controlling his anger. Despite his anger-control issues, Adam scored high ratings on the domain of conscientiousness, which is in direct contrast with the impulsive, under-controlled behavior that one would typically expect from an antisocial criminal. It is in direct contrast to what one would expect from the type of criminal who would walk into a hospital nursery and start murdering newborns, but, you have to remember, he'd gotten away with it at least twice before. Smothered twenty babies in a hospital in Las Vegas and then just walked right out the door unmolested. He did the same in Ohio. On the FFM of general personality, Adam is considered competent, orderly, achievement-oriented, and deliberate. Perhaps it was his characteristic style of careful planning and deliberate execution that enabled him to get away with these killings so many times before.

Exactly how many people has he killed?

I doubt even he knows.

***

Check. Check. Check. This is the first interview with Samantha McCarthy. We are at her private residence. July 19, 2014.

I understand you are the mother of one of the victims, one of the few people alive who witnessed his act. Do you mind telling me what you saw?

I mind. But I've already explained it once in court. I guess I can tell you. It can't make it any worse, I guess. It's just kinda hard. You know? It's still so hard. I still can't believe what that man did. Who does something like that? What kind of man kills babies? Beautiful little babies. I saw it all. It was terrible. It was sick, what that man did. I hope he fries for this. I hope he suffers.

What did you see?

There was a section of the nursery toward the back. It's where they kept, like, the premature babies. The little tiny ones. That's where he started. The babies were all sleeping in these incubators. They were tiny, weak, helpless little things. I didn't know what he was doing at first. I thought he was just a dad, eager to see his newborn. I was like that myself. I wanted to see my baby daughter all the time. That's why I was there. It's just so exciting for a new parent, you know? And he walked in so casually. That smile on his face made it seem like he was there for, like, normal reasons. But he wasn't. When he opened the lid to the first incubator, that's when I knew something was up. Then he . . . then he . . . oh god.

Catch your breath. I know it's hard. Take your time.

Okay. Okay. Just give me a second. This is just . . . I just never thought anything like this could happen. That bastard killed my baby. My little girl. I had just named her. I don't know why it took me so long. I went through all the books of baby names for months. I even had an app on my phone that showed the most popular baby names around the world, minute by minute. Do you know what the most popular girl name in the United States was when my daughter was born? Sophia. Can you believe that? Sophia. Followed by Emma and Olivia. I couldn't see naming my daughter any of those names. They just seemed so adult. Not like baby names, more like the name of someone's mom. I decided to name her Jessica, after my grandmother. She was so beautiful. I never thought anything that beautiful . . . I never thought I could make something so precious.

I'm sure she was a very beautiful baby.

She was perfect. She was absolutely perfect. And he destroyed her. He took her away from me.

Samantha? Can you tell me what he did to them? What you saw?

The little babies, the preemies, needed oxygen tanks to breathe, their lungs weren't strong enough to work on their own. There were these clear tubes that ran up to their noses and constantly pumped oxygen so they could breathe. He took the tubes, wrapped it around the baby's neck a few times, and then pulled it tight. He kept pulling until the knot grew smaller, and smaller, and smaller, until the baby's head just dropped. It was hanging there like it was going to fall off. Her neck was broken, all stretched and twisted. Jesus . . . I was trying to forget all this shit, you know? But I can't forget. I can't stop thinking about it. It's all I think about . . . what that man did.

I'm sorry. If you want to stop, we can.

No. I'm okay. I'm fine. After he killed that first baby . . . after I watched him do it . . . I screamed. I woke up all the babies. They were all wailing at the top of their little lungs. They were scared. They were all so scared. It was like they knew what was about to happen to them. It was like they knew what that man was. I saw Horrowitz curse, he just yelled "fuck," and then he turned and glared at me. I just shut my mouth and stopped screaming. I was scared shitless. I thought he was gonna kill me too, you know?

He checked around for a bit and then picked up the oxygen tank beside the baby's incubator. He didn't need to be quiet anymore. I'd already alerted the entire fucking hospital. Maybe I should have just gotten a nurse quietly, so he wouldn't have known. So he wouldn't have hurried up with what he was doing. Maybe he wouldn't have had time to kill so many. But it was too late. He lifted the tank above his head, and smashed it down on the next incubator. It broke through the glass and crushed the little baby inside. And he went on like that, shuffling down the line, hammering the oxygen tank on their puny bodies. He moved so quickly. I thought he'd get tired after a few but he just kept going.

I wanted to go in and stop him, to slow him at least, but I just had a C-section. My body hurt and I was still carrying around my IV, for God's sake. That's when it occurred to me: where the hell are the nurses? I knew there was supposed to be at least one in the nursery at all times. I found what I was looking for. He must have done it before I got there. Tucked away in the corner, in the shadows, the nurse sat with her eyes closed, leaning against the wall. There was no blood or bruises, like he just choked her or something. So it was quiet. Finally, two other nurses came sprinting down the hall asking me what's wrong. I couldn't speak, so I just pointed. They saw Horrowitz pounding infants with a bloody oxygen tank. They saw the walls, once painted yellow, dripping red. The nurses didn't freeze up like I did, they ran right in. It made me feel guilty in a way. He did the nurses just as he did the babies. The first one ran straight toward him and he turned around and whacked her across the jaw with the tank. She slipped on a puddle of blood and cracked her skull on the tile floor. The next nurse hopped over her colleague's body and charged the guy. They shouldn't have run in one by one like that, or they might have stood a fighting chance. He sidestepped her, and she went crashing into the cribs holding the shattered incubators. They toppled over, and dead infants fell on top of her. She sat up with her jaw hanging open, like she didn't know what she was seeing. Horrowitz stood over her and smacked her jaw loose with the tank. I swear he swung it hard enough to make a dent in the damn thing. The nurse slumped over and rested in the pile of newborns.

He moved on to the healthy babies, pulverizing their defenseless bodies. There was no glass incubator for protection, so their bodies just sorta crumbled underneath the oxygen tank. It was so sick. My own baby girl was just down the line from where Horrowitz was. I didn't even think about it, I ripped the needles from my hand and the patches off my chest and picked up the metal rod that held up my IV drip to use as a weapon. But two doctors grabbed me by the waist and held me back as two orderlies rushed past me. An alarm above us in the hallway was blaring and flashing a red light. I was getting dizzy; the alarm seemed to get louder and louder until I couldn't bear it.

Horrowitz kept walking down the line, like he was fucking playing whack-a-mole or something. And he was getting closer to my baby. I struggled against the doctor's grip; I just wanted a final look at my little miracle. I prayed for the orderlies to stop him. I mean they were men and there were two of them. They should have been able to stop him, right? I mean, he was just a guy, right? He was just a fucking crazy guy.

The alarm blared loud. I couldn't see my baby anymore, I was too dizzy. I listened for her cry, but through the other screaming babies and screaming patients and doctors and the damn alarm, I couldn't make out her cry. I thought my motherly instincts would kick in. Like how animals could pick out the sound of their offspring's chirp or holler in a crowd. But I couldn't. I just couldn't. I had just given birth to her the day before, and I was still so doped up on painkillers from the C-section, I hadn't had time to learn her voice. I didn't know what my own baby sounded like.

I saw the first orderly die. Horrowitz grabbed him in a headlock. He spun the tank around in his palm and slammed the nozzle on the corner of a table. There was a piercing, whistling sound. It was loud enough to rupture the fragile eardrums of those babies. Horrowitz jammed the oxygen tank, still spewing air, into the man's mouth and held it there. It took me a while before I figured out what he was doing. The orderly's eyes bulged, he was scratching at his chest, digging trenches with his nails. Horrowitz pinched the man's nose shut and watched as his victim's lungs burst open. The man fell slack in Horrowitz's arms and then dropped to the floor. When he removed the tank from the dead man's mouth, I saw his chest sink, then blood spill from his mouth.

There was a brief moment of hope when I saw the one orderly—the one that was still alive—knock away the oxygen tank. But that hope was snatched away when I saw Horrowitz snap that orderly's neck. Horrowitz cocked his head, you know, like dogs do when they hear a strange noise. He was standing perfectly still, with his head cocked like that, staring at the babies that were still alive. It was like someone had pressed the pause button on him. Then he just snaps out of it and starts moving again, faster now, more deliberate. He proceeded to twist the necks of the babies he missed. I passed out when he reached into my baby's little bed. I didn't see him kill her. When I woke up, I was back in my recovery room. I still thought maybe she was alive. Maybe someone stopped him before he could hurt her.

When did you find out?

My entire family was around me, just watching me, tears in their eyes. I kinda just knew right then. They didn't need to say anything, I could tell by their looks. I knew I was going to cry. I could feel it coming. The hiccups. The tears right behind my eyelids. But I didn't. You wanna know why?

Why?

Because I got mad instead.

Mad at Horrowitz?

Him too, but not just him. I saw my boyfriend. My baby-daddy. The asshole who promised he'd stay with me after I got pregnant. Do you think he was crying like the rest of my family?

I'm guessing not.

Well, you guessed right. I'll bet that asshole was secretly happy. I'll bet that little fuck was happy he didn't have to pay child support no more. He looked sad, but I knew that fucker was pretending. That's the same face he had when he broke up with me. That same fake, lying, deceitful fucking face. On the inside, that fucker was giddy.

I probably shouldn't have yelled at him. But I needed to get my anger out somehow. Maybe I was just bitter and guilty for not acting during those killings and was taking it out on my ex. I don't know. But I just sat up and started yelling "fuck you!" over and over and over again at him. My mother tried to calm me down, and my dad just grabbed his arm and led him out of the room. And I didn't stop yelling until he left. I don't know, it just felt sorta good. To get it all out. Like I should have the day before.

Is there anything more you'd like to say?

No.

Thank you for your time.

Don't mention it.

(He clicks his recorder off.)

I am now interviewing Adam's lawyer, Isaac Peters. We are at Hunt and Peters, LLC, on July 21, 2014. The time is five forty-nine p.m.

Can you tell me about the time you spent with him?

It was short.

Tell me about the short time you spent with him then.

All right. Well, the court assigned me his case. From what I heard, Adam was passive about the whole thing. Just kind of indifferent. He wasn't making any effort to find himself a lawyer, so the judge picked me.

I only spoke to him a few times before the first hearing. He was always handcuffed and chained before I was given permission to speak with him. The warden required it. To be honest, I wouldn't step into a room alone with him if he wasn't chained up. There's just something about him. The way he looks at you with those cold, dead, emotionless eyes. It's like he doesn't feel any connection at all. Like we're different species.

I know. I feel it too.

Creepy, right?

Yeah.

Anyway, I read his profile before my first meeting with him. And of course, there is only one way to defend something like this. There is really no other logical justification for what he did. We'd make the case that he was insane, mentally ill during his crimes. Usually, *usually,* the jury can be convinced with that argument. I mean, it's pretty messed up to execute someone who didn't know better, right? You just hope you can make the jury find something in the defendant they can empathize with. But I knew this would be a long shot. Whether it was right or wrong to put this man to death, I figured it was my job to make sure he got off, to find a way to make the jury feel sorry for him. Besides, if we did happen to win the case, imagine what that would do for my career.

I'd imagine you'd be famous.

Infamous. But in this profession, it's basically the same thing. Well, I thought Adam would realize that insanity was his only hope, but he didn't. Every time we met he was uncooperative as hell. "I'm not insane. I'm not insane," over and over again. There was no explaining it to this guy. Nobody on the planet would ever agree with him.

Except maybe his father.

Well, he's not the judge. Is he?

But this was what really frustrated me. *He* told *me* what to do. *He* told *me* what to say in court. Who's the professional here? I've never seen an ego that big, before. He told me that what he was doing was for the greater good of humanity. That the end would justify the means when everyone was his descendant, and, therefore, smarter, stronger, faster, better.

His defense was that stopping his massacre was somehow interfering with the natural order of things, that he was the next step in human evolution, and Homo sapiens need to step aside for his offspring. It was a ludicrous argument.

He ended up firing me. He thought he could handle the case himself, that cocky son of a bitch. I was glad to leave, even though I was leaving a high-profile case that could have made me a legal rock star. He scared the hell out of me. The more I spoke with him, the more I began to realize my entire argument was a lie. I've spoken with the psychologist. What was his name?

Dr. Tompkins?

Yes, Tompkins. We both agreed. Horrowitz isn't insane, he's evil.

What about Dr. Tompkins's official write-up?

It's bogus. He probably wrote it so he didn't look like a fool within the psychology community. The truth is, he's a monster. A cold-blooded monster.

I'm beginning to see that. I began this project expecting a silver lining, a possibility of a hopeful ending, but after interviewing all these people, I realize that's not the case.

You authors are always so optimistic. You always need the ideal, happy ending. That's not real life, partner. We learn these things as lawyers. The people we deal with day to day. We're realists.

I think we can wrap it up now. Anything else you might want to add?

No. That's all the interaction I've had with the guy. Thank God.

Thank you for your time.

Wait. I actually have a question for you.

Yes?

Before you stepped into my office, I heard you on the phone with your wife.

Go on.

I understand she is pregnant?

Yes, she is. So?

From what I picked up from the conversation—and I wasn't eavesdropping. But just to clarify.

Sure.

Anyway, from what I picked up from your conversation, your wife is pregnant from a donor sperm?

Yes. This is true. But we have nothing to worry about.

There you go again with your optimism. Here's my card. In case you don't get that happy fairy-tale ending.

I won't need it.

You might.

(He takes the card and rips it in half.) You'll do anything for a client, won't you?

Well—

Good-bye.

(He switches off the recorder and extends his arm to shake the lawyer's hand.)

Second interview with Adam Horrowitz.

Hello, Adam.

How's your research coming? Have you got me all figured out yet?

I confess. You're still a mystery to me.

That's because you don't believe me. How can you do my story justice if you doubt everything I'm saying?

It's an unbelievable story, Adam. But your point is well taken. I will try to keep an open mind. Let me ask you a few more questions. Some things that have been bothering me about your story.

Like what?

Did your father know you were killing people?

I told him. After I killed those guys at the fertility clinic, I told him all about it.

What did he say?

He said I was too emotional. He said that killing those guys was an emotional reaction, not a logical one. I was jealous of them. So he did what he always did when something about my behavior displeased him. He fixed me.

Fixed you?

He took away my emotions. The ones he considered detrimental, unproductive. Hatred. Fear. Envy. Lust. Jealousy. Greed. I don't feel any of those anymore. Daddy made sure of that.

How?

There are genes that determine our emotions the same as there are those that determine our height, weight, and eye color. He isolated those genes the same way he isolated the genes for symmetry and intelligence. Then he altered them, cherry-picking the emotions he thought would be beneficial, like courage and ambition, and eliminating things like fear and empathy that would only get in the way.

That's pretty hard to believe.

But yet here I am. I am living proof that his experiments worked.

So you've said.

Yet you remain skeptical.

It's hard for me to accept that the next step in human evolution is a sociopath, a serial killer. It's hard for me to accept that someone can play God with his own child and decide how he will look, act, and feel.

Father is special. He really is a remarkable man. He may have his flaws but intelligence and ingenuity are not one of them. He made me everything he himself wanted to be: handsome, athletic, artistic, talented, a genius, a leader.

But if what you're telling me is true, then your father made you a serial killer. Perhaps you wouldn't be here right now if your father hadn't experimented on you. Maybe if he'd hugged you more often, took you to baseball games, taught you to throw a football, told you how special you were and how much he loved you, maybe you wouldn't have killed all those people.

(A pause. Someone breathing hard.)

Why are you talking to me like this? You're supposed to be interviewing me. Not trying to turn me against my father. You want answers? Ask some fucking questions!

Are you angry right now, Adam? I thought your father rid you of that particular negative emotion. Perhaps his treatments didn't work after all.

That is it. We're done.

Wait. Let's start over. Tell me about your other efforts to spread your DNA.

Other efforts?

You're an intelligent guy. Good looking. I'm sure you didn't limit yourself to sperm banks and killing babies. Besides, a bunch of mass slaughters like the one that landed you here would have been suspicious. You would have gotten caught much sooner.

(There's a long pause. Then a sigh.)

You are, of course, asking about the women.

Go on.

There were lots of women. Two or three a night. Sometimes more. I'd pick them up in bars, on the Internet, in singles groups. I would have sex with them for days, sometimes weeks, even months, keeping track of their menstrual cycles so I knew when they were most fertile, until I was certain I had impregnated them and then I'd move on to the next one, but I kept tabs on them.

Kept tabs? Why?

To protect my children. To make sure they didn't abort them. One woman got away from me. She had the fetus aborted. I made her pay for that.

Can you tell me more about that?

No.

How did you make her pay?

It's not relevant.

Readers will want to know.

I did not kill her. Not at first. I kept her. I took her to my house. I tied her up. And I made certain she conceived again.

Then I kept her until she was at full term. I delivered the baby myself.

And then?

I took the baby to the fire station. Did you know you could take unwanted babies to the fire station and they will make sure the baby gets to foster care? Wonderful system.

And what about the mother?

I'm sure she is little more than bones now. Dissolved in lye.

Oh my God. That's—that's horrible. Why would you do something like that?

You are editorializing again. You are supposed to be objective. Impartial. Is that not the soul of good journalism? Now, any more questions or are we done?

Yes. Yes. A few more questions. Who else have you killed? I know there are more. There's always more.

As you deduced, I did more than I confessed to earlier. See, like the lion, most predators are territorial. I was spreading my seed far and wide but I felt no satisfaction in that. So I began to narrow my scope, concentrating on one city, one neighborhood.

And what did you do?

I began the same way I did at that fertility clinic long ago, by eliminating competition. I scoped out the best breeding stock through a meticulous process of first setting the boundaries of what was to be my territory and then calculating the number of females in that area. From there I cross-referenced DMV records with medical and birth records to find the number of females of breeding age, which I calculated to be sixteen to thirty-five years old, eliminating the disabled and chronically ill. In no time, I had the number reduced to fewer than seven thousand. Then I began disqualifying them based on things like obesity, poor eyesight, low IQ, poor education, low vocational achievement. In the end, I had narrowed it down to three hundred. Three hundred in a six-mile radius that encompassed more than sixty thousand people. Pathetic.

Then what?
I got to know them. I found out who was married and who was single. Who had children and who was expecting.
And then?
I followed the lion's plan. I eliminated competition.
And how did you do that?
First I made their husbands and boyfriends disappear. Most of the girls were single, so that left a little more than a hundred men. Many of them were dating multiple women in my circle of three hundred. Unbeknown to the women of course. But I didn't have time to break them up. Besides, how would I have known whether causing dissent in one relationship wouldn't have strengthened another or caused the men to court other women in my circle? No, I had no choice but to resort to the old shovel and bag of lye. In one month, I had cleared the field.
What about the police? That many men couldn't go missing in such a short amount of time without someone noticing.
They noticed. They investigated in many cases. In some they assumed the men had simply moved on, in others they suspected foul play. They investigated their spouses and girlfriends, which made things more difficult for me, but it couldn't be helped. That's why I did it so quickly. I didn't give the police time to figure it out. Kill one guy every month or so, and the cops have time to discover bodies, notice patterns, interview witnesses, put together a taskforce. But I overwhelmed their system by killing three, four, five a day. They had no time to react. Then I stopped. It is hard to catch a killer who murders random strangers. Did you know that? It's very hard. And I left them nothing to go on. No fingerprints. No DNA. No signs of struggle. No bodies. They were all just gone.
How did you do it? How'd you kill them and dispose of the bodies so effectively?
I am afraid that is not relevant. It is my secret.

You're in prison. It's over for you. What does it matter?
My secret. Mine alone.
Okay. So tell me more about the women.
The pregnant ones lost their babies. Did you know there is a tea you can drink that produces a spontaneous abortion? There is even a blackberry tea, for women who are in their last trimester, that causes premature labor. The babies that survived their early births I took care of. I went to the hospital and quietly smothered them in their beds. The women who resisted my subtler methods to induce abortions were dealt with a bit more crudely. I chloroformed one and then shot her up with ketamine. Then, using a medical textbook, performed an in-home abortion on her. It was quite a mess.
For Christ's sake!
What? Did something I say bother you?
No. I'm fine.
You forget, I can read your thoughts. I am bothering you. In fact, right now, I can tell that you want to leap over this table and beat me to a pulp. You're expecting a child. Nice. Well, we can stop if you'd like. If you don't want to hear the rest of the story, I'm sure there's another reporter somewhere who would.
I said I'm fine. Continue.
We'll see. Did you know ketamine has hallucinogenic effects? I'm no anesthesiologist so I just guessed the dosage. She woke up halfway through the procedure and mistook me for her lover. "Brendan, how could you? It's your baby! Why don't you love your baby?" Her voice was so pitiful. Then she cried herself back to sleep with my cannula—you know what that is, right? A little tube—still five inches deep. Could you imagine that? Aborting your own baby? That wasn't rhetorical.
I . . . I can't.
Are you holding up all right?
I'm fine.

You're holding back tears. Don't worry; unlike my father, I don't mind seeing a grown man cry. I rather enjoy it, in fact.

Well, I'm not going to cry. Sorry to disappoint. Continue.

From there I proceeded to suck the amniotic fluid, the placenta, and of course, the fetus into the collection jar. I used what was essentially a vacuum for babies. I'd stolen it from an abortion clinic. Smash and grab. It was all over the news. They blamed it on some pro-life organization. The fetus was about the size of the little baby feet pro-lifers wear. Are you pro-life?

Am now. Just finish your story.

I removed the cannula and then inserted a curette to scrape anything from her uterus I might have missed. The smell was something I think I'll never forget. Did you know the blood from inside a woman's uterus has a different odor than the blood say, from when you slit someone's throat? It is a heavier, meatier smell. Pleasant in a way. Suffice it to say I was careful not to damage anything that would prevent her from successfully carrying my seed to term. After that, I visited the women one by one and inseminated them.

You mean you raped them?

No. Nothing so crude. I would have loved to, but that would have taken too much time. Too inefficient, you understand. My method was more systematic. I had been storing my sperm for weeks. I had bottles of it completely filling my little freezer from top to bottom. I drugged the women, without their knowledge of course, and then I artificially inseminated them using a three-dollar turkey baster I bought from the grocery store. I would do ten a day. Systematically. The same way I found them. The same way I got rid of their boyfriends and husbands. It became like a job to me. Eight hours a day with my little bottle of Rohypnol, chloroform as a back-up precaution, and my turkey baster. Then, when I got to the last one, I would start over to make sure it took. In the not-too-distant future, you are going to see a large upswing in the number of births in a certain neighborhood. My territory.

And what neighborhood is that, exactly?

Wouldn't you like to know.

(Recording ends.)

Thanks for agreeing to speak with me, Professor Horrowitz. I can imagine how terrible all of this must be for you.

Yes, well, this is not the destiny I had in mind for my son. He was meant for greater things, to be a leader of men, not a common criminal.

Whatever Adam is, he is certainly not common, Professor Horrowitz. The experiments you did on your son have made him something else entirely.

The experiments? You mean the DNA injections?

Yes. Adam believes those injections made him into something greater than he was. Something greater than any of us. Beyond humanity. He believes you advanced him further along the evolutionary scale.

(Victor laughs.)

Yes. That was my hope. It didn't work though. I knew that after the first round of injections.

Wait. I don't understand.

The DNA injections did nothing. My hope was that the new DNA would bind itself to his genes and change the DNA patterns, altering his physiology on a genetic level. I knew it was ambitious. But I'd had some success with rats and even chimpanzees, so I was confident. At the very least, I figured it was harmless.

So what happened?

Nothing. There were no changes at all. He got stronger but that was just from the workouts he was doing. He was no stronger than any other human being would have been after a similar strength regimen. He looked no different. His IQ was always high. After the injections began, he studied harder, his knowledge increased by leaps and bounds, but intelligence is not about erudition. It is how we process that information, and his IQ remained the same.

If they didn't work, then why did you continue?

Adam's confidence improved after the first round of injections. I didn't see any changes, but he thought he did. He thought he had become more handsome. He had been painfully shy, and suddenly he was talking to girls, going out on dates. I gave him injections of genes meant to make him stronger and faster. That's when he began strength training. He had never been interested in sports before, but suddenly he was taking gymnastics, running track, even taking martial arts, so I continued the injections. Then he came to me, claiming he could read minds. He even claimed his consciousness could travel outside his body.

Astral projection?

Yes. That's what he claimed. We did a few tests, and the results were interesting but inconclusive.

Inconclusive?

We needed a more controlled environment for testing. We were doing the tests in the house and in my private laboratory. He knew those places too well. If I placed him in one room and I picked up an object in another room, it was hard to tell if he was just using his knowledge of the environment and of me, to deduce the objects I was most likely to select. That was the same problem with our tests of his telepathic abilities. It was hard to tell if he was reading my thoughts or just reading me.

How accurate was he?

About 80 percent.

Eighty percent!

Yes. It dropped to around 50 or 60 whenever I introduced new objects he'd never seen before. That's why I am reluctant to say he has telepathic powers. I would just call him highly perceptive and observant. Extraordinarily so, perhaps.

Perhaps? Eighty percent is beyond extraordinary. It's unprecedented! Even if he was just relying on his intimate knowledge of you, that would require an uncanny degree of perceptiveness.

Adam has always been a remarkable boy.

He didn't think so.

What do you mean?

He interpreted your attempts to "fix" him as confirmation that he was flawed in some way, that he wasn't good enough. He believed you were ashamed of him and that's why you were doing everything you could to improve him.

But that's ridiculous. I loved Adam. He knew that. I just wanted him to be better. I wanted him to be the best. Isn't that what every father wants for their son? Isn't it every father's responsibility—

To make sure his son grows up to be a better man than him? Adam told me about that. He also said you believed yourself to be flawed and that you took out your own frustration at not being able to live up to your own idealized standard of perfection on him.

That may be true. I'll accept that. But Adam was happy. The experiments were making him better. Yes, it was a placebo, but the psychological effects were undeniable.

And after he started killing people?

I felt bad about that, but he was my son. I thought I could control him. I guess, ultimately, whether I realized it or not, I started believing in the injections as much as he did. I thought I could isolate the genes that were causing his aggressive behavior and correct them. It was worth a shot.

Dr. Horrowitz, what if the injections really did work? What if he really is what he says he is?

Then he is correct and his genes will become dominant. Humanity as we know it will be forced into extinction by this smarter, stronger, more aggressive species. But I don't think we have to worry about that. It didn't work, and even if it did, that's a process that takes hundreds of years.

In this age? With today's technology? Imagine what

happens when all his children come of age. We don't even know how many there are. But let's say, for the sake of argument, fifty. Those fifty kids make fifty more, who make fifty more, so on and so on. An exponential increase. Assuming they are as aggressive, intelligent, and attractive as Adam, they could wind up in politics, high military positions, CEOs of major companies, areas where they would have a tremendous impact on the world. I don't think we're looking at hundreds of years here, Professor Horrowitz. I don't think we'd have that much time at all.

(End recording.)

Samsara
Sultan Z. White

"When someone seeks," said Siddhartha, "then it easily happens that his eyes see only the thing that he seeks, and he is able to find nothing, to take in nothing because he always thinks only about the thing he is seeking, because he has one goal, because he is obsessed with his goal. Seeking means: having a goal. But finding means: being free, being open, having no goal."—Hermann Hesse, *Siddhartha*

Chapter 1

Tender white hands caress his dark skin. His muscles relax by desire of the feminine whispers, "Let us do all the work." He closes his eyes and feels the nude women around him sucking his nipples, licking his testicles. More women crouch over him, taking turns swallowing his length. More women. Some nibble at his toes, others kiss his chapped lips, drying out the more he sweats. They draw soft silk over his arms and then across his wrists, wrapping it around a polished ivory post; he lets himself be tied down. He looks down at his feet; two pairs of gentle hands delicately tie down his ankles. As he begins to resist, a beautiful woman stoops before him, severing the sight of his bound feet. She wears a silver necklace with a lamb pendant, the only article on her otherwise naked body. Her proportions are faultless. She lingers over him, brown eyes so seductive, and then wraps her lips around his shaft. She keeps eye contact as she takes all of him in, slowly, slowly. He can look nowhere else. She stops at his head, and swirls her tongue, tickling his nerves. With her free hand she strokes his penis with honey, rubbing it through his pubic hair, over his balls, into his ass. He can look nowhere but at her. All around him, the cushions, the blankets, the sheets fall away. The nude women carry away the bedding, yet still he can focus on nothing but the beautiful woman with the silver lamb necklace.

As the covers disappear, the man, tied to a raised cross, is revealed. The beautiful woman ceases tending to his manly parts just prior to his orgasm. He begs for her to finish. Instead, she draws a whip from somewhere beneath him, raises it above her head, and lashes his bare skin. The meat on his thigh quivers as the whip strikes.

"Leave. And never return," she says.

On all sides, naked women incessantly whip his defenseless body. His fists curl up, pulling at the silk; his toes curl, and tears hang at the corners of his eyes. Lines of red appear in flashes across his body. With every thrash, his body convulses. He screams his throat raw until he passes out.

He wakes to honey dripping down his chin. He lifts his head, though a raging ache in his skull protests. He sees the tops of trees, the clouds, the blue sky, and it takes him a while to realize he is suspended upside down. Attempting to move his hands, he is met with a sharp pain. The silk bindings have been replaced with iron stakes. He turns his head toward his hand, bolted to the wood; the bloody wound has attracted insects. They feast at his flesh in a ring around the iron stake. He looks to his left. His other hand is worse. A ring of skin is missing, eaten away by the bugs.

As he returns to his senses, the pain in his hands intensifies. Then he feels pain elsewhere. Another drip from his chin. He looks up to where the honey had fallen from, and his stomach heaves. If his stomach wasn't empty he would have thrown up all over his own face. Flies buzz around his crotch, stopping occasionally for the sugary honey. His penis is blotchy; parts of his skin seem to rise and fall as various insects burrow. A dark-yellow pus, darker than the honey, covers the skin around his pubes. It had begun to fester. He feels a writhing sensation in his asshole and an excruciating itching like he has never felt before. Only after his sphincter stretches open, revealing a torrent of maggots spilling down his back and crotch, does he realize what foreign creature had made a home of his intestines. He watches the insects devour his genitals. He begins to scream. He yanks at the stakes in vain. The inverted cross rocks back and forth as he struggles.

He sat up in bed, the white sheet coming up with him, clinging to his back by his own sweat.

"What the hell are you doing?" Jennifer rolled on to her side so she was looking at Kenneth.

"I just had the craziest dream. It was about—"

"Just tell me in the morning." She folded the pillow around her head, covering her ears, and fell back asleep.

Kenneth looked at his alarm clock, its red light the same color as the rays of the rising sun over the polluted Manhattan skyline. Six o'clock. He rose early from his bed. His alarm was set for seven anyway.

He tiptoed through his daily morning ritual as not to wake his girlfriend. Shower, dress, breakfast. His appetite was small, as he kept thinking of his nightmare. He left the rest for Jennifer to eat and then shuffled over to the bedroom. He stood in the doorway watching her sleep. She was on her side, facing away from him. He watched her shoulder rise and fall as she breathed deeply. The way the sheets hugged her curves, dipping at her waist, rising again at her hips. She was sexy. And for a moment, she overpowered the lingering torment from his dream.

He returned to the bed and snuggled against her back, fitting together like a puzzle piece. He brushed her hair from her face to look at her.

She stirred. "Another dream?"

"No, baby," he said, kissing her. "Remember our mornings last year?"

She arched up slightly to see the alarm clock and then fell back to her pillow with a groan. "I remember. But I have work soon."

He ran his hand down her figure. "You used to go late to work all the time so we could have fun."

She dismissed him. "But I'm tired now. Besides, don't you have some job hunting to do?" She buried herself under the blanket.

He stood up from the bed and walked out, presumably to search for a job. He'd been looking for one since he'd dropped out of college. But in reality, he'd been visiting a rehabilitating teenager named Jason, whom Kenneth had been serving religiously since the accident.

Their apartment above the corner liquor store was only a block from the subway. He walked with his head down, hiding his cheeks from the chilled wind. Faint snow drifted to the street. However, as he passed Radio Shack, its storefront filled with the latest flat-screen TVs displaying the morning news, he saw something profound enough to wrench his face up toward the piercing cold. He stood next to a well-dressed man, one of few pedestrians out this early in the morning, and peered through the glass at the television.

He looked at the saddened face of an anchorwoman. Her distress was peculiar, as he remembered watching the same woman report a gruesome story stone-faced. Kenneth had fallen asleep that night contemplating how she could report this terrible circumstance with such stoicism. He had eventually come to the conclusion that it was a requirement for her job, that the producers paid her to separate emotion from work. She was nothing but a trained messenger to the public. Whatever pulled in the ratings. But this time, her expression was different. As Kenneth watched the sadness on her face and listened to the despair in her voice and the passion of her words through the tiny television speaker, he began to notice quirks in her presentation. Her twiddling thumbs, her sweating brow, the occasional glance off-screen—enquiries of approval to the network producers in the studio.

Then Kenneth saw it. Her pupils dashing back and forth horizontally, like a typewriter. She was reading a teleprompter. Her sorrow, her pain, fabricated. She was an actress. Whatever pulled in the ratings. Kenneth heard a chuckle from the man next to him; he must have noticed it too.

With feigned empathy, the brunette anchorwoman announced the world's most recent tragedy. Then came the image of the burning city of Mecca.

"Now, a live news feed from our first-response copter, on-site in Mecca." At first the camera was blurred by the thick dust and smoke billowing from the flames below, revealing snippets of the destruction. But as the helicopter strafed out of the direction of the wind, the entire gruesome scene fell into plain view. Outside the perimeter of the city, soldiers stood on guard, gunning down any man, woman, or child who tried to escape the burning city. Their weapons were white, their fatigues were white, their helmets were white, yet upon their garments was emblazoned a bright red cross that they had so devoutly sworn to honor.

Mere days ago, pilgrims from around the world embarked on the sacred Hajj, ignorant of the inferno that lay in wait. The camera zoomed to various scenes. The anchorwoman narrated the massacre as if it were the script to a blockbuster movie. Within Mecca's granite walls, families and strangers held each other, suffering as they burned to death. Many exited the city, knowing escape was futile, they chose a bullet from the enemy over the torturous conflagration. Hundreds died inside, making the conscious decision to die on the grounds of the first Revelation than to give their murderers the satisfaction of witnessing their handiwork.

As Kenneth's brown eyes widened in terror, the man next to him chuckled again. His arms were folded over his chest; he stood rigid, indifferent to the cold. Kenneth stood beside him, shivering, pulling the collar to his jacket as high as he could over his ears, taking as many sideways glances as he could to this strange man laughing at the smoldering Muslims. He was a tall, bulky black man. His suit was black. The man stood out, a dark entity embroidered on the dreary and snowy urban backdrop.

Kenneth tried to ignore the man, turning his attention again to the screen.

But then the man spoke to him. "It's beautiful."

Kenneth hoped the man wasn't referring to the killings.

When Kenneth took a while to respond, the man asserted himself further. "Isn't it?"

"I'm not so sure," Kenneth replied, careful not to blatantly disagree with the man, who was taller and more muscular.

They never faced each other while speaking, but they both watched the news and spoke to the glass. Kenneth did not want to turn to the man. He was too intimidating. A turn toward him could be interpreted as a confrontation. The man, on the other hand, was clearly uninterested in Kenneth. Kenneth posed no threat. The man seemed as if he was used to talking to people without looking at them.

"Consider the world devoid of false deities," the man said. "Everyone united under God. Only then would we as humans be great. Our path to this goal is always hindered by those who preach something different, teach something different. And those people must be eradicated."

Kenneth refocused his eyes on the glass, looking at the reflection of the man rather than the images on the television screen. The man's reflection smiled back at him.

Kenneth continued staring at the man's reflection, looking for a change in expression, cautious not to offend him. "Don't you think they'd just find the path on their own? If it truly was the truth?"

"That's too slow. Think of the world you live in. How much it has changed since you were a child. How are we where we are today? Certainly not by pussyfooting around our problems. That's why the church has all the power. That's why they will rule." He unfolded his arms. Kenneth saw a glint of silver on the man's chest in his reflection. It was strangely reminiscent of something, but he couldn't figure out what.

"Don't you agree?" The man pivoted so he was facing Kenneth, looming over him, his chest right at Kenneth's face.

The image from his nightmare, of the bodacious succubus wearing only the silver lamb necklace whipping him until he fell unconscious, hijacked his reality. Kenneth tried to blink away the chilling picture. He took in a quick breath, catching himself before it was too obvious.

The man cocked his head and squinted his eyebrows, noticing Kenneth notice the necklace. He tucked it into his collar. "Problem?"

"No," Kenneth stammered. "No problem. I agree with you, actually. You know, with the church and stuff." Kenneth turned and stared awkwardly at the television, the back of his neck and cheeks turning red.

Kenneth stood trembling in his boots, not from the cold but from fear of the man standing next to him. He wasn't entirely sure what he was so afraid of, but he knew there was something off-putting about him—his words, his mannerisms, something that told Kenneth to run.

The man also turned back to the screen, a tension lingering between them thicker than the falling snow.

And for a while, the news report broke that tension, instead replacing it with dread—for Kenneth, for pride, for the man beside him. Louder than the cracks from the modern-day Crusaders' gunfire, louder than the constant *whop-whop-whop* of the spinning helicopter blades, the wails of the church's burnt offerings filled the air.

Kenneth imagined how deafening it would be if he were there among them. He stood transfixed by what he was watching. Someone bumped into his shoulder, interrupting his stare. Kenneth realized it was late morning, and more pedestrians hurried past him down the sidewalk. It was then he noticed that the man had vanished; nobody else was standing with him watching the news. In fact, every storefront with a television as far as he could see down the block was empty. And every storefront television was playing the same station, the same news story. Apparently rushing to work or getting a morning cup of Starbucks coffee was more important than the slaughter in the Middle East. Kenneth sighed; he knew that if the Yankees game was on, people would stop and cheer, or, at the very least, give a passing glance to check the score.

He melted into the crowd, walking unnoticed to the subway.

The sign on Kenneth's volunteer clinic should have read The New York Clinic for Disabled Persons. However, some plastic letters on the face of the building had long-since fallen away. The sign read: T e New York Clini fo isabled P r ons. The building itself matched the poor appearance of its sign. The paint dirty white; windows were hardly clear, useless to their purpose; ivy grew up the walls, and weeds sprouted from cracks in the sidewalk and along the curb. Kenneth approached the building. A peeling yellow sticker read Caution Automatic Door. He had never seen the glass doors at the front of the clinic perform this function; they have been broken since he started working here, so he pushed them open and walked in.

"Hello, Kenneth." The woman behind the reception desk took her hand away from the family-size bag of potato chips just long enough to wave. She didn't even need to look up to know it was Kenneth. He was one of the last volunteers. "Here for Jason?"

Rhetorical question, he knew. Just like his response was by rote. "Yes."

"Before you go, take this." She held out an envelope.

"What is it?"

"Money. We had a little extra tucked away somewhere."

Kenneth shook his head. "This is a service; I can't accept that."

"Honey, I know you pretend to like this gig, but you'll eventually get fed up of cleaning up shit all the damn time. That's why everyone else leaves." She slipped the envelope into his shirt pocket and patted his chest. "Go on, Jason's waiting."

He turned and walked silently down the hallway to avoid any dispute.

He called into room 110. "Jason?"

He heard two claps from within, the all-clear. Kenneth entered.

Good morning! Jason's freckled cheeks wrinkled into a smile.

Good morning! Kenneth signed back. Jason could understand spoken words but lost his ability to speak when his brain damage worsened. He had received severe trauma to the head after being brutalized by the police. When Kenneth dropped out of college, he spent his spare time learning basic sign language to establish a better friendship with Jason.

"How's it going, buddy?"

I am fine. Thanks for coming. What's that? He pointed at the envelope sticking out from the top of Kenneth's shirt pocket.

"Nothing. Don't worry about it," Kenneth said, zipping up his jacket over his button-down. He sat on Jason's bed. Jason was once a metal-head graffiti bomber, but since his accident, he could at times express his emotions like a child. The slightest hurtful remark could ruin the kid's day.

What about you? How are you doing? Kenneth made

sure to catch each of Jason's hand movements. Kenneth was still learning.

"I'm okay, I guess." Kenneth shrugged. "I had a bit of a rough morning."

Was it Jennifer?

Kenneth laughed. They had spoken about Jennifer before. It was not uncommon for people to dislike her, but Jason seemed jealous at times. "No, no. Other things," Kenneth said. "Besides, what would you know about relationships?" He nudged Jason on the shoulder.

I know my nurse has a crush on me. I'm going to ask her on a date once I'm cured.

Kenneth smiled at the thought of Jason on a date with the overweight receptionist. Then, immediately after, he felt saddened at Jason's optimism. Once he's cured. "You go for it, buddy."

Back to the same topic: Jennifer. *Why would you stay with her anyway?*

"Eh, money, rent, tons of things." He tried to dodge further conversation. "Let's just get you over to the shower."

As Kenneth pushed the wheelchair toward the bathroom, he caught sight of lumps of feces on the tile. He realized Jason tried to hide it by moving his wheelchair over it before Kenneth walked in.

"Sor," said Jason with difficulty. His cheeks were red.

"It's okay," Kenneth replied, rolling the chair into the bathroom. "Take off your shirt, if you can. I'll clean up."

Kenneth pulled some paper towels from the dispenser. He walked over to where Jason tried to hide his accident. As he crouched down to wipe up the mess, he heard the crunch of the folding envelope in his shirt pocket. He closed his eyes and tried to ignore it, when he opened them again he saw his hand, gloved with yellow rubber. He looked up his arm, and then at his entire body. He was wearing a hazmat suit. Not this. The fecal matter on the floor was replaced with blood, and the small hospital room changed into a street corner in the projects. Kenneth couldn't shake the image from his mind—him a cleanup crewmember for violent crime scenes. Kenneth scrubbed in circles, mopping the blood off the pavement on the street corner. He knew who this blood belonged to. It belonged to Jason, the Jason of two years ago, the same Jason who defied order with his slanderous and sacrilegious portrayal of the Almighty. Kenneth couldn't even recall what Jason had painted. It only goes to show how easily any undesired image can be censored by the church. Jason had fallen for a message that had never reached an audience. And when the cops came, Kenneth did nothing to prevent it. He just stood and watched as the police beat the poor kid down.

Kenneth felt a moistness under his palm. He looked down; he was no longer wearing the yellow glove, no more hazmat; he was back in the hospital room. Then Kenneth realized he had been smearing shit into the floor in circles at the same spot. It seeped through the paper towels and onto his hand.

"Fuck," he whispered to himself, and then looked up at Jason, shirt off, waiting patiently in the bathroom. Kenneth finished cleaning. He stood up and helped Jason with his shower.

Kenneth checked the mailbox before walking up the stairs to his apartment. A letter from his father, along with a check. As usual, he opened the envelope and took the check, throwing away the letter without reading it. He already knew what it would say, some sappy congratulatory note about being a college man. He couldn't deal with the guilt any longer. He was no college man, he was just some pushover with no job and a father who'd scorn his own son if he knew any of this. He hadn't yet told his father that he'd dropped out of New York University in September. He'd been failing all his classes—not because he wasn't capable of passing but because he never went to any of his classes. And when he did, he'd end up arguing with the professor. He spent most of his time pent up in the library reading and rereading books that most people ignored. *Utopia, Brave New World, V for Vendetta.* The dust on the book covers suggested they hadn't been checked out in years, and the tabs on the inside covers confirmed it. By the time he quit school, he was convinced he could learn anything he wanted without college, simply by reading. His latest efforts: sign language and caretaking. Besides, he began to think institutionalized learning was a scam—the tuition, the loans—all to exploit the young and dumb.

Kenneth took his time climbing the stairs, thinking of a lie for Jennifer if she happened to nag him about the job search. He lethargically unlocked his front door. He wiped his feet on the mat before walking in.

Jennifer sat cozily on the couch, a bowl of chips on her lap, watching her favorite television show, *Desperate Housewives.* Untouched, the waffles waited on the table. Unread, the love-note on the table.

"You didn't eat my breakfast."

"Sorry, I was in a rush. Woke up late after you woke me up."

He took the plate from the table, dumped the waffles into the trash can—not the garbage disposal as not to interrupt Jennifer's TV time—rinsed the plate, and then placed it in the dishwasher. He also tossed the note into the trash.

"Can you switch to the news? I need to see something." The fact that the television was tuned to something other than the news, let alone *Desperate Housewives*, seemed to disgrace the memories of those Muslims who lost their lives earlier that day.

"Babe, I love this show. Just come watch it with me." She rubbed the couch cushion beside her.

Kenneth complied. He plopped down and glared at the television. He rolled his eyes at the bad sex jokes while his girlfriend laughed. On the screen, five women fought back their midlife crises with makeup and promiscuity. He looked but did not watch, instead reflecting on the events in his day. A deep pain grew inside his chest, but he was unable to locate its source.

Kenneth put his arm around his girlfriend, her head naturally falling to his shoulder. He ignored the pain and focused on the television, replacing his boring reality with the lives of five women in a romantic comedy.

"How was the job hunt?" she asked.

"Fine. I may have an interview soon," he lied.

She raised her eyebrows. "Oh really? Are you sure you weren't just playing around with those retarded friends of yours?"

Kenneth rubbed his face with his hand, tilting his head back and exhaling audibly. "Yes, I'm sure." He wasn't in the mood for an argument. "Here." He handed her his father's check and the envelope from his shirt pocket. "I did a side job for a friend. Made some extra cash."

"This is your dad's."

"Not the other one," he said, pointing toward the envelope.

She forced a smile and placed them on the coffee table. "Let's watch our show."

Kenneth soon grew bored. He kissed Jennifer on the cheek and neck and placed his hand on her thigh.

"Not tonight," she said, "I'm tired. Long day at the coffee shop."

He slumped back into the couch cushions, silently pretending to enjoy the program. When the first commercial came, he spread his arms into the air, faking a yawn. "I'm going to get ready for bed."

"Okay. I'll be there soon." She kept her eyes on the television as she answered.

He grabbed her iPhone from the kitchen counter on his way to the bathroom, typing in search terms with one hand as he undressed with the other. The video buffered as he waited for the shower water to heat up. He cautiously stepped into the shower, protecting the cell phone from the water. Stroking himself with his soapy hand, the thought of his sexless relationship slowly left his mind, like water down a drain. There was a time when he regarded this action a violation of the boundaries of their relationship. But that was also a time when he'd make love to his girlfriend at least three times a week. When he finished, he sat at the edge of the tub, the shower head directed toward his mess, and patiently waited for it to find its way down the drain, just as his memories of happier times had.

He slid into bed wearing only his underwear. He heard the faint murmurs of TV chatter. Jennifer was still in the living room. Kenneth breathed in deeply the lavender-scented sheets. They must have just been washed. He deleted the search history on the cell phone and then lay still under the covers, smelling the lavender, and falling into a heavy rest. Before he dozed off, he felt the cell phone vibrate, a text message. He tapped the screen to life and read the message.

Gerald: Sure, what time tomorrow? ;)

Kenneth looked for any other messages from this man but found none. He found no sent messages either, like they had all been erased.

He threw the phone across the room. It bounced off the wall before resting on the floor. He stood up and paced. The city streetlights cast shadows into his small, dark room; they waved back and forth on the walls in time with his steps.

Who was Gerald?

He stopped and looked out the bedroom door, clear vision of the living room, his girlfriend sitting on the couch. She was the only one here besides him. His only outlet, the only other person for him to take out his anger on.

He walked a few steps forward, almost exiting the room, feeling his rage rise. Then closed the door so he couldn't see her. "No. It can't be." He fell face first into his pillow. And as he slipped into sleep, alone in his bed, he wondered about the frequency of which Jennifer has been changing the sheets. He thought about the increasing time he'd been spending with Jason and the decreasing time with his love. Now, for some reason, the usually pleasant lavender scent of the sheets was off-putting.

Chapter 2

"Look at me!" the hideous woman growls.

He does, for it is all he can do. Trapped in his hogtie, he is forced only to look forward. His arms extend unnaturally behind him, bound to his raised feet. He felt his spine extending, the discs being pulled apart, a terrible agony spreading through his back. A silver lamb swings inches from his face by a thin chain, the woman crouches in front of him, her thigh muscles bulging. She massages the flat blade of a hunting knife, smiling at the helpless man, the veins on her forearms webbing their way up her massive biceps. She sets the knife down and picks up some metal apparatus, clamp-like, something out of a dentist's office. "Open wide." She pries apart his lips and jams the device into his mouth. It pulled in either direction, keeping her victim in an endless yawn. "That should make things a little easier." She picks up her blade and pinches the tip of his tongue between her thumb and forefinger, stretching it as far back as she could. The blade's edge was recently sharpened; his tongue comes off quickly.

His eyes widen, and a gurgled moan erupts from his gory orifice. Blood spatters on the woman's face, as if it weren't already disgusting enough.

She smiles and licks her lips. "Don't want you bleeding to death now," she says. Plugged into the wall beside her is a hair curler, already heated; she'd apparently planned this. With ease, unbothered by the screaming man before her, she directs the heated rod into his mouth, cauterizing the wound, destroying the nerves, sealing the gash, halting the blood flow. It is so professional. He bucks, trying futilely to escape the torturer, burning the roof of his mouth in the process. "Now look what you've done," she says, still grinning. "That could have been much smoother." She reaches for the metal apparatus holding open his mouth and then decided against it. It is probably more uncomfortable to leave it there. Unable to speak, unable to beg, to plea, the man could only cry.

"Your tears are really beginning to irk me." She picks up a spoon from the floor and balances the bowl of it on his nose, laughing. Quickly, effortlessly, she seizes one of his eyelids and cuts it off with her knife. Then the other. He groans, his Adam's apple bobbing with every whimper. She takes the spoon and scoops out an eye. It rests on his cheekbone, hanging by the optic nerve. She removes his other eye too and then cuts the nerves, his eyes fall to the ground in a few mushy bounces.

The laughing woman takes the curling iron and jams it into each of his sockets, cauterizing the red crevices. Her victim tenses, straining at his ropes, his shoulder blades protruding from his back as he wrestles to free himself. "Don't worry; it's almost over," she says, plugging his nose with clay. Calmly, she threads some string through a needle and then ties it off. She sews each nostril shut, holding her palm to his bottom lip, making sure it was impossible for him to breathe through his nose. The man is a useless sack of meat. He cannot see, he cannot smell, he cannot taste, he cannot move. He is essentially worthless to the world, aside from being a plaything for the torturer and the epicenter of screams heard in a mile radius.

Rolling balls of clay between her fingers, the woman speaks again. The last words the man would ever hear. "Leave. And never come back." She shoves the clay deep into his ears. She folds his lobes over his ear canals and sews them in place.

The man's entire existence is pain. It is all he knows. The woman stripped him of all senses aside from the sense of touch. And that sensation is reserved for misery, and misery only. He is incapable of ending his life, ending the torment. She keeps him alive. Having cauterized his wounds, he could not bleed to death. And she comes back to the dirty shed he is kept in to force-feed him and pour water down his throat, his mouth held agape by the apparatus. The pain will eventually subside, and insanity steps forward to become his new bane. For days, his brain is deprived of any stimulation besides the pain that had since faded. No sights, no smells, no sounds, no tastes. The thought-processing center in his brain has begun to malfunction, to shut down, to self-destruct. His mind had been tricked into thinking he was already dead, and it releases toxins into his bloodstream that breaks down his still-living body. The ropes, tight across his body, begin digging into his skin where the tissue had broken down. His teeth fall out. His jaw grows slack, and it eventually falls completely from his face, the metal apparatus coming down with it. His forehead is concave where his skull collapsed. Large sections of skin are missing, revealing the thin muscle and tendons beneath.

Kenneth woke up screaming.

"What's the matter? What's happening?" Jennifer was frightened. The concern in her voice was odd, Kenneth thought. Then he realized she was hardly ever concerned about him. Her worry for him now was inexplicably comforting.

"I—I just had a nightmare," he replied.

"Is that it?" The concern was gone.

He walked to the bathroom sink and splashed cold water onto his face. "Don't worry about it. It's nothing." His pounding heart suggested otherwise. He took a few deep breaths. "I need to forget." He looked at his sleeping girlfriend and his heart rate slowed. "I just need to forget."

He slid back into bed next to her, tickling her sides and waking her up.

"You've been a little brat lately," he said playfully, slapping her bottom. "Do I need to teach you a lesson?" He remembered using that same line when they first met in college.

"Not really, babe." Either she didn't remember or was intentionally dismissing his advances.

"Oh, come on. It's been a while." He slid his leg over her torso and pushed himself up on top of her. He kissed her gently on the chin, neck. He kissed her unpuckered lips; she wasn't returning the affection. "Are you really gonna make me work for it?" He tried to smile but was obviously troubled by her behavior.

Kenneth moved his head down, tracing his path with his tongue. He bit the band of her panties with his teeth and slid them down her smooth legs. He licked his way back up her legs and settled between her thighs. Before he could do anything, Jennifer grabbed him on either side of his head and pulled him up so they were face to face.

"Just fuck me."

"But we always fool around a bit first." He kissed her.

"I want you to fuck me."

Kenneth tried to ignore the way she was acting. "Relax, babe."

He went back between her legs and kissed her inner thighs, trying to taunt her, to tempt her. Then he licked the entire length of her vulva and listened to her quiet moans. She rubbed her slender white fingers through his hair. He knew something was off right away. The smell and taste was unusual. Back when they had an active sex life, he had given her oral pleasure enough times to know something was wrong. Was this another man's smell? Had she snuck out in the middle of the night? But as her back arched and her legs shook, the thought fell to the back of his mind. He needed a release. The lonely sessions in the shower were not sufficient for his desires. And one weird scent was not enough to keep him from making love to his girlfriend for the first time in three weeks. He held open her labia with his thumb and index finger, licking her insides and sucking her juices. He tried to scrape the bitterness off his tongue with his teeth but it stayed. He wasn't used to her current taste. But he still wanted her. He'd been frustrated with her for weeks and needed the satisfaction he deserved. He worked his way up to her clitoris. Holding her legs wide, he flicked her nerves with the tip of his tongue, up and down, side to side. She tensed and moaned, begging for him to come up and fuck her. He complied. He crawled up and hovered over her, easing his dick into her wetness. There was no intimacy, no romance. They did what humans have always done. He felt strange fucking her. He'd always been the type to whisper nice things and hold eye contact, but today a new beast overtook his motions. She screamed his name like she'd never done before, craving more. Clenching his teeth, he held back his own orgasm to pleasure his girlfriend further. She convulsed, gripping the sheets and rolling her eyes.

Kenneth squeezed his kegel muscles and pumped, giving himself over to her. It was not entirely mutual. He fucked her and she received it, enjoying all of it without putting in any effort. Eventually Kenneth envied her. He needed to feel what she felt.

He pulled out and ejaculated on her stomach, clenching his abs and diaphragm, sounds of bliss from his mouth. He closed his eyes and let the orgasm control his body. He fell limp with satisfaction and then rolled over and lay beside her. He took a deep breath, the lavender scent of the laundry detergent rising from the sheets, stronger than the scent of sweat and semen. The lavender.

"Oh, Kenneth. I've never seen that side of you before." She wore a look that Kenneth had not seen for a very long time.

Once shrouded by lust and his dominating sexual urge,

shame now seized his body. The odd taste and smell of her vagina assailed his nose and mouth once more, but just the memory of it. It was accompanied by the sweet scent of lavender, but it tarnished that once-fresh aroma. The lavender was vile, disgusting. It made his stomach heave. He jumped out of bed and puked in the toilet.

He marched to the bed where his girlfriend still lay naked but awake; he wiped the dribble from his lip and then snatched Jennifer by the neck with the same hand. He pulled her in close, so their faces were centimeters apart.

"Are you cheating on me?" His nostrils flared as he spoke.

"No, baby! I'm not! Where did you get that idea? Trust me! I'd never!" she begged, shaking her head from side to side.

Every fiber of Kenneth's being told him not to believe her. Told him that she was a lying, sniveling little shrew. He slightly tightened his grip. Her eyes widened and she clawed at his forearms. He held it for a moment, just so she would get scared, just so she'd know his power, and then dropped her.

"If I ever find out." He shook his head. "If I ever find out." It was all he could say. He left the bedroom, slamming the door.

Kenneth walked his normal route to the subway station, checking the news on his way. Yesterday's headline story was today's forgotten memory. The anchorwoman spoke of the super-mall opening next month. He wished he had watched the news the night before rather than *Desperate Housewives*.

The subway was still fairly empty. Kenneth sat and relaxed on his way to the clinic; he'd usually give up his spot, standing in the cramped train in silence. No thank-yous for his seat offering, no conversation at all, just the tappings against touch-screen phones and the vibrations of text notifications. He'd look down at the row of drooped necks, people looking at their devices, and think of their future back problems. But now it was early enough to sit and enjoy the silence of an empty train car, rather than the silence of an antisocial generation.

He rested his head against the window, waiting for the end of the tunnel, where the train car momentarily went above ground. On days where he could grab a place on the left side of the train car, before it got too crowded, he would see the stunning architecture of a synagogue. Often he'd wonder if the sounds of the subway disturbed temple services.

This time, passing through the back lot of the synagogue, he saw something quite different. Scaffolding blocked his view of the tall brick. Men with orange jumpsuits and hardhats carried relics from the building, piling it on the asphalt. A bearded man stood at the perimeter of the property, watching as the workers heaved a cross up the scaffolding. They placed it above an archway; a faint imprint of the Star of David could be seen behind it. The bearded man slowly walked toward the pile of debris, picked up a dusty *yarmulke*, and placed it on his head. As he walked away another man stopped him. Kenneth pushed his face against the window. He looked familiar: well-dressed, dark skin. The familiar man pointed to the *yarmulke* and then held out his open palm. Kenneth squinted, figuring out the situation, waiting for the result. The train once again descended into the tunnels beneath New York, and Kenneth slumped back into his seat, mulling over where he had seen that man.

"Jason?"

Two claps.

Kenneth walked into Jason's room. The boy's smile ushered away Kenneth's troubles, his ponderings of the past few days. He smiled back.

How are you?

"I'm fine. Actually, I'm good." He paused. "Yeah, I'm good." After a methodical life, forcing his way through college and through his relationship, volunteering had become the highlight of his day.

Good. You seem better than yesterday.

"Thanks," Kenneth said, thinking of yesterday's worry, and then, as he began to expel the disaster in Mecca from his head, more troubles seemed to replace it: the nightmares, the renovated Synagogue, his suspicions about Jennifer. He soon realized there was no escape from the terrors. He preoccupied himself with Jason.

Why do you come here? Jason signed. His arm movements were swift, not shaky as they usually were, as if he had been practicing it for a while. *Why didn't you leave like everyone else?*

"I started coming here in college. Remember the group I came with?"

I haven't seen that group in months. And you dropped out of college.

"Forgot I told you that. I was never able to get a job after college. I still wanted to get out of the apartment every once in a while. So I stayed, I guess." He shrugged.

Jason raised his hands as if to sign something and then dropped them back to his lap and looked down. Kenneth caught his mistake. He made it sound as though he only volunteered because there was nothing better to do.

"But, but, but," Kenneth stammered, "you're my only friend. And my day gets better every time we talk."

Jason looked back up at Kenneth, a silly grin on his face. *Thanks. You're my only friend too. I've really become used to you coming every day. I don't know what I'd do—*

Kenneth pulled a chair in front of Jason's wheelchair and sat down. "It's okay, go on," he said, looking into Jason's eyes.

I don't know what I'd do if you stopped showing up. I remember the first couple of times. We'd go hours without communicating at all. I was always so embarrassed. The job is so personal. I've been humiliated by my condition for years. And I was always afraid that as soon as I opened up to you, you'd just leave me. That's how it always happened. The volunteer works enough hours so it looks presentable on a resume and then leaves. And I just need to make an entirely new relationship with an entirely new volunteer the next day. I hated it. But now you're here. And I'm starting to become dependent on you. Not only because of my condition but for our friendship.

Jason had started crying. The sign language grew harder and harder to read as the tears rolled down his cheeks. His arms were shaking. Still, Jason tried the best he could to keep them steady.

I . . . love you . . . the time when . . . I still think about it all the time . . . You're just so nice . . . thank you so much.

Jason put his hands in his lap. He managed to squeak out a single syllable—"thanks"—through all his hiccupping and sobbing.

Kenneth fought back tears of his own. "Don't worry," he said. "I won't be going anywhere." He smiled. "Besides, I'm here for more reasons than you think."

Really? Jason's hands were wet from the tears he wiped from his cheeks.

"Yes."

Kenneth put a dollar into a homeless man's upside-down hat before he stepped onto the escalator. The man was playing a saxophone and nodded when he saw the money drop into his otherwise empty hat. As Kenneth rode the escalator up to street level, he listened to the notes and melodies echo off the tile walls. With a smile, he thought of Jason, he thought of the beautiful music, and he didn't feel too bad about the world he lived in.

Exiting the subway station, he was met with a scene unlike anything he was used to. The side of the old brick convenience store had been transformed into an artist's canvas. In the center of the mural was a man, dressed in ripped clothing, holding a cardboard sign. It read, "I'll bet you a dollar you saw this sign." All around him were people, noses held high, rushing in various directions. These people were dressed in suits and ties. The man bore an exhausted face, sorrowful. Above the entire image was God, who, just like the pedestrians ignoring the homeless man, had his head turned up from his poor creation.

A young boy in a black hoodie was signing his masterpiece. He kept checking right and left down the street. As he focused on perfecting his signature, a dark-blue Ford Crown Victoria rounded the corner. It slowly approached the teenager, parking on the sidewalk near him. Though the windows were darkly tinted, Kenneth could see the white uniform of the city's police force. He wanted to warn the artist, tell him to run, but his words caught in his throat. Before he had time to reconsider, the officer dashed from the Crown Victoria and bashed the kid across the head with his baton. The teenager had no time to react; as he dropped sideways, a line of spray paint traced his fall to the ground from the end of his signature. Though his subject had already fallen, the officer had no intention of stopping his attack. Kenneth watched with a rising frustration. He remembered the last time he was seized by fear in the face of adversity, idle, a witness to police brutality toward a rebellious youth, a one Jason Lee.

Kenneth's inaction put Jason where he was today. No compensation in court. Kenneth swore to repay him, even though it wasn't his fault, even though no other party knew of his idle presence. Now, every day, he visited the boy to somehow correct the wrongs that the nation had beat into him.

Kenneth saw the white baton redden. With each strike, he felt an overwhelming restlessness expel the hesitation from his limbs. He rushed across the street and snatched the baton from the officer mid-swing.

"The fuck do you think you're—"

Kenneth whipped the baton across the cop's jaw before he could finish his question. His chin slid out of place with two loud pops as both sides of his jaw dislocated. The cop leaned forward and spit out a pair of bloody teeth onto the pavement before falling forward onto his own face.

Kenneth stood tall, looking down at the two hurt men. The red liquid on the sidewalk stained the cement. It looked like Jason's crime scene. Coagulating blood on the pavement. Like stinking shit on a tiled hospital floor. What he had been reduced to.

The police officer held his chin with both hands, rocking back and forth in his own mess. Retribution.

"You know that's not allowed, right?" The voice was deep.

Kenneth turned toward the source and was greeted by the buff black man in the suit, the one he'd recently met watching Mecca on the news. He dropped the nightstick.

"Don't worry. I'm a good guy. I've been observing you. But we should probably flee. You watch the news enough to know what happens to cop killers."

Kenneth was not sure whether to trust the man. Kenneth wholeheartedly disagreed with him on the church's conquest over Mecca, but that alone shouldn't make him a threat. But what of the silver necklace? He could have just imagined it, his nightmares crawling into his daydreams. The man frightened Kenneth, sure, but he had a point. The cops would seek vengeance to the full extent of the law and then some in order to protect their divine image. Kenneth glanced around at the rubbernecks in idle cars and people gathering on the sidewalk. "Yeah, let's get out of here. Do you have a car?"

"Yes. Follow me." The man led him to a Mercedes parked down the street.

"Who are you?" Kenneth asked, settling into the car's heated seat.

"I'm here to protect you."

"Why?"

The man ignored Kenneth's question. "Give me the directions to your home. Don't make it direct. Take a

roundabout way. I need to be sure we aren't being followed."
He sounded legitimate, like he knew what he was doing.

"Do I get a name at least?"

"Call me Roy."

The crowd looked around at each other for a few seconds, then at the beaten teenager and officer lying on the floor beneath the graffiti art. Cars were stopped up and down the block as drivers hung out their window to see what was going on. And for a few seconds, as the sounds of honking horns, screeching brakes, and revving engines diminished, music filled the street from the entrance to the subway, saxophone, jazz. A few people snapped pictures with their cell phones, others simply backed away as if they hadn't witnessed a thing. Eventually the crowd dispersed, and the two injured men blended into the cityscape. People stepped over them to get to their destinations, as if they were stepping over just another bum begging for change. Cars drove by, their passengers shielded from the outside within their mobile cubicle. And the melodic sounds of the saxophone was again lost under the commotion of the city.

As Kenneth gave his final directions to the apartment complex, the man began to smile, as if dwelling over a secret memory. Roy never needed the directions, he apparently already knew this place very well.

"What is it?" Kenneth asked.

"Oh, nothing." Roy's lips were pressed into a straight line. "Where should I park?" He made sure to park his car between two empty parking spaces.

They walked up the steps to his apartment. "Come on in."

"Jennifer, you're home early."

"Lunch break," she said, her back turned. "I take it your job hunt was shitty as usual?" She faced Kenneth and jumped when she noticed the man standing behind him. "Gerald?"

Kenneth scrunched his eyebrows. "I thought your name was Roy." Then he turned to Jennifer: "How do you know him?" It wasn't a question, rather a demand that expected an answer.

"From work." She spat it out quickly, as though it were the first excuse that popped into her mind.

"Really? You called this man Gerald. I've seen a text on your phone from a person named Gerald. Care for an explanation?"

The man stood with his arms crossed, never offering input, simply smiling as he watched the commotion.

"Well. Well. I." She looked back and forth between the two men.

The man interrupted. "I'm fucking your girlfriend."

"What? *What?*"

"Sorry, man." He struck Kenneth on the side of the temple.

Kenneth stumbled backward, hands in the air, trying to block the man. Again, the man punched Kenneth. He moved forward as Kenneth reeled back on his heels, pinned against the kitchen table. He had nowhere else to run. The man continued his attack.

"Please! Don't fight over me!" She ran to them, trying to pry them apart.

"Bitch, I don't care about you," Roy said, tossing her aside with one hand. "I'm here on other business. You're a pawn to me."

She slipped and fell on the kitchen tile, hitting her head on the floor.

Roy gripped Kenneth around the throat with his huge black hands and began to squeeze.

Eyes bulging, lungs burning, Kenneth flailed his hands.

Roy stooped right into Kenneth's face, flaunting his masculinity. As he smothered him, Kenneth's nose was filled with the man's musk and body odor. It smelled familiar. As when he smelled the lavender, he felt he was going to vomit again. That scent triggered an animal within him. Like the beast that fucked Jennifer, this one kills men. Then, blindly, he clutched some smooth ceramic object to the side of him. As soon as he had a firm hold, he swung it around, the plate colliding against his attacker's skull. It shattered into pieces, bits of half-eaten scrambled eggs raining around them. It was the breakfast he'd prepared for Jennifer.

Roy recoiled, releasing his stranglehold. Kenneth still held a sharpened end of broken plate. Without hesitation, he charged the man. He aimed for Roy's chest, lunging forward with his makeshift shank. But Roy blocked it with his arms, the plate wedge digging into his flesh, then sticking between the parallel bones in his arm.

Roy cried out, dropping to one knee in pain. He tried to stand up, but Kenneth caught him before he could do anything. He ripped the plate shank from his arm, chunks of meat flying off, and drove it through Roy's leg.

"Sit the fuck back down." Kenneth saw handcuffs attached to the man's belt loop. This man wasn't a cop to Kenneth's knowledge. He must be some sort of official in one of the many government agencies unknown to the public. He took them and bound him to the heater. "Wait here and watch what I do to this pretty little slam piece of yours," Kenneth growled, turning to his girlfriend, knocked out on the floor in an abnormal position.

Kenneth was not himself; he embodied his nightmare. The tortured becomes the torturer. He picked up a jagged edge of the broken plate and mounted his stunned girlfriend. He raised it above his head then drove it down into her chest. Her eyes opened, and she sprang up from unconsciousness just in time to witness her own death. She looked up at her boyfriend, his face twisted in anger. For a fraction of a second, just before the lights behind her irises faded, Kenneth thought he saw her smiling. She looked happy. Why? Was this the Kenneth she wanted? The Kenneth who killed people, the Kenneth who let his fury dictate his actions. The Kenneth who fucked his woman.

She died with a calm expression despite the pain, imagining her effeminate boyfriend fucking her like an animal, each stab like a thrust in bed. Kenneth yearned for how the relationship was in college, but if this is the man she wants. This is the man she gets. This is the man who kills her.

The man, handcuffed to the radiator, had calmed down. "Killing her doesn't mean anything to me, you know." Though blood dripped from his wounds, he seemed undisturbed. "She was just some slut I used so I could snoop around your apartment when you were away."

Kenneth crouched in front of the man. "I'm better off without her." He dragged the tip of his bloody plate against the man's neck, hooking the silver chain and pulling it up out of his shirt, presenting the lamb pendant. "You're the person from my dreams. Well, not you, specifically, but someone like you. Always wearing this lamb. Always killing me, or whichever person I am. Different centuries, different continents, different ethnicities, but one of you always finds and kills me." He applied pressure to the man's neck, drawing blood. His vein was easy to find for his neck muscles were already bulging. "I want answers, and I want them now."

The man laughed. "Oh? You haven't figured it out yet? Usually they learn their purpose before they start remembering their past lives."

Kenneth gasped. "My past lives?" He still held the man by the shirt collar.

"Yes, your past lives, idiot. You are the Buddha. You know you think differently, you know you are an individual. I ran a background check the moment I had my suspicions about you. Though it'd be extremely hard, since we control every aspect of society, we still can't run the risk of your ideals spreading. One bad apple ruins the bunch. We can't have you being the impetus for free-thinkers. You gave yourself away that time you recognized my necklace. Almost made my job too easy. My necklace shouldn't mean anything to anyone unless he's seen it before. I've been tailing you ever since. And *my* purpose is to kill you before you reach *your* purpose, to become enlightened. Because if I let you become enlightened, I risk the world becoming enlightened. And that's a bad thing." He wagged his finger like a metronome. "That means certain institutions lose their power. And if they lose their power, they lose their money. And my paycheck goes bye-bye. Think of current events, kiddo. Mecca's gone. We run the politics, the consumers, the media. The Jews are converting, everyone is converting. You are the last obstacle. With you dead, that gives us"—he stopped and pointed at the ceiling, at the heavens—"that gives Him another eighteen years or so of free reign before we need to kill the next Buddha." He looked at his watch again. "But it looks as if you've dug your own grave with these crimes. There's no way in hell you'll get off without capital punishment."

He turned his head toward the dead woman. "It's a shame. She was pretty, and you had to ruin her life." He looked back up at Kenneth. "You know, I was really looking forward to torturing you. Took it as one of the perks of the job, besides all the control and the fat payday once I got your head. But, alas—"

"*You're sick.*" He grabbed the man's neck and banged his head against the heater.

"I run this fucking city. Anytime some reincarnated vermin like you is unfortunate enough to be born in my city, I track him down and kill him. Before you go and meddle with the natural order of things. We have always been on top and always will be. There are many more like me. All over the world. No matter which country you are born in, we'll be waiting, and we will kill you. There's no running. There's no hi—"

Kenneth clutched the man's throat before he could finish his sentence, weighing down on his trachea with the full force of his grip.

"Please—killing me won't solve anything," the man managed to squeak out.

"I don't care. I'll kill whoever I have to kill to cleanse this filthy world!"

The man tore his neck away from Kenneth, leaving raised nail scratches. "You sound familiar," he said with a wink.

"*Shut up!*" He bashed the man's skull against the heater a second time. A third time. "You. Fucked. Up. My. Life." Each syllable was emphasized with the man's skull being rammed into the heater. As Kenneth continued the onslaught, two cops kicked down the front door of his apartment. A neighbor must have called after hearing the commotion.

"Freeze!"

Kenneth felt two pricks in his back, and then his muscles tensed and his entire body shook. He'd been tazed. His eyelids sank and he flopped to one side. Kenneth fought to stay awake, at least long enough to see if his victim was dead, if his chest rose and fell, if Roy had died. But he passed out before he could see any signs of the man's death.

Chapter 3

"What's going on?" the nurse asked.

"He's probably having a nightmare." The two nurses, dressed in dreary green uniforms, stood behind the glass door, watching Kenneth toss and turn inside his holding cell.

The sheets on his bed were torn off, the blanket had been thrown to the floor, and he mumbled to himself as he slept.

"What's he in for?" one of the nurses asked.

"Listened to the news on the radio on my way to work. Apparently he just went on a rampage. He killed a teenager on the street and then killed a cop who tried to help. Then he went to his apartment and killed his girlfriend and another guy. Crazy shit, man."

"You really think he did all that alone?"

The nurse looked up and down the hallway before replying. "You know the media loves to exaggerate. And you know the media would never give so much coverage to some whack-job; the government banned media coverage of mass-murderers, claiming it bred more of them, remember? They are trying to slander him, to discredit him. He must know something."

They watched him a while longer.

"He's being held in this psychiatric ward due to the nature of his crime until his trial. The less we know the better."

"Let's come back later after he's awake." The two nurses walked down the white hallway to tend to other patients.

Kenneth fidgeted in his sleep, groaning. There he lay, discomforted, his mind littered with happenings of his past. The moans finally came to an abrupt stop when he rolled out of his bed and fell to the tiled floor. The fall woke him, but he did not get up right away. Rather, he lay on the cold tile floor, shivering as the sweat and tears chilled him further.

"Where am I?" he asked when he finally stopped crying. He sat up, assessing his environment. "Where am I?" He took in his surroundings, the white walls oddly reminiscent. And as he garnered his senses, making out where he could be, he noticed another patient watching him. The patient rolled his wheelchair as far as he could against his glass door and peered across the hallway into Kenneth's cell.

"Jason?"

The patient looked in either direction, a finger pointed at his own chest. "Me?"

"Jason! I'm so glad to see you."

"No, I'm not Jason. You must have the wrong—"

"Jason? Don't you recognize me? It's Kenneth!"

"That's not me. I-I'm someone different. I—" The patient began tapping his fingertips on the armrests of his chair, his eyes darting every which way. Never completely focusing on one object.

"Jason! Don't pretend like you don't know me! Jason! Jason!"

"That isn't me, man. I'm just. Look, man." He took handfuls of his own hair. "Just stop. Stop it."

"No, Jason. Answer me! Why won't you answer me, Jason? I've missed you, kiddo!"

"*No. Stop. Please, I'm not Jason. Stop!*" With wobbling legs he stood from his chair, pounding on the glass. "*Stop!*"

Kenneth continued his badgering. "Just look at me. Jason?"

And so it went. The stranger pounding on the walls of his cell, drowning out the voice of the new patient in the communal psychiatric ward. Both on the verge of tears, they yelled at each other, only eleven white tiles separating the two. Their yells echoed down the hallway, agitating each neighboring cell's inhabitant, the wails counteractive to the numbing drugs, meant to subdue these legally insane criminals. As each patient fell from his blissful high, more throats were turned up to the atmosphere, spewing screams of their own. Hospital gowns, white sheets torn apart. Knuckles bleeding from punching the walls of their holding cell. Tears fell. Deranged prisoners slammed the call buttons on their nightstands.

The two nurses rushed down the hall. "What's going on?"

It's him. That man. Him. Him.

Blaming fingers pointed down the hallway.

The nurses rushed in the direction they pointed, already pulling sedative syringes from their kits.

"Fucking look at me, Jason! I know you can fucking see me."

The mistaken patient sat rocking on the floor, red bald patches on his head from where he had ripped the hair from his scalp.

"*Fucking look!*"

"One day, and look what you've done. Ready?" The nurses nodded at each other. "Get him!" The male nurse swung open the glass door, and as Kenneth rushed from his cell the second nurse grabbed him from behind. "Stop fighting. Calm down." He eased the needle into Kenneth's thigh, pressing its liquid into his veins.

"What should we do with him?"

"Let's put him in solitary confinement." The orderlies looked around at the sobbing patients. "Obviously he's not suited for common holding."

Chapter 4

For the first few nights, images of his former selves plagued his dreams. Each night a ghost of a past life came to visit, retelling the story of its death. Always by the hands of the one who wore the silver lamb necklace. Portraitures of rape, mutilation, and disfigurement were engrained on the inside of his eyelids from the relentless nightmares. The sensation of pain had become all too familiar, had become synonymous with the dreadful words *leave and never come back*. He was almost certain that if someone were to utter those words in his presence, he'd feel physical pain, wrought by the psychological association he'd formed between them. He'd wake up thrashing in bed, turn over to hug his girlfriend, to hug the night terrors away, and then realize she was not there and that he had killed her. Some mornings he'd awake just to puke in the corner. Other days he'd lie motionless in bed, dreading the moment when the inevitability of weariness conquered his mind yet again. *Leave and never come back.* He didn't want to think about it. He just wanted solace, numbness.

Kenneth rolled out of bed and walked to the corner of his tiny cell. He sat cross-legged, staring at the concrete wall. It was the first time since the tall black man, Roy, Gerald, whatever, had told him his true identity that he'd really begun to think about it. Everything happened so quickly. He was too busy suffering to think about his identity.

Seven billion damn people and I'm the one.

He was right.

I'm the next incarnation of Buddha.

Who do I trust?

Those dreams. They've been killing me over and over again for centuries.

What do I do?

Are they still after me?

Fuck. I'm not even fucking Buddhist. I haven't meditated a day in my life.

I'm reaching Enlightenment. How do I know when I'm there?

Signs?

Am I supposed to save the world? I can't save it if I'm not yet enlightened myself.

I just fucking committed murder. Off to a shitty start.

Seven billion damn people and I'm the one.

Why me?

He sat and thought. For hours he sat and thought. The barred shadows of his window arched across the room as the day wore on. Midday. A nurse cracked open the door and slid an aluminum tray across the floor. "Your meal." The green beans, chicken nuggets, and mashed potatoes sat on the tray. Almost as motionless as Kenneth. The heat dissipated into the air.

Kenneth sat and thought, waiting for something to come. But nothing came. The day changed to night and Kenneth still sat in the same position, waiting. He grew weary, his head rested against the wall, and eventually sleep sneaked inside him, waiting for something to come. But nothing came. And for the first night in a while, no dreams came either.

*

He woke with the odd sensation of a fretless night. "Babe?"

He patted to his side, expecting the tender flesh of his girlfriend's skin but felt nothing. He forgot she was dead. He forgot he had killed her. He forgot he hated her. And he then realized waking up alone in his cell was the same as waking up at home beside her.

For the time being he felt a sort of happiness. Though imprisoned in his small ten by ten cell, the mere absence of his night terrors was enough to bring joy. But after a while, the feeling began to dull. Just like everything else. He'd live boring days and sleep dreamless nights. And his life became so mundane that he fell into a deep depression. He no longer had a purpose. Even if he did, he was trapped. An empty feeling inside him. His body was absent.

He had time he never knew he had. Time became his friend and enemy. Lots of it was spent thinking of Jason. Their sessions together throughout the year, the laughs they shared, but inevitably, day after day, his mind wandered to their last meeting. The poor child put his soul on the table, declared his love, his dependence, and Kenneth was gone the next day. Usually the nightmares kept thoughts of reality at bay, but with their absence, Jason's image presented itself evermore. There was never an hour where Kenneth did not think about the kid. It became haunting in a way. The sense of betrayal tore heavily at his heart, until there eventually came a time when he hated being awake and longed for sleep. His failure became a living nightmare, a constant reminder of his now meaningless, unfulfilled existence.

The weeks bore on. Restlessness hung on his every limb. Thoughts of death crept into his brain, and he began to curse every rounded edge of the room and high ceilings, anything he could use as an instrument for his own death. For a time he thought he may waste away, perish not by any physical harm but by the shear desire of wanting an end. Sitting in the corner, waiting for the end.

But then a lawyer saved him. And for the first time in a month he was graced with the presence of a fellow human being. Each day the lawyer would visit and they would converse for a few hours, and then he would leave. Those few hours became the only thing worth living for.

He tried explaining his entire situation to the lawyer. That he was the next Buddha, that he was becoming enlightened, that he had a mission to enlighten the world. But of course the lawyer never believed him. In fact, his ranting seemed to support the case he was trying to build. "You will plead insanity at the time of the crime," the lawyer always said. And he had said it so many times that Kenneth began to believe it was true, that he was indeed crazy.

"That's our case," the lawyer said, "and we're sticking with it." He stood up and adjusted his tie. "See you in a few months."

The next day when the lawyer did not return, Kenneth cried. And he finally understood what Jason felt. Like his friendship was led on. Like he was betrayed. And at this very moment, though his eyes were shrouded with tears, he saw, with clarity, himself for the first time. When the lawyer left, he took part of Kenneth with him.

After Kenneth detached himself from his ordinary life, from Jason, the center of his personal universe, he consequently detached himself from whatever path to self-discovery he may have been on. That is why the dreams had since faded. He was no longer remembering his past lives. The Buddha within him died, without anyone physically killing it. Kenneth had severed it through his own choices.

Kenneth wiped the tears from his eyes and crawled to the corner of his cell, cradling his knees to his chest. This was his new existence.

Kenneth sat staring into the corner. The door behind him opened. He waited for the aluminum tray with bland food to slide across the floor, just as it had every day for the past three months. Instead, the nurse walked in.

"Hey. Put this on." He tossed a suit onto the bed. "Your lawyer sent it to you. Your trial is in an hour."

A nurse on either side, they gripped Kenneth's triceps and led him to the elevator at the end of the hall. He was giddy with the thought of leaving this place. As the elevator descended, the length of time between each *ding,* signaling a new floor, grew exponentially.

When at last they reached ground floor, a nurse turned a key in the elevator control pad to open the doors. With only his first step, a sudden realization of where he has been overpowered him. The white walls. The tiled flooring.

"Hey, Kenneth. Never took you as the murderous type." The same obese receptionist sat behind her desk. "All that time you spent volunteering, now it looks like you're the one who needs help." She chuckled, her neck fat rolling as she reached for the Big Gulp on the counter.

Kenneth ignored her. His eyes wide, he took in the familiar place. This entire time, only a couple of floors from what he once knew.

"Are we leaving now?"

"The car isn't here yet," the nurse said, looking through the window in the lobby at the parking lot. "Five minutes, tops."

"Then can I visit an old friend? I know which room he's in. I just want to say hello."

The two nurses looked at each other. "I'm not sure we're allowed," one said after a pause.

The receptionist chimed in. "I know the kid. Let him go. He used to volunteer here. It should be fine."

The taller of the two nurses gripped him tight by the arm, reeling Kenneth around. "Fine. Make it quick. And we're going with you. Don't try anything stupid."

"Jason?" Kenneth called into the room.

Jason took a while to respond. Maybe he was sleeping. Or maybe he didn't believe he actually heard that familiar voice. Two claps.

Kenneth crept into the room. He didn't want to startle the boy.

The nurses stood by his side, making sure he wasn't attempting an escape. But Kenneth truly wanted to see his old friend, to talk to him, to apologize.

"Hey, remember me?"

No answer.

"I know you're angry. And I just want to say I'm sorry."

Still no answer. Just a blank stare. The brakes in his wheelchair were pulled up, his arms folded. No intention to move. No attempt to greet his old pal.

Kenneth's cheeks turned red. The nurses were clearly doubting he even knew Jason. Kenneth needed to fill the silence before he was dragged out of the room by the nurses. "I'm not sure what stories you have heard about me, but I want you to know that I still care about you. You're my friend. I thought about you a lot."

Jason pressed his palms into the armrests, balancing himself as he struggled to stand. His knees were shaky, and he looked as if he could topple over at any second.

Kenneth took a few steps forward to help, but Jason stood up quickly and raised an open hand, halting him.

"Do you forgive me, Jason?" Kenneth's voice wavered, sounding pitiful.

With the patience of a sage, Jason raised an arm, his fingers curling inward, revealing a lone index finger pointing toward the door from which Kenneth had entered. "I don't know why you left me, and I don't want to hear you make excuses. All I know is the mockery they made of you on the news. That you thought you were The Buddha. That you sought enlightenment for the world. But you snapped and killed lots of people instead. Let me tell you first, if you hadn't figured it out for yourself, you were wrong. You promised me companionship and you broke that promise. Maybe this little retard right here, sitting in front of you, is what you've been looking for all along. That you could learn everything you've ever wanted from a person who couldn't even speak. Have you ever thought of that? Have you ever even considered that? Or did you become obsessed with some other destiny? That obsession blinded you, which is why you went fucking psycho. You had tunnel vision. Whatever you wanted you thought you could achieve with a straight and singular path. But you were wrong. You forgot about the world the path set through. And like a fool, I waited for you to return. That was one of the worst mistakes I've ever made, aside from spray painting that wall." He kept his outstretched arm, index finger, once pointed, was snarled into a nasty hook. "Leave. And never return." His voice was strong, dominating, unmerciful. It was the first time Kenneth had ever heard him speak with his voice, not his hands.

It couldn't end like this. Kenneth couldn't follow that command. He couldn't passively obey that order just as he had passively watched Jason get beaten. So he spoke up. "I feel somewhat responsible for your brain damage. I never knew the right time to tell you this, but I guess we've known each other long enough." Kenneth looked at the ceiling, thinking of what to say next, as if the words were written up there.

The two nurses took Kenneth by the shoulders and led him backward, Jason pointing the way. The old friends held eye contact as Kenneth was dragged away, Jason's eyes receding into unforgiving squints, Kenneth's eyes watery with the tinge of the forlorn.

"The day you were jumped by those cops, I was there. I saw them knock you over and continue to beat you even though you were down."

The nurses kept dragging him away, and as they pulled him farther, Kenneth yelled the rest of his apology. "But I was too scared to do anything. I couldn't stop them. So I stood and watched. When I found out you landed in here, I took it upon myself to try and make your life happier. As some form of repayment. I hope you can forgive me. I'm so sorry."

As the nurses carried him away, Kenneth took in the last he would ever see of Jason, the one person he truly loved. He took in the final sight of the ward where he had spent so much time. The smooth flooring with missing tiles. The bleak white walls, empty as the minds of the people they enclosed.

The drive to the courthouse was a one-way conversation. The lawyer sat beside Kenneth, reminding him what to say, what to plea, the details of his case—that he was legally insane at the time of the crime—but Kenneth said not a word. He silently stared out the window, watching the city roll by. Every pedestrian, every driver, and every passenger he saw sitting in other cars bore the face of Jason. Kenneth closed his eyes and pretended to sleep the rest of the way. He knew why the dreams had stopped. He knew what he had become. He knew why Jason had no desire to see him. He knew that with the knowledge of his differences, his insight, his concern, his enlightenment he was simultaneously ignorant. He knew he had already died yet lived on, trapped within the shell that is skin and organs and flesh. He was not the next incarnate, not anymore, not since he let the pressure of the world's burdens collapse on him. He snapped; he reached his edge, his limit. He killed people. And with that, he had killed himself. He knew everything yet knew nothing.

"Please be seated," the judge said, walking up to his seat. "All persons are innocent until proven guilty. You have the options to plead guilty, not guilty, or no contest. You have the right to obtain counsel. If you cannot afford an attorney the court will appoint an attorney for you." His words were monotonous. He had said that same statement hundreds of times on hundreds of different days. Though it was nine a.m., and his first case of the day, he was obviously not happy to be there. "Please come forward."

Kenneth watched his opponent step to the stand. He didn't recognize him or the people sitting at the table.

The judge addressed the plaintiff. The bailiff swore him in.

Kenneth walked to his stand afterward. Then, after the judge swore him in, he said to the courtroom, "We are here today to try the case regarding the murders of Jennifer Constantine, Shawn More, Officer Joshua Sanchez, and Officer Frances Ratzinger, with a maximum consequence of death."

Kenneth carefully listened to his charges. The only name he recognized was his girlfriend, Jennifer. Shawn must have been the graffiti artist. Kenneth knew for a fact that he did not kill him. Officer Sanchez was the one who beat Shawn. Kenneth knew also that his hit with the baton could not nearly have killed that cop. Officer Ratzinger. That must be the old black man, his hunter. He finally had a name. Everyone in the courtroom could smell the pungent foul-play, but no one risked addressing it

"And I have to take the blame for all of this?" Kenneth whispered to himself.

"Shhhhh." Kenneth turned his head to see his lawyer's glance of disapproval.

"Mr. Kenneth Hatta, how do you plead?"

Kenneth adjusted his weight from the balls of his feet to his heels and back again, rocking to and fro. He thought about Jason, who no longer loved him. He thought of the world that seemed to reject his very being. He was refuse, blowing in the wind with all the other garbage littered throughout the world.

Kenneth cleared his throat. "I plead guilty."

The lawyer shot out of his seat. "No, no, no, no. No, no, no. He does not mean that. We've been over this."

"Sit down, please," the judge said, raising his gavel. "Sit down, now."

Kenneth turned and growled at his lawyer. The lawyer slumped back into his seat, his face reddening, Kenneth watching him until he was fully settled into his chair.

He looked up at the people in the crowd, then his opponents, and then back at the judge. "I plead guilty. I'm guilty of destroying myself when I thought I was destroying the enemy. I'm guilty because I sought too hard for something that I never knew I already had. We all have it, and none of us see it. We're all guilty of the same thing. I'm just the one who dies for it."

The judge raised his gavel but hesitated. "The crimes. No sweet talk. Are you guilty of the crimes?"

Kenneth felt his words carried no weight. He sighed. "Yes. I plead guilty to the crimes."

The judge slammed the gavel on the wooden pad on his desk. The polished scale, held by the bronze statuette of Lady Justice on the judge's desk, rocked gently.

The light was bright. His body illuminated for the families of the victims. Tight leather bands restrained him. He saw Jennifer's parents. He saw his own father, his disappointment. He saw crying faces, angered faces, all people dressed in black. The needles were already in his veins, connected to tubes, now empty, soon to be filled with his cause of death.

"Last words?"

Part of him wanted to stay silent. Die wordlessly. It wouldn't matter in the end. In such a short time, he acquired vast knowledge and lost great wisdom. He only wanted to sleep a dreamless sleep. "Even if I was who I thought I was, there is nothing I could do to save the people I love. It would be difficult for even the one person who is awake in this sleeping world. We are a ruined kind. And there is nothing we can do about it. I should have known that. I should have just lived my life, caring for the person I loved without obsessing over external circumstance. At least I would have been happy. At least he would have been happy. That is all."

Kenneth watched as the tube in his left arm filled with liquid, the sedative. He peered through the glass separating him from the vengeful family members watching his death. Most had stopped crying; it was the first time they'd seen someone die. A temporary fix. The least he could provide. He felt drowsy; his eyelids drooped halfway shut. Before he slipped into his final sleep, he saw one distinct face in the crowd: A massive black man in a pressed suit. He smiled at Kenneth, a silver lamb necklace hanging from his neck, and mouthed the words, *It's not over.*

Kenneth was ripped from his drowsiness. Every muscle in his body tensed and then locked into place. He tried to move but was paralyzed. He focused on turning his head, from tearing his eyes from the man sitting in the crowd, but couldn't. He couldn't even force his own eyelids down. That would be his last image, his final reminder never to return to this damned world. Through his unblinking stare, his eyes began to tear up, and Kenneth found it a blessing as it obscured his vision of the man in the suit. But when the tears fell, it left lines of red down his cheeks. Kenneth felt a stinging sensation in his esophagus, his acid reflux. Vomit wretched its way upward to his clenched jaw, a dam blocking the putrid river. He couldn't open his mouth and gagged on his own fluids, his body beginning to writhe uncontrollably as he drowned. A frothy red dribbled from the corners of his mouth, first slowly, and then it spewed as the pressure pried through his locked jaw.

"What's going on?" the doctor screamed. "We need to help him!" He waved his hands before Kenneth's eyes, searching for a response. "He's suffering! I don't know what to do!"

"Let him squirm." A cop stood at the one entrance to the room. "Criminals like him deserve the cruelest form of death." He spit on the floor.

Twin streams of blood fell from Kenneth's nose. Bubbles formed at his nostrils in sync with his laboring lungs, his chest rising and falling in great differences. The restraints across his body prevented him from breathing in fully. His earlobes were stained red from the constant dribble from the canals, like wearing ruby earrings. The front of his prison uniform was stained, a red blemish over his crotch, puddles forming at the bottom of his pant legs.

"Someone's tampered with the machine!" the doctor cried, checking the fluid pump attaching the tubes to Kenneth's arms. He rushed to the cop, who smiled at the entire scene. "Wipe that stupid grin off your face and shoot the man. He can't go out like this. Nobody should."

"No."

"Fucking shoot him!"

The officer pulled out his pistol with a sigh, nudging the doctor out of the way with the butt. "Fine, punk." He closed an eye and peered through the crosshairs, leveling the barrel on Kenneth's head, and pulled the trigger. The shot went low. It tore through his Adam's apple without taking out any major arteries. Just another bloody gash, adding to his pain.

"Are you fucking kidding me?!" The doctor threw his hands in the air. "You're ten feet away! Who the hell hires these guys?" He pointed at Kenneth's head. "Shoot him again, *now!*"

"I can't! The gun's jammed!" The officer held the gun between his legs, fumbling with the metal frame.

Kenneth focused on the man in the crowd. *Leave and never come back.* The man exaggerated the motions as he mouthed the words.

"Christ!" The doctor took a scalpel from off the table and ran up to the bleeding patient. "I've never killed. I'm sorry." Tears built up in his eyes and then fell when he brought the blade down on Kenneth's head. It cut deep, but he wanted no mistakes. He tore it from his skull and drove it down again, deeper, again, deeper, again, deeper, digging into his brain long after he had died.

The doctor dropped the scalpel and then collapsed to his knees in front of Kenneth, kneeling in the blood. He sluggishly looked up at the man he had just killed. Kenneth's neck had fallen limp, and, drooping forward, he seemed to look down at his savior with lifeless eyes.

The doctor wiped the tears from his eyes, and gazing up, the blinding industrial hospital light created a radiant corona around the dead man's head.

Fallen Apple
Sultan Z. White

"Open the fucking door."

I hesitated, fingers around the knob, as I caught the scent of alcohol on my father's breath, so strong it seeped through the thick cedar. Father banged on the door with his first row of knuckles, not knocks but punches. I slowly unlocked the door, standing on my toes to reach the top deadbolt and working down, because I knew that if I waited until my father was finally able to fumble the key into the lock it would make the beating worse. I opened the door, demolishing the barrier between us, revealing my father, ripe with the odor of a night of drowned sorrows. The stench of booze hit me hard, with a fist behind it.

I fell to the floor, my bloody nose dripping down my face, like the putrid fluid that saturated Father's piss-stained jeans. Father got completely shit-faced that night at the local bar; he had been kicked out by the owner and stumbled home muttering obscenities at mannequins in shop windows. I knew that tonight would be bad. I curled up into a ball, desperately trying to soften the ceaseless blows. Some tiny twisted thought told me to forgive Father, that he's only doing this because Mom died, that he only became an alcoholic to cope with the longing. But as I caught sight of Father's bulge, an erection straining against the zipper in his pants, getting harder with every strike to the side of my temple, I knew Dad didn't actually miss Mom but was pissed off that he hadn't gotten laid in more than a year. That's when I knew I'd never forgive him. That's when I knew I'd never give Father the satisfaction of taking out his sexual frustration through vicious drunken abuse.

The bus screeched to a stop, its brakes wailing as it decelerated the metal mass, crying out for the under-funded public transport in this area of town. I stepped onto the sidewalk, endless desert across the street; behind me a flickering neon sign, *Master Toddy's Muay Thai*, struggled to stay lit. I was on the outskirts of Las Vegas. I walked toward the gym, less than a quarter-mile, yet had to ignore a drug dealer asking, "Hey, wanna hit?" and a block later a hooker asking almost the same question: "Hey, baby, wanna hit?" this time accompanied with the flash of a loose and overused pussy. I considered heading back home to the nice suburban area of Vegas, but that would be heading back to more nights of helpless assault. By the time I grabbed the door handle to the gym, wet with who-knows-what, I had already made up my mind.

"Four hundred a month," the short man said. I wasn't sure if I heard him correctly, maybe it was the accent. A thick Thai accent, with extraneous syllables and drawn-out vowels.

"Four hundred?"

"Yes."

I considered. *Where could I get that kind of money?* I figured I could steal it from Dad; he'd be too wasted most of the time to realize anything was missing. "Deal."

"Today's your first day. Do you have workout clothes?"

I was taken off guard. The short Thai man was already nudging me toward the mats. "Um, no."

"Then buy." The short man pointed me toward a dinky equipment store in the corner of the gym.

Looking at a pair of Muay-Thai shorts, the price tag hanging from the waistband displaying its ridiculous amount, I started to fume. *This guy's trying to rip me off because I'm a kid.* But as I approached the hanging Muay Thai shorts, gloves, and shin pads, I realized the posters covering the walls. The short man was Master Toddy, just much older than in the pictures. I calmed down and did as he said.

The going was tough. I (well, Father) would be paying $400 a month for thorough ass-kickings. But unlike the free ones I received at home, I was being trained how to fight back. I'd be exhausted the entire bus ride home, always getting a row to myself as the smell of sweat repulsed any possible seat-partners. Drifting in and out of consciousness I dreamt that my sparring-mates were my father, finally getting a chance to defend myself against the onslaught. I learned the movements of the ancient Thai art. "The deadly art of eight limbs": two fists, two knees, two elbows, two shins. My bruises came in pairs as well, pouring out my fury on hanging leather bags until the skin on my knuckles thinned, the skin on my shins and my knees and my elbows thinned. No more bruises from Dad, his beatings waned as I gained weight and muscle. I was stronger and more intimidating. No longer was I approached by the whore on the street corner or the drug dealer nearby. For an entire year, everything went smoothly.

I felt strong walking home. My trips home from the gym were swift, eager to rest for the next day of training. I remember when I'd drag my feet the entire walk home from school, unsure of whether or not my father was falling into an oblivion of Bud Light. As I held the doorknob, I noted my firm grip and the veins surging under the skin in my forearms. I opened the door—

"You've been stealing my money." My father punctuated his sentence with a beer-induced belch.

And I instantly became the scared child of my past.

He chucked a bottle at me, which exploded into shards against the wall near my head. Some pieces sliced into my cheek, drawing blood. He ran toward me as I held my palm to my face to stop the bleeding. However, instead of goring me into the wall like he had done before, I took a step back and front-kicked him in the chin. He landed on his back, the glass on the floor digging into his flesh.

"I'm not taking your shit anymore, Joe."

My dad tried standing, propping up onto his elbows, but I kicked him in the forehead and his head snapped back to the floor. I mounted him, my knees touching the floor on each side of his body.

"Son, I'm so sorry."

"No you aren't. That's what you'd say whenever Mom threatened to leave you, but you never meant it. You'd beat her again within the next week." I punched him in the nose, causing the back of his head to smack the floor. It was so satisfying. Master Toddy always taught to stop fighting once you've disabled your attacker, but the beating my dad was about to receive was long overdue. And it was way too satisfying to stop.

I continued striking him, left, right, left, right, left, right long after he had lost consciousness. His loose chin slopped to and fro with each hit. Puke dribbled out of the corner of his mouth. The scent of liquor enraged me even more. I kept punching his limp body until my arms grew tired.

I rolled over to the hardwood floor, panting hard, and I looked at my still father. I focused on his chest, watching for the up and down oscillation of breath. There was none.

"Dad?" I crawled to his side. "Dad? Dad, wake up!" I shook him by his shoulders. He did not wake up. I stood up and backed against the wall, feeling the hot sensation of tears behind my eyes. I fought them back, forcing myself not to look at my dead father. For a full minute I was fine, but when I felt the erection pulsating in my jeans, I fell to the ground, ashamed, salty tears pouring from my eyes.

I was fourteen and there were no witnesses. I claimed I acted in self-defense, yet I always thought back on the pleasure I took from beating my father. The alcohol in his system and testimonies from neighbors helped paint dear old dad as the villain.

Dad would always try to haunt me. Therapy never worked, so for the next three years I defeated the haunting the same way I had when he was living: with Muay Thai. As the years rolled by, the memory of Dad became less scary and more exhilarating, almost erotic in a way. I looked forward to when he'd make his next appearance—always in the ring— so I could relive the day when I killed him. Nothing was better than a day's work of beating back the past. I became a local favorite in the amateur kickboxing scene.

Tonight was my bout for the amateur title. The venue was Master Toddy's gym, one last match-up at home court before I went professional. The crowd was amped, cheering and clapping. I knew I had to give them a show.

My opponent stood across from me, baring his teeth and beating his chest with leather-bound hands. The audience yelled louder as they saw him display his masculinity, as they saw the athlete ready to fight, but I grew quiet, with a steady fury thriving within me. Because I saw someone different. I saw Joe, my father, ready to abuse me again. The bell rang and we warriors rushed to the center to battle. The title match was scheduled for five rounds, unlike the three for under-card bouts, but I didn't expect it to go past one. I always knocked out my competitor before then.

This guy was a different story. He manhandled me for the first four rounds as if he were a father teaching his son a lesson. And I would stand for none of that. The final round began; I ran across the ring and jump-kneed the roaring kickboxer in the face. The crowd stood up and cheered, louder than ever. I landed on the balls of my feet in front of him, grabbed the back of his headgear, and kneed him in the face again and again and again. This was technically illegal in amateur matches, but the referees usually let it slide because the spectators loved it. However, the fanatic cheers morphed into boos as the members of the crowd realized I wouldn't stop. I repeatedly kneed him in the face, rearranging his features. The audience started throwing their concessions into the ring, showing their disapproval at the sight of the man with a crimson river flowing from his mouth and nose. But what I saw was my drunkard father and his dislocated chin spilling out alcoholic vomit.

The referee pushed me in the corner; the boos of the crowd filled my ears and mind. I roundhouse kicked the referee in the solar plexus. He fell to the floor gasping for air, making wretched croaking sounds. Silence descended upon the entire gym.

I hopped over the ropes and trudged through the crowd; every person made sure to get out of my way. No one made a sound. I walked directly to the temporary bar in the corner of the gym and took a forty off the rack. I promised myself I'd never drink, but fuck it. I downed it right in front of the bartender without buying. He didn't say a word. Then I exited the gym, making sure to slam the door.

He stomped his way toward the bus station, until he caught a familiar sight.

"I'm not even gonna bother, you always ignore me anyways," the same prostitute from his first visit to the gym said, rolling her eyes and batting her long fake eyelashes.

But Tony wasn't the frightened little boy he once was. This time he went directly to her. "No, slut," he spat through clenched teeth as he took a handful of her weave and directed her to the alley behind the gym.

Tony scrambled to pull down his pants, one hand holding the struggling hooker against a dark-green dumpster, the other fidgeting with his waistband. He forced her head down so that she was doubled over, her mini-skirt riding up her stomach on its own, exposing her panty-less privates. Tony guided his erect cock inside her, grabbed hold of a bony hip with his right hand, left hand still grasping her weave, and began pounding relentlessly, dulling his anger with each thrust. The top of the prostitute's head clanged into the metal dumpster at a quickening pace. She gritted her teeth and held in her screams, every once in a while lowly squealing if the tip of her rapist's dick happened to collide with her cervix. Not even a scream. As if she were used to this kind of treatment. The everyday life of a whore in North Las Vegas.

Tony fucked faster and faster, a tingling sensation shooting up his spine, and he knew he was close to coming. He tore his eyes from the pimpled back of the whore and tilted his head back to the sky, letting the ecstasy drown away his rage.

But when he looked back down he saw nothing but horror. He saw his mother. He saw Dad pinning Mom to a filthy dumpster, screwing her until she cried, mascara dripping from her cheeks.

Tony reeled back on his heels just as he came, wetting the hooker's thighs with his jizz. A look of terror was plastered across his face as he gazed upon what he had done. His mother lay before him, huddled against the metal in a pile of garbage, shaking, sobbing. Tony reached forward to apologize, but she kicked at him. Tony knew what he was. Tony had become the very man he despised. He had become his father.

Amber Alert
Wrath James White

Prologue

Martin James had never experienced racism before, not until Maria left him, but he'd read about it. He'd studied African American history at Harvard. There he'd learned all about the trans-Atlantic Slave Trade, the Civil Rights Movement, how the "War on Drugs" had become a war on the young black male, and a new term, at least for him, "institutionalized racism." His black studies professor had even shown him footage of Civil Rights marchers being beaten and attacked with dogs and fire hoses and then compared and contrasted that with footage of Rodney King being beaten by the LAPD. Martin had gotten angry. He'd joined several activist groups on campus and became one of the loudest voices against racial injustice, attacking it wherever he saw it or imagined he'd seen it. But he'd often felt like a fraud.

Martin's only experience of African American culture came from what he read in books and saw on campus. He'd grown up in comfort and privilege in a predominantly white upper class neighborhood in Las Vegas. His adopted parents were both white and relatively affluent, each making well over a quarter of a million a year. He'd gone to the best schools. In fact, it was attending Andover Repertory Academy that had gotten him into Harvard. The school had cost his parents $40,000 a year, almost as much as they were spending on Harvard. In contrast, his friends in Men of African Descent (MAD) and The Third World Alliance were mostly scholarship students from the inner city who had experienced racism first hand. He felt like a hypocrite when his white parents came to visit him and so he discouraged their visits and removed all the pictures of them from his dorm room. Then he'd met Maria Scolletta, an Italian-American from South Philly, and his world had changed. He'd fallen in love.

Maria was the most beautiful girl he'd ever seen. She had long curly hair, big brown eyes, a brilliant smile complete with dimples, long legs with thick thighs and breasts the size of his head. At first he had felt guilty. He thought he should have been dating a black girl. He had even tried to keep their relationship a secret. But then he had given in to his emotions. His parents were both New Age Spiritualists, Pagans or Wiccans or something, and one thing they had taught him was that some things were predestined, the will of the cosmos and that's what he felt like his relationship with Maria was, the will of the cosmos.

Slowly, Martin had pulled back from his involvement in Men of African Descent and The Third World Alliance. He had never fit in there anyway and now he no longer had to pretend. He introduced Maria to his parents on spring break and then Maria had promised to introduce him to hers. Everything had seemed perfect but then something happened. Maria stopped calling.

A few days before he was supposed to accompany her to her parent's home in Boston she had stopped returning his phone calls. When he finally cornered her on campus she had been cruel and dismissive.

"Look, I'm just too busy right now, okay?"

"What's going on?"

"I've just got a lot on my mind."

"Then let's talk about it."

"Martin, I didn't want to do this right now."

"Do what?"

"I think we should see other people. Maybe we should just be friends."

Martin was devastated.

"Why? I thought we were in love. Why are you doing this?"

"Martin, you're a great guy. Really. You are. And I do love you. This just isn't going to work."

"But why? What did I do wrong?" Martin was in tears and his voice was getting a desperate panicky tone to it. People were starting to stare and he could see that it was making Maria uncomfortable, but he didn't care.

"You didn't do anything wrong, it's just that we come from two different worlds. Look . . . " She lowered her voice and pulled Martin in closer so he could hear her without making a scene. "My father doesn't want me to see you anymore. He wants me to date an Italian boy. Maybe you should just find yourself a nice black girl."

Martin felt like he'd just taken a knife to the chest.

"What?"

"It's just not going to work between us. I'm sorry."

She turned and walked away, leaving Martin standing in stunned silence, his mouth hanging open and tears streaming down his face. This was his first experience of genuine racism and it made his stomach revolt.

Martin ran to a nearby trash can and threw up. He had just been dumped because he was black. He couldn't believe it. He refused to accept it.

Martin continued calling Maria, stopping by her dorm, sending flowers and notes, emailing her, waiting outside her classes to speak with her until she called campus security and they warned him to stay away from her. After he ignored their warning and tried to pull her out of class he'd been sent to the Dean's office and sent home in disgrace. His Harvard career was over. Since then he'd been working on his own solution to the race problem. He had set out to make one race. If everyone on the planet looked the same there would be no more racism.

Martin's adopted father was a genetic research scientist, but he was also an occultist. Martin found this no more odd than Christian biologists and archeologists of which there were more than a few. His father had books that he had collected over the years from all over the globe, rare books on Paganism and spirituality, dozens of books on Wicca and some darker books on spells and demons. Martin read through them all as he continued to mourn the love of his Maria and dream of a better world. He then began reading through his father's books on genetics and stem cell research. Finally, he found his answer in an ancient tome written in Latin called *The Book of A Thousand Sins* and a textbook called *Recombinant DNA and Genetic Engineering*. Between the two of them Martin held the keys to a new race of man.

Chapter 1

My name is Spencer Logan. I'd been a volunteer with Operation Rescue for over two years when I got the call. In that brief time I'd been on over four dozen searches. A lot of kids go missing in Vegas. Sin City draws predators and irresponsible parents in equal numbers. Our recovery rate was greater than fifty percent. That made us one of the more successful such programs in the country. Most of the missing kids we managed to locate were the ones who'd just wandered off and gotten lost or decided to run away for some reason. When a kid got snatched off the street by a pedophile or a gang or a pimp our success rate dropped to thirty percent. Only ten percent recovered alive. The bodies we found still haunt me. Every one of them. But some more than others. Some are full-fledged nightmares.

Doing this kind of volunteer work exposes you to the most heinous and horrific aspects of humanity. There is no limit to the terrible abominations people will commit to satisfy their perversities, for the sake of sexual release. I have seen innocent children mutilated beyond all sane imaginings, found their bodies scattered across playgrounds, crushed into sewers pipes and tucked into trashcans. I would have quit long ago, saved myself the nightmares, except not helping makes the nightmares worse. I can't stand to think that there are children out there, lost, in the hands of some pervert, that I could have helped find. So I look for them. I volunteer for every search. I am the hero. I wish I could stop.

I started carrying the gun over a year ago. After I was gut shot by a guy who'd kidnapped his own daughter and was holding a gun to her head when we found him in a park a mile from his house. His name was John Brown and he'd reportedly gone crazy when his wife died a week after their baby was born. He kidnapped her from her grandparent's house after they'd won custody of the child.

John Brown didn't look like a pervert or a lunatic to me. He looked disturbingly mundane, right up until he pointed the gun at his daughter's head, until I rushed in to try to stop him from killing her and he turned the gun on me.

He got away that day, left me bleeding in the playground sand under the swings, praying that the bullet hadn't hit my spine and turned me into a paraplegic. I was okay. The wound was through and through. When we discovered his daughter's body a day later, decapitated with her heart ripped out and bible pages stuffed in her chest cavity where her heart should have been, I felt guilty for having spent those twenty minutes waiting for the ambulance, thinking about myself instead of her. I think about her now though. Every night.

Every time I see an Amber alert, it's her face I see as I pull myself out of bed to hunt through trash cans and public parks. It's her I keep hoping to find. She was only six weeks old when she died. In my dreams she's every age from twenty-five to two months. All the ages she never got to see. Her father had the decency to shoot himself too. At least that's something.

Just before John Brown shot me he'd said the same thing to me this guy said. That's why I pointed my gun at him. That's why my finger tightened on the trigger and I thought about shooting him in the face. I didn't want to get shot again.

"You don't understand. Nobody understands. She's not human! She killed Mellissa, my wife! Drained her dry. I've got to kill her."

It wasn't verbatim, but it was close enough to make my skin crawl and bring back all the fear and anger of that day, watching John Brown point a snub-nosed thirty-eight at my stomach. The parallels don't end there either. This guy also lost his wife weeks after she gave birth. Just like John Brown's wife, his wife died of massive blood loss. The doctors said she must have hemorrhaged during child birth and continued to bleed little by little for days. I knew all about him. I do research now. I look up everything I can about the children and their families before I go out on a search. I don't want any surprises.

"She's not human, man. I swear. I'll show you."

I warned him not to move and cocked the hammer back on my Sig-Sauer .380. I could feel my legs and hands begin to shake as the adrenalin flooded my system. This guy didn't have a gun. He had a knife. I had the gun. Still, I was terrified. I kept thinking about how close I'd come to dying the last time I confronted one of these nuts by myself. I kept thinking about the ten-foot rule and wondering how fast this guy could cover the ten feet between us with that knife before I squeezed off a shot. I looked around to see if any of the other thirty or forty volunteers had caught up to me yet. But I was on the other side of the park in back of the public restrooms and behind the dumpsters. I'd followed a hunch and strayed away from the rest of the search teams.

"Don't fucking move, dude."

His daughter's name was Naima. She had tan skin and thick curly brown hair, big puffy cheeks with dimples and eyes as black as the night surrounding them.

"You've got to believe me. Somebody has to believe me. Let me show you what she is."

When he started sawing his daughter's arm off I almost shot him. My pulse rate rocketed and I began to hyperventilate as my bloodstream filled with adrenaline. I felt my finger tighten on the trigger. I clenched my teeth and squinted my eyes and prepared for the report and the recoil, but then I hesitated. Something was wrong. The child wasn't screaming. I could feel myself getting woozy. Everything was closing in on me, my vision was narrowing to a pin-dot. All I could see was the blood. There was so much. It seemed impossible that something so small could contain that much blood. Then the baby started to laugh and it was full and deep and throaty and not human at all. It sounded mechanical, like the laugh of a full grown man put through a synthesizer, or the roar of an engine. Her father began to shake. He seemed absolutely petrified and only then did I realize that it wasn't me and my little gun he was afraid of; it was the chubby little child in his arms with the curly brown hair and shiny black eyes and rows and rows of needle-like teeth behind huge billowy lips like suction cups on a guppy or a leech.

"What tha fuck?"

"You see it don't you? You see it. She's not right. She's some kind of monster."

I couldn't trust myself then. I couldn't trust what I was seeing or hearing. I wasn't about to make any decisions based on any of the things that were happening in front of me because none of them could have been real. Babies didn't laugh like that. They didn't have teeth like piranhas and eyes like sharks. And their arms didn't grow back when you sawed them off despite the fact that I was now watching the little girl's arm regenerate even as her father attempted to saw through her humerus.

"That's enough! Stop it! Put her down now!"

He shook his head back and forth. There were tears streaming down his face and his mouth was open as he tried to find the right words that would convince me to kill the child or let him kill her or whatever he wanted from me. But he complied. He laid the baby down on the asphalt and backed away. Then the thing started scampering toward me.

"Oh shit! Oh shit!"

The baby was on all fours. Not crawling like a normal baby but hunched over so that its legs were straight and its arms were touching the ground in front of it as it crossed the distance between us faster than it should have been able, grinning and giggling, its needle-like smile getting closer to me. I stumbled backward and began firing, missing three times until the thing was almost on top of me. Then it leapt.

This baby, just weeks out of the womb, crouched low like a cat and sprang into the air until its face was even with mine. It's jaw unhinged, opening wide like a snake, until I was looking straight down the thing's throat. The last bullet went straight into its mouth shattering teeth before blowing out the back of the thing's head. It fell to the dirt squealing and screaming and snarling, blood and saliva foaming from its mouth. Legs and arms twitching and convulsing like a dying cockroach, then it righted itself, returning to that bizarre four-legged crouch, only now the top of its head was missing from just above the nose. It sniffed the air as if searching for me, then it smiled again and once more leapt into the air. I cracked it with the butt of the pistol, beating it back down into the grass, pulverizing what was left of the thing's head until it lost all cohesion, disintegrating into formless strawberry pulp.

"What the fuck was that?"

"That was my child." He looked down at the ruin I'd made of his offspring and breathed a long sigh, all the tension draining out of his face and posture. He looked calm now, at peace. He dropped the knife and it landed in the grass with a dull thud.

Chapter 2

His name was Daryl Thompson, and I had just murdered his infant daughter. I had come there to rescue her, to save her from a father that I believed had gone insane. Instead, I murdered the child myself. I was still breathing hard, sweating, heart pumping like a heavyweight boxer. I had killed this man's child. Only we both knew that what I'd just destroyed was definitely not a child. Not a human one anyway.

"What tha fuck was that thing!" Now that it was over, my mind was failing to make sense of everything and that was driving me into a panic.

"I'll tell you the whole story, but right now we'd better get out of here. Those gunshots have got everybody in the park scrambling and you're covered in blood."

I looked down at myself and sure enough my arm was saturated in red all the way up to the elbow and my face and chest were splattered with flecks of crimson.

"Come on!" he yelled.

We jogged deeper into the park, the darkness swallowing us up as we circled back toward my car.

I was still trembling when I climbed behind the wheel. I was thinking about the shell casings I had left behind and wondering if the cops could somehow trace them to my gun. I knew you were supposed to pick up your shell casings but wasn't exactly sure why. I assumed they could trace them back to the store where I'd made the purchase with my own credit card. None of that really mattered anyway. A baby had been shot and bludgeoned to death in the area where I was supposed to be searching for her, and I had left the scene of the crime. I would be a suspect before they ever ran any ballistics. Either that or they'd figure that Daryl had kidnapped me. Either way they'd be looking for my vehicle. I pulled the car out of the little gated community and onto the freeway. Then I pointed the gun at Daryl. My adrenaline was still pumping hard. I was scared, confused, and angry at being made a child murderer even if I had no choice.

"What the fuck is going on!"

"My wife was abducted."

"I thought you said she bled to death after giving birth?"

"Before that. She was abducted from our bedroom in the middle of the night. It was aliens, man. Some kind of creatures from space or something. I watched them take her, but I was paralyzed. I couldn't stop them. They hit me with this green light and it made my muscles freeze up. I couldn't stop them. When she came back the next day she was pregnant. They put that thing in her."

It was insane. I would have thought it was all bullshit if I hadn't seen that thing scamper across the grass at me, grinning at me with those needle-like teeth.

"What were they? What did they look like?"

Daryl pulled out a cigarette and lit it up, inhaling deeply and blowing it out slow. He didn't even ask me if it was okay to smoke in my car and as much as I hated the smell of cigarette smoke I let it slide under the circumstances.

"I couldn't really see them. They were wearing black hoods."

"Hoods?"

"Yeah. They had these big black hoods on their heads and they were wearing long robes."

"So how do you know they were aliens?"

"Because of that paralyzing thing they did. That had to be some alien shit right?"

"I don't know."

I drove for another mile, thinking about what he said. We

passed another Amber alert bulletin about his daughter. This one had the description of my car including the license plate number.

"Shit!"

We needed to get off the freeway.

"So what do we do?"

"We need to get a new car."

"I mean what do we do about these aliens? They could be kidnapping and impregnating women all over the place."

"I'm not sure I believe this is some kind of invasion. I mean, I believe you about the abduction. I just think it might have been something else."

"Like what?"

"I don't know . . . something."

Daryl stared down at his lap and seemed to be struggling with something.

"There was something else too . . . the reason I tried to kill my daughter. The night before my wife died I heard voices."

"Voices? Where?"

"Coming from the baby monitor. We had one in her crib with a receiver by the bed and I woke up at about one o'clock in the morning one night because I heard whispering coming from the baby monitor. It sounded like two people talking real low. I thought I was still dreaming. I tried to go back to sleep, but then I heard the whispering again."

I swallowed hard. "What were the voices saying?"

"They were saying things like, 'Kill the whore and her weak husband. Eat them up. Feed the litter. Strip the meat from their bones and suck out the marrow. We need food to grow strong.' I ran into the bedroom and for a second I thought I saw someone standing over Naima's crib. It was like a shadow but more solid. Then it turned its head . . . or what looked like its head and it looked right at me and just faded into the darkness.

"I turned on the light and there was no one there but me

and Naima. She was awake and just staring at me. She didn't cry. She didn't smile. She just stared at me. It freaked me out so bad that I just backed out of the room and turned off the light.

"I couldn't sleep all night. The sun was rising before I finally drifted off. In the morning I woke up and the bed was saturated with blood. My wife was dead. She had bled out during the night. Then I looked beside the bed and Naima was sitting there with blood smeared all over her face. I kept thinking about what I'd heard the night before while I watched the guys from the coroner's office take my wife's body and I just snapped."

I thought about John Brown pointing a gun at his daughter's head. Perhaps I had misjudged him. That made two women who may have been kidnapped and impregnated and if there were two there may have been more, perhaps even many more. Dozens? Hundreds? Thousands? Las Vegas was a big town.

"I need to make some calls. I've got some friends on the force."

"Cops? They're not going to believe you! They'll lock your ass up and mine!"

"Cops are people too, Daryl. If I believe you maybe they will."

"But you don't believe me!"

"I told you, I believe you about the abduction and the impregnating. I'm just not sure we know who or what it was that did this. I'm just not ready to say they were little green men from Mars."

Daryl shook his head and then dropped his forehead into his palms, drawing his knees up to his chest and continuing to shake his head back and forth.

"No. No. You only believe me because you saw it! They won't believe shit!"

I turned to look at Daryl.

"If I saw it maybe one of them has seen something weird

too. I mean, I doubt you're the only one this is happening to. They might know something."

Daryl paused. He was rocking back and forth in the seat with his knees still drawn up to his chest, nibbling his fingernails and staring out the windshield.

"Okay. Okay, but don't tell them where we are."

I dialed my friend Detective Ramon Chavez. He worked in Missing Persons and had been on more than a few child searches with me. We'd had beers together a few times when the searches had turned up something bad. He answered on the first ring.

"Hello, This is Chavez."

"Hey, Chavez. It's Spencer."

"Spencer? Fuck, where are you, dude? Everyone thinks Daryl Thompson kidnapped you. You okay? Why did you take off like that? They found the Thompson kid dead."

"I know. Daryl is sitting right beside me."

"Oh shit. Is he holding you hostage? Where are you?"

"I'm not a hostage. You need to listen to me. I saw something today, something that has me all freaked out. I think I'm losing my mind."

Chavez paused on the other end of the line. When he finally spoke he sounded tense.

"What exactly did you see, Spencer?"

There was a tone in his voice that I couldn't quite put a label on. It sounded almost threatening, as if he were warning me not to continue. I dismissed it as my own paranoia. I told him everything. His response surprised me.

"Shit, then they're real."

"What do you mean, they're real? You've seen them too?"

"I was on a call last week. A couple that worked at one of the software companies downtown hadn't shown up for work in weeks. The woman was out on maternity leave, but the husband should have been at work. She'd had her child a month before, at home, with a midwife. Nobody had seen or heard from her since. Her parents lived out of town and when they didn't hear from them and couldn't reach either of them at work, they called us. We knocked a few times and nobody answered so we kicked down the door. It was fucking terrible."

I swallowed hard. All the saliva in my mouth had dried out. My voice cracked when I spoke.

"What-what did you see?"

"Bones. That was all that was left of the three of them. Just bones, man. And by the time we busted in there it had already started cracking them open and sucking out the marrow. The floor was tacky with congealed blood."

"It?"

"You know what the fuck I'm sayin' here! The goddamn baby! It was eating its parents and the damned midwife."

I didn't know what to say.

"Fuck. So what are the cops doing about this? Are the FBI involved?"

Chavez snorted derisively.

"The goddamn feds swooped in and took over the whole case. They tried to make me and my partner look like we had imagined the whole thing."

"What happened to the baby?"

"I shot the damn thing. It came after me. The thing jumped onto the wall and was sticking to it like a damn spider. It came scrambling toward me and then it leapt off the wall and attacked my partner Dave. I kicked it off of him and put ten bullets in the thing. I blew its head off and it kept trying to get at me. There was nothing left but the bottom part of its jaw. The top half of its head was gone, but it was still clawing at my ankles and trying to gnaw at my shoe. I started shooting it in the chest. I nearly cut the thing in half before it finally died. I called it in and I had half the damn homicide unit there in about fifteen minutes. The CSU guys showed up and started taking pictures of everything and filling their little fucking ziplock bags. The homicide boys started interviewing me and Dave and that's when I realized that I was now one of the victims. Some techs showed up from the coroner's office and began collecting pieces of the thing's skull and sticking it into one of those little body bags they use for kids along with the rest of the corpse. Then the damn Feds showed up and locked the whole thing down. They kicked everyone out. They took the case over before we could even get the body to the morgue. The M.E. never even got a chance to look at it so it was me and Dave's word against the Feds. Dave had these bite marks on his face where the thing had tried to tear his cheek off. Its teeth had broken the skin and a chunk was missing, but they all acted like it was none of our business."

I shuddered as a chill ran through me. Feds? Was this some kind of government experiment that had gone wrong?

"And I'll tell you what's weird as fuck," Chavez continued, "normally, when there's an officer involved shooting, there's all kinds of paperwork, an investigation, a visit to the shrink. I killed a kid, man, and there was none of that. The FBI did this bullshit little interview with me to verify my story. They didn't even write anything down. I felt like they were just trying to find out how much I knew and when they realized I didn't know shit they just started ignoring me again. My office, didn't ask me a single question. Nothing. They didn't even want me to write a report. I didn't have to justify the bullets I fired. My captain just handed me ten bullets to replace the ones I used and told me to let it go and get back to work."

"Weird."

"Yeah, weird as fuck. They just made the whole thing disappear. There wasn't a word of it on the news or anything."

I had to think about this. Maybe it was some sort of experiment but that didn't seem likely. Not involving US citizens in the middle of a major metropolis. Maybe Daryl was right and this whole thing did have something to do with aliens. Some sort of government cover up. Some Area 51 type shit.

"Hey Chavez, this thing has got me completely freaked out. Can you meet with us? We need your help. Right now Daryl is accused of kidnapping and I'm going to be facing a murder charge if I can't get some answers. I just killed a kid, dude, and unless I can prove that it really was some sort of alien or something, I'm going to prison or the damn gas chamber."

"My shift isn't over yet, man."

"Fuck that, I need you!"

There was silence from the other end of the phone. I could hear Chavez covering the phone and cursing out loud.

"Listen, do you know where I live?" Chavez asked.

"No. I mean, I was there once when we watched the fights together, but I can't remember."

"I live in Green Valley. Warm Springs and Eastern. It's a gated community called The Pinnacle. The gate code is 6673. My address is 126 Legendary Drive. Go there and wait for me. Just park in the driveway and wait."

"All right, I can do that. How long will you be?" I asked.

"Does it matter? What the fuck else do you have to do? Just sit there and wait. I'll be there when I'm done and we'll figure this all out."

He hung up and I told Daryl what he said as I continued south on the 15 freeway toward Green Valley.

"Well, how long do you think he's going to be?"

"I don't know and he's right. It really doesn't matter. We've got nowhere else to go."

Chapter 3

We pulled through the gates of The Pinnacle. It was a small gated community of single family homes. The builder had been more creative than most in Vegas and had designed it so that no two homes would be alike. There were at least eight different floor plans with three different elevations and apparently the exterior paint color and stonework was optional as well. With all of those choices it was a bit of a letdown when we pulled up in front of Chavez's home.

His house was a single story with gray ceramic roof tiles, gray paint, and purple, blue and gray slate stonework around the garage and front door. His driveway, which was composed of red cobblestone, was the most colorful thing about the house. Even his landscaping was composed of a tan stone the color of the desert sand with yucca, sage, and rosemary planted here and there. Not a dash of color anywhere. Either Chavez was colorblind or had some sort of aversion to vibrant colors.

I pulled the car to a halt and sat there trying to put together some kind of plan.

"Hey, Spencer?"

"Yeah?"

"You believe me now, right? I mean, this cop pretty much confirmed everything I said and everything you saw back there."

"Yeah, I guess."

"Then how about taking that gun off of me?"

I hadn't realized that I had still been pointing my pistol at him the entire time. I lowered the weapon.

"Thanks. So what now?"

"Do you have any idea how this happened? I mean, your wife? Her pregnancy was normal and everything? They didn't see anything unusual on the ultrasound?"

Daryl shook his head.

"Everything was normal. We had regular checkups. We even did one of those 3D ultrasounds. She just looked like a regular little girl."

I hesitated a second before I asked the next question. Daryl noticed my apprehension.

"What?"

"I hate to ask this but why didn't you have an abortion? I

mean, if you knew they had put an alien or something inside of her then why did you go through with the pregnancy?"

Daryl looked out the car window and shook his head.

"We didn't know for sure. It could have been my baby inside of her. Besides, we're Catholic. We don't believe in abortion."

"Better to give birth to a monster?"

"I told you, we didn't know anything was wrong with it. All the tests came out fine."

"But even if there was a chance . . . "

"If there was a chance it was my kid I wasn't going to murder it."

There was no sense in arguing with him. It was a matter of faith and that was something I didn't understand. If there was a chance in hell that my wife might have been carrying a baby that was implanted into her by aliens or demons or something there would have been no power on earth that could have persuaded me from getting her an abortion. But I am not and never have been religious and after years of hunting for lost children in my spare time, I was running short on hope and faith.

We sat in silence for a while. I stared out one window and Daryl stared out the other. I kept seeing that little infant scampering across the grass on all fours and then leaping at me. I could still see it charging forward with half its skull blown apart. I reached out and turned on the radio.

There was a hip-hop song playing, violent, misogynistic, just what I wasn't in the mood for. I turned to a soft-rock station and wallowed in my own misery as some whiny annoying band like Journey or Air Supply sang about love. I wanted to shoot myself, but I just wasn't in the mood for anything hard. After another three minutes and a Queen song, I turned to a jazz station. Ten minutes later Chavez showed up.

He was dressed in a sweaty blue shirt that looked like someone had used it as a napkin. His red tie looked only slightly cleaner. There was a big yellow stain on it that looked like old mayonnaise.

The detective walked by our car and waved for us to follow him as he marched up to his front door. I tucked my gun back into its holster and left the vehicle. Everything felt surreal, like some clandestine meeting between spies or underground revolutionaries. What was worse was the way Chavez hadn't even looked in my direction when he walked past the car. It made me feel like a criminal, something I had never been or ever wanted to be. It almost felt like we were going to do a drug deal and I began to worry, perhaps irrationally, if maybe Chavez was wired and after we'd told our stories the Feds would come busting in and arrest us all for kidnapping and infanticide.

Daryl and I followed Detective Chavez to his front door and waited as he turned off his alarm system and put his Rottweiler outside. The dog hadn't made a peep the entire time we were parked outside or even when we walked up to the door with the detective. That creeped me out for some reason. It was like the dog was lying in wait to ambush us had we been foolish enough to try to break in.

Chavez looked Daryl and I up and down. He paused on Daryl and stared at him for a long, hard moment. He looked at my holster and his eyebrows furrowed. I know it sounds weird but I had never really thought of Chavez as a cop until that moment. Not like the assholes that stop you for going a couple of miles over the speed limit or having an expired registration. Chavez was just a guy who was committed to finding lost kids just like I was. I had always looked at him almost as a social worker. But now I was seeing him as suspects saw him and it was intimidating.

"Sit down."

We took a seat on the couch and Chavez sat across from us on a recliner. He didn't recline but leaned forward, staring hard at both of us.

"So, you said that some guys in hoods broke into your house and kidnapped your wife?"

Daryl nodded slowly.

"But you didn't call the police? I checked and there's no report."

"I didn't file one."

Chavez leaned forward.

"Now, why would a man watch his wife get carried out of their marriage bed by men in hoods and robes and not call the police?"

"They paralyzed me. I couldn't move. Then I passed out and when I woke up my arms and legs felt all weak and goofy. I tried to get out of bed and fell right on my face. Then Jessica came out of the bathroom. She was crying, but she refused to talk about what happened to her. A month later her OBGYN told her she was pregnant."

"So, she never told you what happened to her that night?"

"No. She would yell at me and burst into tears whenever I tried to bring it up. She was terrified when she found out that she was pregnant though. She told me that it was them. They had put a baby in her, but when I asked her what she meant by that she locked herself in the bathroom. After we had the ultrasound and they did some sort of DNA test for down syndrome and everything looked fine she relaxed. But then the thing killed her."

Daryl's eyes were filled with tears but they didn't fall from his eyes. It looked as if he was starting to run out of tears.

Chavez's features relaxed a bit. He reached out and put a hand on Daryl's shoulder.

"I know this is hard, but can you tell me about the birth?"

Daryl looked as if Chavez had splashed water on his face. He sat straight up. His eyes widened and his mouth dropped open.

"It tore her apart!" It was exactly what he had told me. I shuddered to think what he meant by that.

"I'm so sorry. I know this is tough for you, but I'm going to need to hear all of it, all the details."

Now the tears spilled from Daryl's eyes. I felt a tightening in my gut. Something fluttered in my stomach. I didn't want to hear this. My imagination was already doing a number on me. The last thing I wanted was to hear the gruesome details. Daryl closed his mouth then opened it again but nothing came out. His eyes looked far away, filled with horror and dread. He shook his head slowly as more tears raced down his face.

"I need to hear it."

I wanted to tell Chavez to leave Daryl alone. The man was obviously hurting. Recalling what happened to his wife was destroying him.

"I was in the hospital with her. I watched that thing come out of her. I didn't know what was normal and what wasn't, but it just looked like too much blood to me. Her . . . her vagina . . . it just ripped. It tore open when the baby came out. She hadn't dilated enough, but it just came anyway. It tore open her cervix, her vagina, even her rectum. After she died they said that there had been massive internal damage that the doctors hadn't caught. The coroner's report said that some of her organs had been eaten from the inside. She just bled to death. She was in so much pain. That week before she gave birth she was in terrific pain all the time and even after the birth. She just never recovered. They tried to stop the bleeding at the hospital. They stitched her up and packed her full of gauze and then they . . . th-they just sent her home to bleed to death."

He fell into a fit of sobbing and weeping. I didn't know what to do. I felt like I should have hugged him or something, but I didn't really know the guy. I patted him on the shoulder and so did Chavez. I looked up at the detective and he motioned for me to follow him into the next room as he rose from his recliner.

"Take a moment and pull yourself together. I'm going to brew us some coffee. I don't think we're getting any sleep tonight."

I stood and followed Chavez as he walked into the kitchen. I felt nervous as if I was a school kid being called to the principal's office.

"What do you think?"

"I think we've stumbled our asses into some really deep shit," Chavez said.

"Do you think this is some sort of conspiracy?"

The detective paused, deep in thought. I shifted from one foot to the other as I waited for his reply.

"It could be. Something ain't right here. I think the Feds know a lot more than they're saying."

It wasn't what I was hoping to hear. I was hoping he would tell me that I was exaggerating, that this was all easily explainable, that he knew exactly what to do to make everything right again. One look at his face would have dispelled such naïve optimism. Detective Chavez looked frightened and perplexed.

"So what do we do?" I had to ask it. Even though I had a feeling Chavez didn't know the answer.

"We need to find these guys . . . the guys who kidnapped Daryl's wife. We've got to find out who they are and arrest these fuckers."

Really? Kind of stating the obvious. I wondered if he really thought it would be that simple.

"And how do we do that?"

"I have no fucking idea."

Even though I knew it, I damn sure wasn't ready to hear it.

"I've been thinking," I began, "I think we should just sit right here and wait until we hear about another kidnapping or missing child then we go and see if this is some sort of epidemic."

"You mean just wait until the next Amber alert?"

"We'll listen to your police radio and anything that sounds weird we go check it out."

Chavez shook his head.

"This is Vegas, man. We'll be rolling out every ten minutes. Do you know how much freaky shit happens in this town?"

Daryl walked in and sat down at the kitchen table. I took a seat across from him.

"Then we'll go to all of them. These things killed my wife. They put that creature inside of her! We'll go to every fucking call until we catch these bastards!" Daryl said.

"You guys aren't going anywhere."

That stopped us cold.

"I can't have civilians showing up to crime scenes with me. Especially with APBs out on both of you."

"You're off duty," I said. "We can just go in your car. We'll change clothes. I'll even shave my head. We'll both shave out heads. That should disguise us enough to get a quick look. Besides, no one will expect us to be running around with a cop. You can just say we're guests of yours from out of town, old college buddies, and we were all hanging out in the area when you heard the call."

"That might work the first time, but how am I going to explain showing up at ten or fifteen different crime scenes with you guys?"

"You don't explain it. At least not tonight. Who's going to know how many crime scenes you've been to unless all the calls happen in the same police district?"

"Some of them are going to be in the same district. Same cops. We'll wind up running into the same guys three or four times in one night. Especially if they're missing persons cases. There's not a lot of us over there. We could run into the same detectives on every call."

"Then we need to try to get there before the other detectives do so we don't have to answer too many questions. If they're already tied up on one call processing a crime scene when the next call comes through it should be easy for us to beat them there. You might have a lot of explaining to do in the morning but hopefully we'll have some answers by then."

There was a breathless desperate tone to my voice that I hated but couldn't seem to get rid of. I *was* feeling breathless and desperate.

"Yeah, easier said than done." Chavez grumbled. "There are razors in the bathroom. Shave your faces too."

Chapter 4

Martin James sat in the center of his pentagram surrounded by *things*. He didn't know what exactly they were even though he had created them. He had been watching them grow for months and they had become increasingly hideous and terrifying. When they broke out of their cages Martin had hastily drawn a circle of protection, muttering half-remembered spells from *The Book of A Thousand Sins* and then completing the pentagram once safely in its protection. Then the things had begun to speak to him and Martin thought he was losing his mind.

"Father? Are you afraid of us, father? Aren't you proud of us? Aren't we beautiful?"

The things surrounded the pentagram, regarding Martin with curiosity and amusement. They shouldn't have been able to talk, not this soon. They were all less than a year old. And they shouldn't have been so . . . *big*! Their physical appearance was all wrong too. They didn't look human. Martin had wanted to advance human evolution to its next step, beyond race, not create a new species. But these things didn't look remotely human. They looked like . . . demons.

Since he'd begun his experiments combining recombinant DNA and sorcery, Martin had found others who believed in his cause. Black militants from the north side of Las Vegas. He had recruited them to help him with his experiments and they had volunteered to find him test subjects—Guinea pigs.

He had begun collecting semen and eggs, altering their DNA with a genetic virus he'd manufactured in his lab and then mutating them further with spells before placing them in the bellies of crackwhores his friends gathered, bribing them into participation with drugs.

Then the whores gave birth.

Their babies looked normal even though they had each killed their mother during birth and displayed a penchant for cannibalism along with unusual strength and dexterity requiring them to be caged. Martin didn't know if he had succeeded or done something truly awful, but his friends, members of a radical black militant group called the Black Revolutionary Militia, thought he had succeeded just fine. Their leader, Asad, a tall, handsome light skinned man with green eyes, thin lips, and a slender nose, who wore his hair in an afro and sounded like one of Martin's Harvard professors when he spoke, had decided to continue with the second phase of their experiment and soon he was bringing Martin three, four, five women a night to be impregnated by these things. Martin had argued that they should wait to see what happened with the babies they had in the cages which seemed to be growing at an accelerated rate. But Asad was impatient.

"We can't wait. You have done it, my brother. You created a new breed of man. A dominant breed that will take over the world and bring an end to strife and division. This was your vision. One race! Well, you did that shit, man! The next step in the evolution of the species. You created a race that will wash over the globe, replacing modern man the way *Homo sapiens* replaced the Neanderthal.

"We tested your little zygotes on Latinos, Caucasians, blacks, Asians, Middle Easterners, Pacific Islanders, and even Native Americans and look! No matter what race or nationality their parents were, no matter what pigmentation their skin is when they are born, they all eventually turn the same color. Black. You have created a new dominant race. A new black race!"

His eyes were filled with madness and despite his own fears, Martin could feel the same madness boiling within himself. A race of black super humans ruling the planet inspired deep feelings of racial pride within him. So Martin had continued the experiments and he had watched his monsters grow. Now they were slathering and growling just beyond his pentagram. His babies, all grown up. But, though they were black, they didn't look like his dream of super humans. And though he was sure that they would do just what he had created them to do and replace *Homo sapiens*, he no longer saw it as a cause for celebration. What he'd created were abominations. He shuddered to think of what these monsters would do to the world once they were unleashed.

Martin tried to remember how many women he had impregnated with these things in the past months. A hundred? Two hundred? Three hundred? He couldn't recall. And in the last few weeks Asad had begun taking some of these older monsters with him to impregnate women the old fashion way.

"What have I done?" Martin whimpered as the creatures began to break through his circle of protection.

Chapter 5

Without hair my head looked ridiculously pale. Sort of a wrinkled grayish color like something that had been pickled. You could see every scratch and scar standing out lividly against my scalp. Without a mustache and my ever present five o'clock shadow I looked like a teenager. Daryl looked even worse. He had a big bulbous head that looked like a gumball that had been sucked and spit out. With his goatee gone his weak chin just disappeared into his neck. It was hard to suppress the urge to laugh as we drove to the scene of the first call.

Less than ten minutes had passed from the time we turned on the police scanner to when the first "unusual" call had come in. It was a domestic dispute in the northeast. A man claiming that his wife was possessed by Satan had barricaded himself in his home with his wife and newborn child. It sounded so close to the scenarios we had been discussing that a chill raced up my back as we heard the dispatcher relay the information. Daryl was excited, but that haunted look continued to darken his features. I knew that no matter what happened, tonight that guy was never going to be okay. Maybe none of us would.

Detective Chavez grabbed an extra clip for his Glock 40 cal. and strapped a snub-nosed .38 to his ankle. I still had my gun, but I was low on ammo. Daryl was the only one of us who remained unarmed. He had asked the detective for one of his guns and Chavez had simply set the burglar alarm and walked out of the house without replying. Daryl didn't bring it up again which was probably for the best.

None of us spoke as we headed toward the center of town. The air in the car felt heavy, saturated with dread. Chavez was staring straight ahead at the road, gripping the steering wheel so tight his knuckles were turning white and the veins in his forearms were bulging. His jaws were clenched tight and the chords in his neck stood out prominently. I imagined that NASCAR drivers probably looked much the same way as they lapped the track at 200 miles an hour.

In contrast, Daryl looked like a man on his way to death row. He was sweating and swallowing hard. His eyes were lowered, staring intently at his own hands as they fidgeted in his lap. Looking at the two of them I felt as if I should have been more nervous but somehow the whole thing seemed so unreal to me. That baby scurrying across the grass at me. The demonic voice that had come out of it after Daryl had tried to cut one of its arms off. It just didn't seem real. But it did give me an idea.

"Devil worshippers."

"What?" Daryl and Chavez asked in unison.

"The black hoods, the demon babies, it has to be some kind of occult thing."

Chavez scoffed, but he kept his eyes on the road and his grip on the steering wheel tightened. I had seen the prayer candles in his bathroom when we went in there to shave. I knew that he believed in angels and spirits which meant he probably believed in demons as well, even if he refused to admit it.

"Devil worshippers? But what did they do to my wife?" Daryl asked from the backseat where he'd been sitting in a near stupor.

"I think they put some kind of demon inside her."

"Bullshit," Chavez declared. "That's just bullshit. That thing wasn't a damn demon. It was flesh and blood. You killed one and so did I. You think you can just blow a damn demon away with a few bullets?"

I shrugged. "I'm no demonologist, but I heard that thing laugh and it wouldn't be hard to convince me that it came from hell. It kept coming at me even after I'd blown its damn head off!"

"I think it's some kind of genetic experiment. Some kind of government biological weapon or something," Chavez said. He sounded insincere, as if he doubted his own words.

"The government is kidnapping women, impregnating them, and then sending them back home? That doesn't make sense. They would do it in an underground lab or a military base somewhere no one would hear anything about it. This is too sloppy, too reckless. Whoever is doing this doesn't seem to give a fuck if we know or not. They seem to want those things to get out into the population."

"So then you think it might be terrorists?" Chavez asked.

"I don't give a fuck who or what they are," Daryl whispered. Something had changed in his voice. It had hardened. It sounded cold now. I turned around to look at him and his eyes had taken on the same hardness that was in his voice. It was that thousand-yard stare that war veterans, convicts, and hookers got after years of seeing things, surviving things, that no one should ever have to experience.

"I just want to kill every damn last one of them," Daryl said. "My wife was the only thing I had to live for. I loved her and I never treated her right. I cheated on her. I complained about her weight. I drank too much and yelled at her. Called her names and shit. After she got pregnant I wouldn't even touch her. I was a fucking asshole and she was never anything but good to me. Now she's dead and I never had a chance to apologize to her and show her how much I loved her. Those fuckers took all that away from me. They need to pay for that. They're going to pay for that shit even if I die trying."

"This isn't a revenge mission. We're going to find out what's going on and then we're going to arrest these sons of bitches. They'll stand trial and go to prison like any other criminal. You hear me? We aren't killing anybody."

"But these aren't like other criminals are they? I think we can all agree on that. Whoever did that to Daryl's wife, created those demon-baby-things, wasn't just some street chemist. Whatever we're about to find, it's not going to be anything like any of us have ever seen before."

That pretty much ended the conversation. We all sat there trying to imagine what it was we were about to see when we arrived at the scene. We didn't have long to think about it. Chavez exited the freeway at Washington Blvd.

We raced down the boulevard, then turned onto a side street, whipping back and forth through a maze of cul de sacs. We were now less than a mile away. We turned onto Raeburn Street where the dispatcher had said the man was holding his wife. Any hopes we had of being the first on the scene were dashed by the black and whites blocking off the street, another cul de sac. This one filled with cops.

"You guys are going to have to stay in the car. It looks like a full-blown hostage situation."

Detective Chavez flashed his gold shield as he drove past the black and white patrol cars. One of the officers pointed him to the house as if there was any doubt which one it was. All you had to do is look which way the guns were pointed.

SWAT showed up a few minutes after us. I was hoping they didn't kill the guy. I had to know if his wife had been kidnapped too. Maybe she would be willing to tell us where they had taken her and what exactly they had done to her.

Chavez parked behind the other police vehicles.

"Stay in the fucking car. Let me find out what's going on."

He climbed out of the car, popped the trunk, and took out a Kevlar vest and a shotgun. He hung his badge and ID from a lanyard around his neck and jogged over to a group of detectives assembled directly across from the suspect's house, leaning against an unmarked car.

Half an hour went by before Chavez climbed back into the vehicle.

"Was it one of those demon babies?"

"I don't think so. The guy is just some speed-freak who thinks his wife has been having orgies with demons. No mention about anything weird with the kid, but we'll keep checking in. I think SWAT is about to go in. In the meantime we've got another call. A guy reported his wife missing, then called right back to say she had come home. No one else is going to look into it so I figured we might. It's probably nothing, but you never know. Then there's a call up at Sunrise Mountain. A woman says she was kidnapped and gang-raped."

Either one or both of the calls could have been an abduction like the one Daryl's wife had experienced. They could also have been nothing, just another day in Sin City. Detective Chavez turned the car around and drove us back through the police barricade. We decided to go to Sunrise Mountain first. There was no rush to get to the other call because we would be the only ones investigating it.

It took us just over ten minutes to get there. There was a

black and white parked out front, but Chavez was the first Detective to show up. We climbed out of the car with him and walked together to the front door. A uniformed officer, a tall Asian guy with hair that looked like it had just been styled at a salon, opened the door for us. Chavez flashed his badge.

"Detective Chavez. What do we have here?"

"James Taylor," I said, offering my hand. I was hoping that Daryl would pick up my cue and make up a name as well.

"Richard Murphy," he said, shaking the officer's hand.

The officer nodded and never asked me and Daryl for our IDs.

"Officer Mike Cho. You guys with Sex Crimes?"

"Missing Persons. We heard there had been a kidnapping?"

"Yeah, but she's back now so she's not really a missing person anymore."

"We'll check it out anyway."

In the living room the victim sat on a couch with a small black officer with hair cut almost as short as mine. He looked like a kid barely out of high school.

"These detectives are from Missing Persons. They want to have a word with Mrs. Ditmar."

The young cop stood up and shook all of our hands, introducing himself as Chad Jones. He was the first black guy I'd ever met named Chad and I had to stifle the urge to say so. He closed the notepad he'd been scribbling in and gave us a raised eyebrow and a shake of the head, then cut his eyes sideways in the direction of the victim. He obviously thought she was nuts.

The woman on the couch looked to be in her late forties or early fifties, but she'd had so much work done that it was impossible to tell her age. She could have even been in her sixties. She had enormous, ridiculous-looking fake breasts that resembled flesh-toned basketballs glued to her chest. Her face was a mask of plastic surgery scars that made her skin look tight and shiny. Her lips were so full of collagen that they looked like two big sausages. She was wearing a sheer nightgown with just a bra and panties underneath and her legs were tan and muscular. She had a six pack, but there was an obvious liposuction scar just above her panty line that I couldn't help staring at. It was evident that she spent numerous hours in the gym fighting to regain her lost youth. There was something both sexy and hideous about her. The kind of woman you'd fuck if she came on to you strong enough but would gnaw your arm off the next morning trying to get away from.

"Mrs. Ditmar? Is it okay if we ask you a few questions?"

"Please, come sit down, boys."

Her voice was deep and scratchy as if she'd been smoking two packs a day since age twelve. It was almost an Eartha Kitt, Cat Woman purr but raspier and with more bass. I wondered if perhaps Mrs. Ditmar was really a man. I'm not a detective or a psychologist, but the immodest way she was dressed said anything but gang-rape victim.

Chavez sat down and we sat beside him.

"My name is Detective Chavez. Can you tell me what happened to you this evening?"

"Ellen Ditmar. You can call me Ellen."

"Okay, Ellen. What happened to you tonight?"

Mrs. Ditmar reached out and took one of Chavez's hands pulling it to her chest, right into her cleavage as she closed her eyes in some exaggerated expression of anguish. She dropped his hand to her lap and held it there on her thigh. Chavez looked like he was about to crawl out of his skin. Obviously, Mrs. Ditmar was not his type.

"Well. I was asleep in my bed. I had just taken a Xanax so I was sleeping pretty deeply which probably explains why I didn't hear them break in. They were all over me when I woke up. Their naked bodies were pressed against me, crushing me into the mattress."

"Did you see what they looked like? How many there were?"

"They were black and there were six of them. Big, strong, muscular, black men with big long cocks thick as my wrist. They ravaged me right there in my bed. They took me one at a time and then all at once. They sodomized me. They made me swallow their cocks and then they ejaculated all over me."

She began rubbing the Detective's hand over her nipples and then down between her thighs, grinding her clit against it. Chavez snatched his hand away and leapt from the couch as if he'd been electrocuted. Even Daryl had to turn away to keep from laughing.

"I think we've heard all we need to."

"But I didn't tell you about them blindfolding me and driving me to their dungeon."

"I'm sure it would make a lovely story, but I think these two can handle it." He shook his head and rolled his eyes as he turned to the two officers. "Good luck, boys."

"Wait! You can't go! They put something inside of me! I can feel it growing in me. It's inside of me!"

Chavez turned and stormed out of the house red-faced. Daryl and I followed behind. I giggled nervously at the absurdity of it all. Daryl smiled back mirthlessly. Under different circumstances seeing that old chick try to fuck Chavez's hand would have been hilarious. But after Daryl had just watched his daughter tear its way out his wife's womb and then stood by helplessly as the woman he loved bled to death, then seeing his child transform into some type of demon and get her head blown off, I wasn't surprised that he couldn't find any humor in the situation. Remembering what had happened at the park I found all the humor draining out of me as well.

When we returned to the vehicle reality hit us. We had been to two 911 calls now and we were no closer to figuring this thing out.

The next call was in Green Valley about twenty miles away on the other side of town.

"Are you sure this is the best way? There's got to be more

we can do than just follow these random calls hoping to get lucky and find a lead."

"I think this is the only way. What else can we do?" Daryl answered.

"It may take us dozens of calls before we find a real lead. That's police work, my friends. Clues don't just fall out of the sky into your laps. It's tedious, boring, exasperating work sometimes, but if we want to find out what's going on and keep you two out of prison than we need to stick with it," Chavez said.

Mark and Valerie Trevor lived in a big two story house that overlooked a golf course. There was a guard gate and Detective Chavez paused at the gate to ask if the guard had seen anything unusual tonight.

"Did you notice any strangers coming through here, any vans or large SUVs with tinted windows?"

"A lot of SUVs came through tonight. Almost everyone who lives here drives an SUV."

The guard was a muscular Latino guy in a black beret. His uniform had stripes on the shoulder and he wore a gold badge. Chavez quickly dismissed the guy and continued through the gates to the Trevor's home.

Mr. Trevor was waiting at the front door in his pajamas and robe when we pulled up in front of the house. The guard had called ahead to let him know we were on our way. Mr. Trevor's eyes were bloodshot and his hair was disheveled. He was smoking a cigarette and there seemed to be a slight tremble in his hands as he raised it to his lips.

"Mr. Trevor?"

"Yes?"

"I'm Detective Chavez, Las Vegas Metro Missing Persons Department. Do you have a moment? We wanted to discuss the emergency call you placed earlier."

"Thank you for coming. Please come in, detectives."

I had been expecting him to tell us that his wife had been in the home all along and that it had all been a mistake, but he seemed eager to talk to us about something.

"I understand that your wife is home now?"

"Yes, she is. But something isn't right."

Chavez turned and looked back at Daryl and I. We were all thinking the same thing. Maybe this was what we had been looking for.

Mr. Trevor walked us through an expansive entryway with a slate floor and into his great room which had a twenty-two foot ceiling and a fireplace as tall as me. We sat on a big plush couch made of some sort of soft tan suede. The couch had gold tassels hanging from it and looked like it should have been in a showroom and not in someone's living room where strangers like me might sit on it and scuff or soil it. I was actually nervous about sitting down and brushed off the back of my pants before I did so.

Daryl looked just as uncomfortable as I was and had squeezed himself into one small corner of the couch as if trying to minimize his impact on the furniture. Chavez plopped down onto the couch with utter disregard and for one horrible second I was afraid he was going to rest his feet on their stained-glass and brushed nickel coffee table. Then he appeared to think better of it and crossed one leg over the other. Mr. Trevor sat down on a loveseat across from us. He crushed out his cigarette into a nearby ashtray and immediately lit another one.

"I'm not supposed to smoke in the house. I had stopped smoking for a couple of months. I was using one of those electronic cigarettes that give off water vapor. But then this happened and I grabbed the nearest pack I could find."

"What happened?" It was Daryl who asked first.

"I woke up in the middle of the night and Valerie was gone. I heard the front door slam and a couple vehicles pull out of the driveway?"

"A couple?" Chavez asked.

"Definitely more than one. Maybe even three or four."

"Did you see what they looked like?"

"I couldn't. I couldn't get out of bed. I felt paralyzed. I just laid there listening to my wife being driven off by God knows who. I laid there like that for an hour or two and then I . . . I'm ashamed to say it but I . . . I fell asleep. When I woke up four hours had gone by and I could move again. I jumped up and grabbed the phone and called 911. I told the dispatcher everything that happened and she said she'd send a patrol car. When I hung up the phone I heard the shower running. I ran into the bathroom and Valerie was there taking a shower. She was crying and there was blood and welts all over her. It looked like she had been whipped. I asked her if she was hurt and she just started sobbing louder. She screamed at me, said she'd been raped. Then she told me about being pulled out of her bed by men in black leather, black men. You know? African Americans."

"Black guys?"

"Yeah, she said that they were black guys and that they had taken her to some type of church and poured goats blood on her and dripped candle wax all over her, that they said it was made from the fat of an unbaptized baby. Then they injected her with drugs and they raped her with . . . " He swallowed hard and his bottom lip trembled. "With this . . . big statue thing shaped like a penis while they played drums and prayed and chanted. They forced her to have intercourse with a bull."

"A bull? You mean like a male cow?" I asked. Just the thought of a woman being fucked by a bull bordered on absurdity. I was rather certain that the bull was probably one of her black male captors. I was almost just as certain that this was another bullshit call. Whatever this chick had been involved in, it had probably been voluntary. Her story sounded more like some sort of sexual fantasy than a real crime.

"Yes, a bull, a goat, and then a snake."

"A snake? How do you fuck a snake?" Daryl asked and Chavez gave him a mean look and shook his head. It was an insensitive question given the circumstances, but I wanted to know too. Then Mr. Trevor explained and his explanation brought to mind even more absurd images.

"They strapped her down and slid the entire thing up inside of her. She said she could feel it writhing around inside of her . . . you know. Then they made her drink blood. They said it was demon blood."

"Sir, I hate to say this but—"

"I know. It sounds crazy. That's why I called you guys back and told you not to come. I figured she was either lying or high or sleepwalking or had just gone crazy. But there was all of that blood on her and when you guys showed up I figured I might as well talk to you."

"Where is Mrs. Trevor now?"

"She took a painkiller and an anti-depressant and went to sleep. There was one other thing she said though, before she went to sleep."

"What was that?"

"When they used that big stone statue on her, the phallus, she said it ejaculated inside of her."

"It what?" Chavez asked. His patience seemed to be giving out and this was looking like another dead end. We were wasting time.

"She said the statue ejaculated. It came inside of her."

Detective Chavez shut his notepad and stood up. He turned his back on Mr. Trevor and began walking toward the door.

"Well, that's it for me. If you want to file an official report just come down to the station, but we have another call to get to."

"That's it? You don't want to interview his wife?" Daryl said, looking almost as confused as Mr. Trevor.

"Well, she is sleeping. I wouldn't want to wake her if you don't think it's necessary," Mr. Trevor said.

"See? She's sleeping and we're done. Let's go."

With that we all filed out of the room. Mr. Trevor's face was turning red as he held the door for our departure but I couldn't tell if it was from anger or embarrassment.

Back in the car we were all silent. Chavez was gripping the steering wheel again in that white-knuckled choke hold and his jaw muscles had tightened. He was getting increasingly annoyed, and I was worried that he was going to give up and just take Daryl and I into the station and turn us in. As much as I didn't want to go to jail I was even more worried about what was happening to these women.

My imagination began running wild and I wondered if women were being kidnapped all over the state or maybe even across the entire country. What if it was happening around the world? What if hell had risen? Come to earth through the birth canals of these poor women? I imagined a world overrun by those little demon babies. Then I had an even more troubling thought. What do they become when they grow up? Images of old Ray Harryhausen movies came to mind with marauding monsters the size of skyscrapers.

Daryl was chewing on his fingernails, tearing them off in long strips and spitting them to the floor, then doing the same to his cuticles. He was going to draw blood at that rate. I looked over my shoulder at him and his eyes were wide and fidgety. He looked like he had something he needed to say.

"Something bothering you, Daryl?"

"You mean aside from my wife being dead and you shooting my daughter's head off after she tried to kill you?"

He stared at me with cold humorless eyes and for some absurd reason I kept waiting for him to smile or something to let me know that he was just kidding and didn't blame me for his child's death. His expression never changed.

"Yeah. I mean aside from that."

"Mr. Trevor's story . . . I mean Mrs. Trevor's story it . . . it sounded pretty close to what happened to my wife . . . I mean, what I know happened to her. And that other lady, the horny old broad . . . her story was pretty similar. They both said they got kidnapped by big black guys."

"Everyone says that," Chavez interrupted. "Black guys are the generic default bad guys. Saying that you were attacked by a bunch of black guys is the same as saying I don't know who attacked me."

"But the stories were so close."

"You know, I hadn't thought about it, but Daryl's right."

"No. He's not. Look, that old chick said the guys were wearing leather, Daryl and Mr. Trevor said their wives were kidnapped by guys wearing robes, which I admit is pretty similar but not unusual. People watch those horror movies about devil cults and that shapes what they think they see. That old chick said she was raped in her bed. Neither of you said that happened to your wives. Mr. Trevor said the guys never touched his wife. She said they made her fuck a bull and a snake . . . "

"And a goat," I added for no particular reason.

"Yeah, and a goat. No gang rape. You said you were awake when your wife was taken and there was no gang rape involved."

"Well, maybe they're just getting the details mixed up. I mean, you see how that old broad was. She'd fuck any swinging dick that came through the door. She was probably upset that they *didn't* gang rape her and so she made that part up or maybe they did and she just embellished on it. Maybe it was Trevor's wife who made up all that shit about fucking snakes and bulls and ejaculating statues to mask the fact that she'd been gang raped by a bunch of big black guys in black robes. Maybe she liked it a little and was embarrassed about it. Getting gang raped by big black guys is a pretty common fantasy among white chicks."

I didn't even want to know how Daryl thought he knew that.

"So, are you saying we should go back there?" Chavez asked.

"Maybe we should."

"What do you think the odds are of the very first calls we go on being connected to what happened to Daryl's wife?"

"It depends on how frequently this is happening," I said,

giving voice to my fears. "If this is happening to hundreds or even thousands of women then our odds are pretty good."

I kept my worries about what these things would grow into to myself.

"Let's just see what else happens tonight. Maybe we'll find something that will tie everything together," Chavez said, shutting down the conversation and sending us all back to our own introspections.

The next call we overheard was a multiple homicide. A man had killed his twin sons claiming that they had attacked him in his sleep. His wife had to be rushed to the hospital due to severe bleeding, complications from childbirth. The twins had been only two weeks old.

"I think this is what we've been looking for."

It was beginning to look more and more like an epidemic. I couldn't help wondering how many of these babies were out there right now running loose.

Chapter 5

The house was an abattoir. There was a trail of blood from the master bedroom to the master bathroom all the way to the front door. The blood looked chunky as if it contained bits of meat. My stomach rolled and I got a little dizzy. I had to turn away and lean against a coffee table to keep from falling over.

"That's from the mother. I guess she'd been bleeding ever since she left the hospital," Detective Martin Link said. He was an old homicide guy that Chavez knew from back when he first made detective. He was a hulking 6'5" and well over two hundred and fifty pounds. He had a large belly, but he also had biceps the size of my head stretching the fabric of his brown sports coat. As odd as it felt to say this about another dude, there was something majestic about him, like a military general or a ruler. There was a hardness about him that made you wonder if he ever smiled, ever thought of anything but enforcing the law and catching criminals. Chavez had the same hardness but in Link it was tenfold. He was clearly not a man to be fucked with. I wondered what would have happened if he had found out that Daryl and I were wanted for the kidnapping and death of a child. I definitely didn't want to find out the answer.

Apparently Chavez had once considered going to homicide but had changed his mind at the last moment and chose missing persons. He wanted to help people who were still able to be helped rather than merely avenging those who were past saving and bringing justice to their murderers.

He had introduced Daryl and I as material witnesses on a case he was working with a similar M.O. to the killings. That satisfied Detective Link, but he still didn't look too happy about civilians poking around his crime scene. Chavez explained to him that it might help jar our memories if we could see the crime scene while it was still fresh and that we might even be able to spot something that could help him with his case. Detective Link looked doubtful, but he allowed us to stay.

We borrowed shoe covers and latex gloves from the CSU boys so we wouldn't leave footprints or fingerprints and we were ordered to leave the shoe covers with CSU when we left in case we wound up with some valuable piece of evidence sticking to the bottom of them.

As I looked around I spotted blood spatter on the walls that I at first assumed had come from the baby, but a closer inspection revealed them as tiny bloody footprints and hand prints. Something had crawled across the wall. I remembered Detective Chavez's description of the baby running down the wall toward him and a shiver ran through me.

"Where are the bodies?" I asked.

Detective Link looked at me and then at Chavez who nodded, indicating that it was okay for him to show me the corpses.

The father had apparently been gunned down by the police when they responded to the call. His body lay crumpled in the hallway leading to the master bedroom. His bullet ridden carcass was being photographed as we shuffled past it on our way to the master bedroom. There must have been thirty or forty bullet holes in his body.

"He wouldn't drop his weapon." It was all Detective Link offered as an explanation.

Chavez knelt down and took a close look at the body. I followed his eyes. There were claw marks on the man's face, chest, and arms and what looked like a huge bite had been taken out of his upper left thigh. I met Chavez's eyes and I could see the fear growing there. I could see my own terror reflected in them as well. He rose and we all walked into the bedroom.

The twins lay in a tangled mess on the master bedroom floor riddled with bullet holes, bludgeoned, and lacerated with cuts. I could distinguish little or nothing of their facial features. Both of their skulls had been crushed. The broken shards of a lamp and a large mirror were mixed with the blood pooled around their corpses. One of the CSU guys was stuffing a large work boot caked with blood into a plastic bag. Obviously the bullets hadn't been enough.

Detective Chavez knelt down and examined the baby's closer. He examined the corpses, picking through the remains with his rubber gloves. He grabbed one of their legs and stretched it out. It was roped with striated muscle and seemed much too long and the muscles seemed to go in odd directions, not just up and down but at angles. Rigor mortis had not yet set in and when Chavez bent the leg at the knee it went easily in both directions. Bending backwards like the legs of a dog or more like a grasshopper or kangaroo.

"What the hell?" Detective Link asked.

"And look at this."

Chavez peeled back the other twin's lips revealing rows and rows of sharp needle-like teeth.

"What the hell are they?"

"We don't know. Every time I've tried to examine one, the Feds have swooped in and locked us out. They've completely shut us out of the investigation. If you don't mind, I'd like to get some pictures before they show up here and believe me they will."

"What is this? Some sort of government experiment?"

"I don't know. I doubt it. The government is definitely trying to cover it up whatever it is."

"Well, no one is going to take this case from me."

Chavez nodded solemnly but didn't reply. They both knew it was just bravado. When the feds swooped in, Link would have no say-so in the matter.

"What about the wife? Is she able to talk?"

"She's in ICU right now. She's had some massive internal damage and they had to rush her into surgery."

"When will she be conscious?"

Detective Link shrugged.

"It could be hours."

"Were you able to get a statement from her?" Chavez asked.

"Yeah, but I don't know how much sense it makes."

"Can I read it?"

"Well, I haven't written the report yet, Ramon."

"Can I read your notes?"

"Sure."

Daryl and I crowded around Detective Chavez, reading over his shoulder as he rifled through Link's notes. The woman's name was Margaret Ellington. She was thirty-one years old and had been awake watching Jay Leno when what she described as monsters with dark black skin, black eyes, and fangs like a wolf slipped into the house without making a sound. They walked upright and wore what had at first looked like hooded cloaks but were actually part of their skin. Their hands and feet looked like alligator claws. They didn't speak and when she screamed they shot her with some sort of tranquilizer dart. She said it was a blow gun or something, but she didn't see it. She heard a puff of air and then the dart was just there, sticking out of her chest. She said it looked like a slender piece of bone that had been whittled down and sharpened. When she woke up she was strapped to a table and the "monster men" as she called them were sliding some sort of hose attached to a machine up inside of her. She said that there were doctors there too, human doctors. They were checking her vitals on a computer and examining her, taking blood, taking her blood pressure and pulse. When they were done they brought her back to her house.

"Some crazy shit, huh?" Link said.

Chavez didn't reply. His eyes were wide and he swept them slowly from the notepad down to the infant's corpses.

I leaned over and whispered to Daryl.

"Actually, of all the stories we've heard tonight, this one somehow seems to make the most sense."

"How the hell does monster men make sense? How the fuck does that explain what happened to my wife and child?" Daryl asked.

"I don't know. It's just like Chavez was saying, this might be the story that somehow ties everything together."

Daryl thought about it for a minute.

"It does sort of tie the other stories together in a way. I mean, if the kidnappers aren't black dudes but some kind of mutant freaks artificially inseminating women for whatever reason, then I suppose that would make more sense than Satan worshippers making these chicks fuck bulls and snakes. But just about anything makes more sense than that shit. On second thought, no, that shit doesn't make more sense. That shit is even crazier."

I shook my head. I didn't think it was. Something about this story made sense to me. It fit the facts of the case better than all the others. We knew the babies were some kind of monsters so why wouldn't the people who were creating them be monsters too? Maybe I had just seen too many Sci-fi flicks, but I could easily imagine a bunch of genetically altered mutant scientists or alien researchers with women strapped to a gurney while they fertilized them with turkey basters filled with mutant sperm. Yeah, it did sound crazy. Perhaps I was losing my mind. I just nodded my head, agreeing with Daryl. Then I let the matter drop for the moment. I was almost certain we would be finding out the truth soon enough.

We looked around a little more. There was blood everywhere, the bed, the floor, the walls, even the ceiling. I looked back down at the shredded and broken bodies of the infant twins and I felt an overwhelming sadness sweep over me. More dead kids. I had killed one earlier tonight and now there were two more lying dead at my feet. I had found more than my share of dead children in my years as a volunteer but never more than one in a single day. Now they were beginning to stack up like cords of wood. I was surrounded by the bodies of infants.

The room began to blur and the floor beneath my feet felt unstable like I was riding a skateboard. I staggered through the crowd of detectives and police officers, making it outside onto the front lawn just before everything went black. I felt the cool grass against my cheek as my face hit the lawn. Seconds later I woke up in my own vomit. I rolled over onto my back and saw that I wasn't the only one throwing up. There was an officer on his knees beside me giving up his lunch to fertilize another patch of lawn.

"That is fucking awful. Who would do that to their own kids?"

My thoughts were completely different. Whose kids were these? Who or what was creating these little monsters. I had to find out before I lost my mind. Before the next Amber alert sounded and I had to look at another twisted little body or see another woman bleed to death, another family destroyed.

I had just crawled to my knees when Daryl and Chavez came rushing out of the house.

"SWAT just busted down the door over on Raeburn Street where we got the first call. The hostage just gave birth to . . . *something*."

"Something?"

"That's what the Sergeant on site said. Something. And whatever came out of her is tearing shit up over there."

Daryl helped me to my feet and we raced over to Detective Chavez's car. Chavez drove back across town as fast as he could without killing us. None of us knew what to expect when we turned the corner onto Raeburn Street.

"What the fuck?"

"Oh, shit."

It was all I could think to say. All hell was breaking loose.

Chapter 6

Cops were shooting in all directions. A bullet shattered the windshield and burned a furrow along my neck an inch below my carotid artery.

"Ow, shit! I've been shot!"

Another bullet hit the engine and then another came through what was left of the windshield. Chavez whipped the steering wheel sharply to the left sending the car into a tailspin. He stomped down on the brakes as the car fishtailed and the tires squealed. Chavez's car slid across the asphalt sideways and slammed into a parked patrol car. Bullets continued to whiz past the vehicle.

"I'm bleeding!"

I slapped my hand to my neck and it came away wet. Blood trickled down my neck and stained my shirt. Chavez leaned over and checked the wound as I began to whimper and hyperventilate. I heard myself whine and felt like a punk as I fought back tears. I didn't want to die.

"It just grazed you. You're fine."

I was overwhelmed with relief. It didn't last long. The three of us looked out of the car window and this time I screamed. The cops were under attack. There were more than a dozen of those little demon babies and they were tearing the SWAT team apart. They scampered on all fours across the hoods of nearby cars, hopping like frogs, springing at the police officers and lacerating them with razor-like fangs and claws.

A plain clothes officer ran past the car with one of the things clinging to his head, its legs wrapped around his throat like some sort of submission hold as it cannibalized the detective's face. Blood spurted from his head and rained down around him. His screams were horrible. As we watched, he aimed his pistol at the baby and fired. The bullet went through the baby's back and into the detective's own head, killing him instantly. The man's body crumpled to the street where it lay there convulsing as the baby continued to eat his face, heedless of its own injury, lapping greedily at the fountain of blood spurting from the fresh bullet wound in the detective's head.

The baby was no more than a newborn. It still had its umbilical cord attached and its skin glistened with amniotic fluid and blood, though most of the blood had come from the detective. Its eyes were black sunless pits and those same needle-like teeth we'd seen on the dead twins bit into the detective's nose with a sickening crunch. The detective's nose and upper lip stretched and ripped then disappeared down the infant's throat. It bit down again, cracking the detective's skull like an egg, and began scooping out tiny fistfuls of the man's brain and cramming it into its mouth.

Chavez stepped from the car and fired three more shots into the baby, point blank range, nearly tearing the little creature in half. The thing yelped and then hissed at him. Chavez fired one more shot into the thing's brain, finally silencing it. I pulled my own weapon and stepped from the car.

There were less gunshots now as some of the police ran and others died. A sudden volley of automatic weapon's fire drew my attention and I turned in time to see the last of the SWAT team laying down a hail of bullets at a group of cloaked figures at the end of the block. Apparently the guy who'd taken his wife hostage wasn't the only one on the block whose house had been visited by dark men in black hoods. Daryl, Chavez and I stood and watched, waiting to see if SWAT would take them down and we'd finally get to see who or what they were.

The babies that had not already been killed rushed toward the SWAT team and were shredded by M-16 rounds. Their tiny bodies reduced to lumps of bloody meat. That's when I heard the roar. The shrouded figures at the end of the block opened what I first thought were hooded cloaks but were actually flaps of skin, some sort of vestigial wings. They creatures dropped down on all fours the same way the babies had and attacked. Only they were bigger than the demon babies, stronger, and much more terrifying. The minute I saw them, I knew those policemen were doomed. A few bullets were not going to stop those things. I wasn't sure I could think of anything non-military that would. A grenade launcher maybe?

They looked like prehistoric dogs or wild boars, yet there was something reptilian about them. Their hands, feet, and faces were layered with obsidian scales, glistening with some foul unctuousness and a thick layer of black hair that covered their arms and legs and bristled along their backs like enraged hyenas. They had the arms and torsos of men, and they had been walking upright until they had dropped their hoods. Their faces had tusks, over-sized fangs that jutted from between their lips. Their eyes were wide empty chasms blazing with a fiery red and yellow luminescence like candles in the eyes of Jack o' lanterns. As they charged forward their heavy clawed hands raked the asphalt, their mouths opened revealing even more rows of serrated teeth and I could understand why the one woman had said they looked like alligators. There were no comparisons to any earthly creatures that did them justice. They looked like exactly what they were . . . demons. I was certain of it.

The SWAT officers held their ground, raking the demons with gunfire. One of the creatures went down with the top of its skull shorn off, then rose just as quickly to continue the attack. When they reached the police officers they tore them apart. Limbs and heads were viciously amputated, organs and intestines were ripped out and consumed. I was screaming long before I was aware of it. I wanted to curl up into a fetal position, shove my fingers into my ears to muffle the agonized shrieks and the sounds of tearing flesh, close my eyes and wish it all away. I wanted to wake up in my own bed and for someone, my mother, to hug me and tell me it was all just a bad dream.

I still had my gun in my hand. It felt small and useless. I looked over at Daryl who had wet himself.

"Oh God. Oh Jesus. Oh fuck." He repeated. Struck dumb by the brutal carnage taking place in front of us. Chavez looked no better. He was pointing his gun at the demons and sobbing uncontrollably. A pool of urine had formed at his feet and the crotch of his jeans was dark and wet. Chavez had started out on the Narcotics and Gang Taskforce, had faced down submachine-gun-toting youths who had no conscious and no fear of death. He'd been in gunfights with murderous drug dealers and seen his fellow officers gunned down in front of him. He'd gone under cover on drug deals wearing a wire knowing that discovery would mean death. None of that had prepared him for this. What he saw attacking those officers was proof that hell was real. He now feared as much for his soul as his life.

I grabbed Chavez and Daryl and pulled them into the car, falling back into the driver's seat and pulling them down on top of me. I received a few knees and elbows to the chest and stomach as they scrambled over top of me into their seats. I was screaming, my mind fighting for sanity, as I pushed Daryl off of me and into the back seat.

I sat up behind the wheel and threw the vehicle in reverse, stomping down on the accelerator. I could hear the screams of the SWAT team even above my own as they were dismembered, brutally eviscerated right there in the street by beings that looked like something from a Renaissance portrait of Inferno. I had been right. Hell had risen.

Chapter 7

The radio blew up. There were frantic calls coming from all over the city. What was happening on Raeburn Street was happening all over Las Vegas. I whipped the car into a 180-degree turn, then shifted into drive and rocketed forward. Behind me, Daryl was screaming desperately.

"The whole SWAT team is dead. They're coming! Those monsters . . . they're coming after us! Go! Go! GO!"

The things I saw in my rearview mirror, galloping toward us on hooves and claws, bearing tusk-like fangs stained red with the blood of the fallen police officers, threatened to switch my mind off completely. I could feel the cracks in my sanity as they formed one by one. I forgot all about the kidnapped women, the mutant babies, all I could think about was saving my own ass. The only mystery I wanted to solve was the mystery of how we were all going to survive this.

I stared in the mirror at the creatures bearing down on us in a full sprint, those eyes crackling with the flames of hell raging just beyond the rear bumper, and saw nothing in them that suggested mercy or compassion or any consciousness at all. It was like looking into the furnace of some engine of destruction. I stomped down on the accelerator, pushing it to the floor, desperate to put as much distance as possible between us and the voracious demons. We turned onto MLK blvd. at 70 miles per hour, tires squealing and smoking. Ahead of us, were more mutant demon babies and more of the demons in black hoods. Much more. The entire street was filled with them. They were pulling people out of cars and slaughtering them. I slammed on the breaks.

"What do we do?"

Chavez was wild eyed. In his eyes I could see the same cracks in his sanity that were forming in mine. This shouldn't be happening. None of this. It just shouldn't have been. But if we wanted to survive we had to do something and fast. Chavez looked up at the street sign and then to the left.

"Pull the car onto the sidewalk. Get around these things. If you can make it to the corner there's a gun shop down the street. Maybe we can find something in there to stop these things."

"Like what?"

"I don't know. There's got to be something."

"That's what they always do in those zombie apocalypse movies, they find a gun shop. In every invasion movie or end of the world flick they do that. The survivors break into a sporting goods store and load up on weapons. If it works in the movies why not try it? Besides, I don't know about you, but I'd feel a whole fucking lot better with a big ass assault rifle in my hands even if it doesn't kill these things. Maybe it will at least slow their asses down long enough for me to get out of dodge," Daryl said.

"Hey, I'm not arguing. I certainly don't have a better plan," I said.

"Then we do it. Something has got to be able to stop these things. Just drive. Let's get there quick and get our hands on some heavy artillery."

"But what if we don't make it to the corner?" Daryl asked. "What if those things stop us?"

Chavez looked at him with eyes full of terror. He didn't need to answer. We all knew.

I whipped the car onto the sidewalk and pushed the

speedometer up to one hundred. I was determined to ram through anything that stepped in front of us. The car was parallel to where the beasts and the other cars had converged in the street and for a moment it looked like we would sail right past when two of the larger demons turned to cut us off. I pushed the car up to one hundred twenty miles per hour, its maximum speed, trying to beat them to the corner, but at that speed I knew the vehicle would roll if I tried to make the turn. I would have to slow down and when I did they would get us.

Chavez, as if reading my mind, pointed his Glock at the two approaching demons and fired. I couldn't see if he hit them or not or what damage he'd done if any. I was occupied with trying to make sure I didn't wreck the car and kill us or leave the car crippled and us a helpless meal for the monsters. I breathed a sigh of relief when we sailed past the demons easily. Chavez had slowed them down just enough. I stomped down on the breaks and spun the steering wheel to the right. The car went up on two wheels and I said a prayer, hoping that it wouldn't roll. I stopped breathing until the wheels finally touched asphalt again and we made the turn in a cloud of burning rubber.

Chavez may have slowed the things down, but he hadn't stopped them and they were right behind us as we sped down the street. Our luck held and another vehicle, a big red Ram truck, came rocketing out of a side street with three of the little demon babies clinging to its windshield and barreled into the two monsters that were chasing us, driving them into a row of parked vehicles on the other side of the street. I kept my foot firmly planted on the accelerator, figuring they would shake off the blow and be after us again. I was surprised when I looked back and saw that one of them was struggling, severely injured, stuck between the mangled truck and a minivan that had been parked on the street. The creature appeared to be in its death throes, blood squirted from its wounds and its arms flailed wildly at first and then began to slow as it lost more blood. The other one was limping. One of its legs apparently shattered. It may take a hell of a lot to damage them, but just like the babies, they could be wounded and even killed. That was good to know.

I turned back to focus on the road as one of the babies that had been clinging to the driver's windshield, the only one still alive, crawled its way into the front seat and began to feast on the unconscious driver. The baby was quickly joined by the large demon with the limp. There was movement in the back of the truck and that's when I realized that the driver had his entire family in there. They were all being butchered and there was nothing I could do. I was considering turning the car around to try to help when Chavez, sensing my thoughts, put a hand on my forearm to get my attention and then slowly shook his head.

"They're dead, Spenser, and we will be too if we go back there. The Gun Shop is right on your left on the next block. Let's get there and get ourselves armed."

I nodded and tried my best to avoid looking in the rearview mirror again.

The Gun Shop was like a mini-supermarket filled with rifles and pistols. When I spotted it I slowed the car, but Chavez shook his head.

"Do you think the door is open? Have you got a fucking key? Ram this thing right through the front of the damn place! Get us inside. *Now!*"

I turned the car toward the front of the building and stomped down on the gas once again. The vehicle rocketed across the street through the parking lot, over the walkway and through the front window, taking out the security gate and setting off the burglar alarm. The airbags exploded, knocking the wind out of me and blinding me for a few panicky seconds during which I was certain we would be attacked. When it finally deflated I took a few rapid breaths to calm myself.

The siren blared and a silent alarm sent a signal to a

private security firm who called a phone that rang somewhere in the back of the store. Soon they would be calling what was left of the police. I doubted they would get much of a response.

I unbuckled my seatbelt and checked myself for cuts and bruises. I was fine. My next thought, even before checking on Chavez and Daryl, was about the car. I hoped it hadn't sustained too much damage from the impact because even fully armed I had no desire to face these things on foot. The windshield was completely shattered and the front of the car was smashed inward and steaming. I wasn't a mechanic, but I was pretty sure the radiator was a loss. I didn't know how far the vehicle could get us with a busted radiator, but the engine was still running so I took that as a good sign. I reached for the keys and was about to turn the car off, then I thought better of it. I wasn't sure whether or not it would start again and if those things attacked us and we had to make a quick getaway, I wanted the engine running.

Chavez groaned beside me. He was a few inches shorter than me and the airbag had caught him right in the face, bloodying his nose. Otherwise he looked okay. I looked over my shoulder and Daryl was already opening his door and stepping out. He didn't even look rattled. He stumbled over to the rack of rifles behind the counter and tried to yank down an H&K USC .45 caliber semi-automatic rifle. The rifles were all locked up with a thick chain, but Daryl continued to yank on it as if he thought he would somehow find the strength to snap steel links.

Chavez stepped out of the car, wiping his bleeding nose with his shirt sleeve. He pulled his gun and walked over to the rifle rack. The detective placed the barrel of his pistol against the chain and fired, snapping it in two, allowing Daryl to claim his H&K. Then he proceeded to pull down two Mossberg 12 gauge shotguns and two Colt M-16 9mm assault rifles. He smashed the display case with the butt of his pistol and replaced his Glock .9mm with a Desert Eagle .50 cal. He tossed me a shopping bag and pointed me to the shelves behind the display case closest to me.

"Start filling it with ammo. We need nine millimeter ammo full-metal jacket, some Black Talons if you can find them, and some Glasers. Get me some fifty caliber ammo too and some forty-five caliber as well. Fill a couple of bags. This is going to be a long night."

I got busy loading the bags and Chavez and Daryl started loading the shotguns and looking for larger magazines for the semi-automatics. Even with the guns I had very little confidence that any of us would survive the night.

We got all the guns loaded and were just about to climb back into the car when the babies came. There were six in all and behind them was one of the men in the black robes, only at this distance it was clear that the thing was nothing close to human even before it opened its long flaps of black skin and attacked. It looked like we were about to find out if we had wasted our time breaking into the store. We lifted our weapons and unloaded on them as the demons scrambled through the shattered storefront window.

The babies were torn to shreds. A rain of bullets poured through them, punching fist-sized exit wounds in their young flesh. They were ripped open like pinatas, organs spilling out onto the hard vinyl floor. The thing with the black wings was not as easily dispatched. It continued coming forward as we pumped it with shotgun shells and Chavez raked it with 9mm bullets.

"The damn thing won't die!"

"Aim for its face!" I yelled as the thing closed in on me.

It was almost on top of me when Chavez and Daryl blew its skull open and it came crashing down on the hood of the car.

"Okay, so what the fuck do we do now?"

"I think we need to get out of town. Whatever is going on seems to be happening all over the city."

We walked cautiously around the dead demon thing and

climbed back into the car. Chavez put it in reverse and we backed out of the store.

"You think we have enough ammo?"

Our guns were empty, but we still had shopping bags full of bullets.

"I don't want to fight any more of these things. We just need to get the hell out of town. Then we can get the National Guard or somebody in here to get rid of the rest of these fucking monsters," Chavez answered.

"Chavez! Chavez, are you there?" It was Detective Link and he sounded excited.

Chavez grabbed the radio from the dashboard.

"Link? Is that you?"

"Yeah, and I got something you should see. Can you make it back over here?"

Chavez snorted.

"You do know what's going on over here right?"

"It's happening all over the city. I just had to shoot my way out of a suspect's house. We got a call on the radio from someone who said they were about to be eaten by demons. But you need to hear what else he had to say. He's still alive, for now, but I don't think he's going to last much longer. Those things were tearing into him when we got here. We lost a few of our men too. I think this is the guy responsible for all of this."

"Do you think he knows how to stop it?"

"I don't know. He wasn't able to stop them from damn near killing him. I don't know what he can tell us."

"Where are you? We'll get there."

"How the hell are we supposed to get over there?" I asked. "What happened to getting out of town?"

"If we can stop these things then we have to, man. They killed my fuckin' wife!" Daryl yelled. "Fuck that! I'm stayin' and fightin'! I'ma kill all these mutherfuckers!"

"We're all going. Unless someone wants to get out and walk?" Chavez said.

I kept quiet and began loading one of the shotguns. The matter had been decided.

"I'm still up at Sunrise Mountain, on Falling Sparrow and Desert Inn. You'll see my car when you turn the corner. We've got half the precinct over here," Detective Link said.

"In case you guys haven't figured it out yet, you have to shoot for their heads. We lost an entire SWAT team over here," Chavez offered.

"Yeah, we figured it out. See you soon. Good luck."

Chapter 8

The ride back to Sunrise Mountain was littered with the dead and dying. The bodies of demons lay strewn about the streets amid piles of human remains. The entire city was becoming one big graveyard.

We turned on Desert Inn road and Chavez stepped down hard on the breaks.

"What the fuck?"

What looked like a group of gang members were walking down the middle of the road followed by three of the large creatures. The main thug, a tall light-skinned black man with a shoulder-width afro, pointed at our car and the creatures charged.

Chavez threw the car in reverse as we began firing our weapons at the creatures in a panic. Daryl was firing the H&K in rapid bursts and one of the creatures went down, its head torn nearly from its shoulders. One of the other creatures had nearly overtaken the car when I hit it with three quick shots from the Mossberg, removing the upper part of its skull and sending its brain flopping out onto the asphalt. Daryl and I concentrated our fire on the remaining creature. A bullet whizzed by my head. The gangbangers were firing at us.

Chavez pulled out the Desert Eagle and returned fire as

he continued to pilot the car in reverse. The guy with the afro went down hard with two in his chest and the guy immediately behind him took one in the gut and screamed. The other three thugs quickly scattered.

I ran out of ammo and ducked back into the car to reload. Chavez and Daryl finished off the last demon-thing before I managed to load the first round. Its skull came apart under the assault and it collapsed in a lifeless heap.

Chavez stopped the car and we all sat there, breathing hard, totally freaked-the-fuck-out.

"What the hell is going on? Gangbangers teamed up with demons? What tha fuck?"

Daryl was freaking out.

"How do you know they were gangbangers?" Chavez asked.

"They took a fuckin' shot at us! They were controlling those things!"

Daryl was practically screaming. I was too terrified to speak.

"That sounds like something a bit deeper than your average drug-dealin', gun-tottin', scumbags doesn't it?" Chavez said sarcastically.

He was right. Something wasn't adding up.

"Let's go see your friend, Detective Link. Maybe he knows what's going on."

Chavez nodded his head, turned around and headed back up the road, weaving in between the bodies of the fallen demons. I looked at the bullet hole in the window. It was mere inches from where my head had been. For the fifth or sixth time that evening I had almost been killed.

We made it to Falling Sparrow Lane just as the sun began to rise. The entire block was cordoned off by a dozen police vehicles and several dozen officers. Two ambulances sat on the sidewalk with three overworked EMTs rushing around, tending to wounded officers and civilians.

"This looks like a fucking warzone."

"That's exactly what it is. We're at war here," Daryl said. He had gone all solemn and serious again.

Chavez flashed his badge and one of the officers ushered us through the barricade and up to the house where Detective Link waited along with a fourth EMT who was covered in blood.

"Chavez, get your ass over here. He's lost a lot of blood and I don't think he's going to make it much longer."

"Who?"

"He said his name is Martin James. He says he created these things."

"What?" Chavez said.

"He said what?" I asked.

"He has a whole laboratory set up in his basement. He's some kind of rich trust-fund kid or something. There must be a couple hundred thousand dollars worth of equipment in there, maybe more."

"But why? Was this some kind of experiment gone wrong?"

Detective Link shook his head.

"He did it on purpose and he said it was more than just science. He said he used some kind of black magic."

"Why? Why would he create those things?"

"Let's go ask him."

Detective Link led us into the house, down into the basement where a man lay on a gurney wrapped in bandages. His arms and legs had been amputated. He was little more than a torso. I was pretty sure he hadn't always looked like that. The demons, his creations, had done this to him.

"Martin James?" Chavez asked the man.

"He's on a lot of drugs. I don't know if he'll wake up again," the EMT said.

"Then fucking give him something to wake him up!" Link barked.

The EMT reached into his medical bag and came out with a syringe.

"It's adrenalin. It'll wake him up."

He swabbed the man's neck with iodine and injected the adrenalin into the largest vein he could find.

"That ought to do it."

"Martin? Martin James?" Chavez asked. He reached down and slapped the man lightly on both cheeks to wake him up.

"Who is it? Let me sleep."

"Fuck no, motherfucker! You ain't sleepin'! Wake your ass up!" Daryl shouted and that seemed to clear the cobwebs from the man's head.

"Who are you?"

"We're the police. Now, what the fuck did you do?"

He turned to look at Daryl.

"I did it for us, bro. I did it for all of us."

"What the fuck are you talking about, you fuckin' piece of shit. You killed my wife!"

Daryl lunged at him and Detective Link and I had to hold him back to keep him from ripping Martin James's heart out with his bare hands.

"I did it for us, man! This was my way of ending it once and for all. No more racism. No more hatred. Just one master race."

"Them? Them! That's your fucking master race!"

"It got out of control."

"Damn right it did, motherfucker!" Daryl was still struggling to get at the man, but his efforts were weakening. "I watched that thing you created . . . You created! I watched it tear its way out of my wife. I watched her bleed to death. And then I had to kill it. He had to kill it!" Daryl pointed at me and I felt an irrational pang of guilt.

"Tell us how to stop them," Chavez said. "You've got to end this."

"I-I don't know how."

"What the fuck do you mean, you don't know how? You created these things. You must know how to destroy them."

"I-I didn't design them to be stopped. I designed them to breed and kill. To keep going until they were the only things left, the dominant life forms. A new race of humanity."

"Those-those aren't human. That's not us."

"No more war. No more hate. No more us against them. One race." Martin smiled, then slipped peacefully into a coma.

We all stood there, staring at Martin James as if we were expecting him to say something more, to give us some answer that would save us. He said nothing.

"So, what does this have to do with the feds?" Chavez asked.

The answer came to me immediately. It was obvious. They knew.

"What do you think you would do if you were the government and you found out that someone was creating demons in his basement?"

Chavez nodded.

"I'd find the people involved, shut them down, and then I'd militarize the entire operation. I'd turn the fucking things into weapons."

"Yeah." Detective Link nodded his head. Chavez was right.

"That's not gonna happen now though. Not with him dead."

"Nope," Chavez said, still staring at Martin's corpse, a look of grim resignation on his face.

"So then what will they do?" I asked for no particular reason. This answer too, was obvious.

"A military strike. A cleansing. Hopefully they'll get all of those things. Kill them all before they can spread. If not, if any of those demons get out . . . "

"Then Martin's dream comes true," Daryl said.

"What do we do now?" I asked. No one answered. When the shooting began outside, I barely had the energy to grab my shotgun. I was spent, defeated. The screams were horrible, but I was already getting used to them. The sun was almost fully risen and with it came a new dawn. The dawn of a new race. A new master race. No more war. No more hatred. No more division. I saw it in Daryl's eyes before he ran up the stairs to join the fight. He understood why Martin had done it.

I finally cocked the shotgun and ran up the basement steps to join him with Detectives Chavez and Link at my rear. We all knew we were running to our death. I didn't want to die, but I understood.

About the Authors

Sultan Z. White was born in 1994 in San Francisco, California. He sat through many a parent-teacher conference over the contents of his writings and doodles throughout his schooling. At age 7, his story *Evil Monsters Everywhere* was published in the children's horror anthology *Dark Offspring*. Throughout high school he continued to concern his teachers with the culmination of his senior project, which (supposedly) threatened to pop the so very delicate "Exeter bubble". When he is not writing he is running in circles on a track, bboying with his crew, and not partying and not drinking at Middlebury College because he is still a minor and follows the rules.

Wrath James White is a former World Class Heavyweight Kickboxer, a professional Kickboxing and Mixed Martial Arts trainer, distance runner, performance artist, and former street brawler, who is now known for creating some of the most disturbing works of fiction in print.

Wrath is the author of *The Resurrectionist, Succulent Prey, Yaccub's Curse, Sacrifice, Pure Hate*, and *Prey Drive* (*Succulent Prey Part II*). He is also the author of *Voracious, To The Death, Skinzz, The Reaper, Like Porno For Psychos, Everyone Dies Famous In A Small Town, The Book Of A Thousand Sins, His Pain* and *Population Zero*. He is the coauthor of *Teratologist* co-written with the king of extreme horror, Edward Lee, *Orgy Of Souls* co-written with Maurice Broaddus, *The Killings* and *Hero* co-written with J.F. Gonzalez, and *Poisoning Eros I* and *II* co-written with Monica J. O'Rourke.

Made in the USA
Coppell, TX
12 May 2023

16702089R00132